# Reprint Publishing

FOR PEOPLE WHO GO FOR ORIGINALS.

www.reprintpublishing.com

# Uncle Sam Trustee

Yours sincerely
Leonard Wood

# Uncle Sam Trustee

*By*

## JOHN KENDRICK BANGS

*" Peace hath her Victories no less renowned than War."*
*—Milton to Cromwell.*

New York

RIGGS PUBLISHING COMPANY

MCMII

This

Volume is Dedicated

With Sentiments of Affectionate Esteem

to

Brig.-Gen. Leonard Wood

Maj. William M. Black          Maj. William C. Gorgas

Maj. E. St. John Greble          Lieut. M. E. Hanna

Maj. Louis V. Cazíaro          Col. Tasker H. Bliss

Lieut. Frank R. McCoy

# PREFACE

*T*HE time has come when the people of the United States are to relinquish to the people of Cuba the control of their own affairs. Believing that the incidents of the past four years in so far as they have to do with the relations of the United States to Cuba form a page in history which reflects high honor upon the American people, and noting in some quarters a disposition to exalt one branch of the public service at the expense of another, it has seemed proper to me to present in this form some of the results of my observations of the efforts of the United States Army in Cuba, in no wise attempting to minimize the value of the achievements of the Navy. In order to make the presentation of the subject as comprehensive as possible I have ventured a brief sketch of the history of Cuba, some consideration of the relations which for a century or more have existed between the people of that island and our own, a statement of the results of the Spanish-American War in so far as it involved Cuba alone, and a general statement of conditions prevailing at the beginning of the American occupation. I acknowledge my indebtedness in the preparation of this book to the officers of the United States Army in Cuba who have placed

# PREFACE

such information as I have required at my disposal; to Mr. Franklin Matthews and Mr. Charles M. Pepper for valuable material gleaned from their books, *The New Born Cuba,* and *To-morrow in Cuba,* to Messrs. Houghton, Mifflin and Company of Boston for their courtesy in permitting me to quote at some length from the pages of *The Discovery of America,* by the late John Fiske; to the War Department at Washington for much valuable material placed at my disposal; to the Hon. Henry Cabot Lodge for his acquiescence in my request to quote liberally from his work on *The Spanish War;* and to Messrs. Harper & Bros., N. Y., for their kind permission to include in these pages pictorial and other matter originally contributed by myself to the columns of *Harper's Weekly.* My only claim for the story which follows is that it is as clear and comprehensive a statement of conditions in Cuba as they exist at the moment of the transfer as it is possible to provide at this early period. When I have found a portion of the story better told by other pens, as in the quotations from Lodge, Fiske, Packard, Sanger and others, I have not hesitated to quote with liberality. The main point has been to have the story told, and I trust that I have not failed.

My special acknowledgments for material assistance

# PREFACE

rendered are due to Maj. Wm. Murray Black, U. S. A.,
from whom I have received a vivid statement of the conditions prevailing in the last year of Spanish control and
the first of American; to Lieut. Frank Ross McCoy,
U. S. A., of the personal staff of Gen. Wood, for interesting and illuminating notes upon subjects of
importance, and to Mr. T. E. Tomlinson, who accompanied me on my trip to Cuba, and whose memoranda of
things seen have been of great value.

JOHN KENDRICK BANGS.

YONKERS, N. Y., *April* 15, 1902.

# CONTENTS

## CUBA IN HISTORY

PAGE

I. Discovery, Natives and Early Settlement........ 1

II. Further Settlement, The Spanish Colonial Theory 19

III. Slavery and Piracy........................... 38

IV. Insurrections in Cuba......................... 60

V. Relations of United States and Cuba until 1898.. 79

VI. The Year of 1898 and Its Results............... 105

## THE TRUST

I. Brig.-Gen. Leonard Wood at Santiago........ 123

II. A General Survey of Cuba at Close of War.... 142

III. The Department of Public Works.............. 161

IV. The Department of Charities and Correction, I.. 203

V. The Department of Charities and Correction, II.. 217

VI. The Department of Public Instruction, I........ 231

VII. The Department of Public Instruction, II...... 251

VIII. The Custom House and the Post Office.......... 268

IX. The Police and Administration of Justice........ 287

X. The Department of Sanitation................ 312

XI. Conclusion ..................................... 338

# ILLUSTRATIONS

| | | |
|---|---|---|
| LEONARD WOOD | *Frontispiece* | |
| THE PALACE, HAVANA | *Facing p.* | 6 |
| MAJOR GENERAL JOHN R. BROOKE, U. S. A. | " | 14 |
| MAJOR EUGENE F. LADD, U. S. V. | " | 22 |
| BRIG. GEN. ADNA R. CHAFFEE, U. S. A. | " | 30 |
| LIEUT. FRANK ROSS MCCOY, U. S. A. | " | 42 |
| OFFICERS' QUARTERS, CAMP COLUMBIA | " | 52 |
| MILITARY ROAD OF AMERICAN CONSTRUCTION | " | 52 |
| SCHOOL ROOM FOR BOYS | " | 62 |
| A SMALL CUBAN FAMILY | " | 62 |
| BRIG. GEN. WILLIAM LUDLOW, U. S. A. | " | 74 |
| CAPTAIN HUGH L. SCOTT, U. S. A. | " | 100 |
| BENEFICENTIA AT HAVANA | " | 124 |
| MATERNITY ROOM AT BENEFICENTIA | " | 124 |
| THE BENEFICENTIA LAUNDRY, 1900 | " | 128 |
| THE BENEFICENTIA LAUNDRY, 1902 | " | 128 |
| THE KITCHEN, BENEFICENTIA, 1900 | " | 132 |
| THE KITCHEN, BENEFICENTIA, 1902 | " | 132 |
| THE SHOE SHOP, BENEFICENTIA | " | 136 |
| THE TAILOR SHOP, BENEFICENTIA | " | 136 |
| MAJOR WILLIAM MURRAY BLACK, U. S. A. | " | 142 |
| VAPOR STREET, HAVANA, IN JANUARY, 1900 | " | 150 |
| VAPOR STREET, HAVANA, IN JUNE, 1900 | " | 150 |
| LUDLOW PLACE, 1898 | " | 156 |
| LUDLOW PLACE, 1901 | " | 156 |
| CALZADA DE JESUS DEL MONTE, 1899 | " | 164 |
| CALZADA DE JESUS DEL MONTE, 1901 | " | 164 |
| AGUILA STREET, HAVANA, 1900 | " | 172 |
| AGUILA STREET, HAVANA, 1901 | " | 172 |

# ILLUSTRATIONS

| | | |
|---|---|---|
| ESCOBAR STREET, 1899 . . . . . . . . . . . | *Facing p.* | 178 |
| ESCOBAR STREET, 1901 . . . . . . . . . . | " | 178 |
| PALATINO ROAD, 1899 . . . . . . . . . . . | " | 186 |
| PALATINO ROAD, 1901 . . . . . . . . . . . | " | 186 |
| THE SEA WALL OF LA PUNTA . . . . . . . . | " | 192 |
| LA PUNTA, 1902 . . . . . . . . . . . . | " | 192 |
| COLON PARK, 1899 . . . . . . . . . . . | " | 198 |
| COLON PARK, 1901 . . . . . . . . . . . | " | 198 |
| MAJOR E. ST. JOHN GREBLE, U. S. A. . . . . . . | " | 204 |
| SOME RAW MATERIAL FOR THE SCHOOLS . . . . . | " | 208 |
| THE SCHOOL ROOM AT GUANAJAY . . . . . . | " | 208 |
| CALISTHENICS AT THE GUANAJAY SCHOOL . . . . | " | 210 |
| GYMNASIUM AT THE GUANAJAY SCHOOL . . . . . | " | 210 |
| THE SHOE SHOP AT GUANAJAY . . . . . . . | " | 212 |
| SOME OF THE WORK OF THE BOYS AT GUANAJAY . . | " | 212 |
| SCHOOL ROOM . . . . . . . . . . . | " | 214 |
| FIELD DAY AT GUANAJAY . . . . . . . . . | " | 214 |
| THE BLACKSMITH SHOP . . . . . . . . . . | " | 216 |
| THE CARPENTER SHOP . . . . . . . . . . | " | 216 |
| THE GARDEN AT ALDECOA . . . . . . . . | " | 218 |
| AT ALDECOA . . . . . . . . . . . . | " | 220 |
| THE CHAPEL AT ALDECOA . . . . . . . . . | " | 220 |
| SEWING CLASS AT ALDECOA . . . . . . . . | " | 222 |
| AT MAZURRA . . . . . . . . . . . . | " | 222 |
| INSPECTION AT THE LEPER HOSPITAL . . . . . . | " | 224 |
| IN THE LEPER HOSPITAL OF SAN LAZARO . . . . . | " | 226 |
| THE DINING HALL AT MAZURRA . . . . . . . | " | 226 |
| A VIOLENTLY INSANE PATIENT AT MAZURRA . . . . | " | 228 |
| TRAINING CUBAN NURSES . . . . . . . . . | " | 230 |
| SCENE AT HOSPITAL NO. I, HAVANA . . . . . . | " | 230 |
| LIEUT. MATTHEW E. HANNA . . . . . . . . . | " | 232 |

# ILLUSTRATIONS

| | | |
|---|---|---|
| COMPOSTELLA BARRACKS, HAVANA, IN 1898 . . . . . | *Facing p.* | 238 |
| COMPOSTELLA BARRACKS, HAVANA, IN 190: . . . . . | " | 238 |
| THE COMPOSTELLA SCHOOL CHILDREN . . . . . . | " | 242 |
| DAILY DRILL AT THE COMPOSTELLA SCHOOL . . . . | " | 242 |
| A GROUP OF CUBAN NURSES . . . . . . . . . . | " | 250 |
| THE COOKING CLASS, COMPOSTELLA SCHOOL . . . . | " | 250 |
| PARADE OF SCHOOL CHILDREN . . . . . . . . | " | 256 |
| RECESS . . . . . . . . . . . . . . . | " | 256 |
| A GROUP OF CUBAN TEACHERS . . . . . . . . | " | 264 |
| CLASS ROOM FOR GIRLS . . . . . . . . . . | " | 264 |
| COLONEL TASKER H. BLISS, U. S. A. . . . . . . . | " | 270 |
| THE HAVANA CUSTOM HOUSE . . . . . . . . . | " | 278 |
| DRILLING RAW RECRUITS, HAVANA POLICE . . . . . | " | 278 |
| THE VIVAC, HAVANA . . . . . . . . . . . . | " | 292 |
| MAJOR LOUIS V. CAZIARC, U. S. A. . . . . . . . . | " | 294 |
| A SERGEANT OF POLICE, HAVANA . . . . . . . . | " | 300 |
| A MOUNTED POLICE OFFICER, HAVANA . . . . . . | " | 306 |
| AFTER A SHOWER IN HAVANA . . . . . . . . | " | 316 |
| A TYPICAL HAVANA RESIDENCE BLOCK FROM TWO POINTS OF VIEW . . . . . . . . . . . . . | " | 316 |
| MAJOR W. C. GORGAS . . . . . . . . . . . . | " | 332 |

# PART I

## CUBA IN HISTORY

# CUBA IN HISTORY

## Chapter I

DISCOVERY—ITS NATIVE POPULATION—THEIR CHAR-
ACTER, RELIGION AND HABITS—EARLY SETTLE-
MENT BY SPANIARDS—OVANDO—VELASQUEZ.

*B*Y virtue of the divine right of Christopher Columbus to annex to Spain all new lands discovered by himself in the Western Ocean, conferred
upon that worthy explorer by proxy, through the
bull of May 3, 1493, issued by Pope Alexander VI,
which invested with certain active and retroactive juris-
dictional powers their sovereign Majesties Ferdinand and
Isabella of Spain, Cuba became at the moment of her discovery the territorial possession of the Spaniard. The
island was discovered on Sunday, October 28, 1492, a
fortnight after the first notable achievement of Columbus
as an explorer of western waters, and while he was cruis·
ing about in search of more convincing evidences of the
existence of a westerly passage to the fabled fields of
Asia than he had yet secured. The point at which he is
supposed to have made his landing is in the section now
known as the Bay of Nuevitas, on the North coast of the
Province of Puerto Principe, lying a trifle to the east of
the centre of the island, but the precise spot is unknown.
The waters of this portion of the coast are filled with

countless small islands and lines of reef of coral formation, making navigation difficult, and identification of any particular point of historic interest in uncharted times impossible. What is definitely known, however, is that the discovery of the Island of Cuba followed close upon the heels of Columbus's first achievement, in the locality of Nuevitas, now a city of 4,228 inhabitants, and that somewhere hereabouts Columbus raised the standard of Spain and took possession " in the name of Christ, Our Lady and the reigning sovereigns of Spain," christening the island Juana in honor of the well beloved Prince John of pleasant memory. " As he approached the island," says Irving, " he was struck with its magnitude and the grandeur of its features: its airy mountains, which reminded him of Sicily; its fertile valleys and long sweeping plains, watered by noble rivers; its stately forests; its bold promontories and stretching headlands, which melted away into remotest distance."

At the time of its christening Cuba was enjoying that which it lost with the entrance of Spain into its territory, and for the restoration of which it has been struggling ever since: a form of government which was its own, which sufficed for its needs and was dependent for its powers upon no forces outside of its own borders. The natives, variously estimated in number at between 200,000 and 1,000,000 were red-men, for the sake of convenience called Indians, in disposition gentle and friendly, simple in their methods of life and having a religion of their own, "devoid of rites and ceremonies, but inculcating the existence of a great and beneficent Being and in the immortality of the soul." It is said as evidence of the latter that during the second visit of Columbus to Cuba he was approached by one of the venerable native chiefs who, after greeting him warmly and presenting him with a basket of fruit, said to the visitor: "Whether you are divinities or mortal men, we know not. You have come into these countries with a force, against which, were we inclined to resist, it would be folly. We are all therefore at your mercy; but if you are men, subject to mortality like ourselves, you cannot be unapprised that after this life there is another, wherein a very different portion is allotted to good and bad men. If therefore you expect to die, and believe with us, that every one is to be rewarded in a future state according to his conduct in the present, you will do no hurt to those who do none to you." This according to report was duly interpreted to Columbus by a native whom he had taken to Spain, and who had there acquired the Spanish language. The truth of this version is attested by Herrera and other historians whose credibility we may accept or reject according to our choice.

The natives were singularly free from the abhorred vices of their neighbors of the adjacent islands. They expressed themselves with a certain modesty and respect, and were hospitable to the last degree. Reading between the lines of the records of history, it is manifest that after their own rules and estimates, their lives were chaste and proper, though it was admissible for kings to have several wives. Moreover, though living in a state of nudity, they religiously observed the decencies of life, and were more outraged by Spanish lasciviousness than can be clearly expressed.* They were governed by nine independent chiefs, *Caciques,* ruling as many independent principalities, whose word was law; and, in those primeval days, were living in peace and amity with each other and with their neighbors, contentedly and happy. The cannibalism of the other islanders was not practised by the Cubans of those first known days and the testimony of those who lived and worked among them is that they were industrious and orderly to an almost Utopian degree. They lived mainly upon fish, fruit and Indian corn. They built huts for themselves of enduring construction, and of a type still preserved by the poorer Cubans of to-day, using the materials that lay to the hand, bark, leaves and palm. Their fields, such as they had under cultivation, produced cotton, corn, potatoes, tobacco, pineapples and manioc; and in the fashioning of articles with the hand they had produced a certain kind of rude pottery, and stone weapons for possible use against the chance enemy that came their way. Of domestic animals they had none save the dog. Others such as the horse, the mule, the ox

* Due South, by M. M. Ballou.

and the cow were imported later by their Spanish con-
querors, with, singularly enough, the orange, the lemon
and the sugar cane. Everything they had was of their
own make. Everything they ate was of their own raising
or catching. Their fish nets and hooks were of their own
devising. Their religion was the outgrowth of their own
spiritual needs, and their contented prosperity was due
wholly to their own industry and simple faith in the
efficacy of their own hands under the guidance of their
chiefs, and protection of their Great Spirit.

To them then entered Columbus with the civilizing influences of the old world in his train, and the woes of
Cuba began with the "pacification" of these happy
islanders under Spanish rulers, using Spanish methods to
teach them the error of their ways. The great admiral's
first contact with these simple folk at their best, was
through two envoys whom he despatched, shortly after
his landing, under the impression that he had reached the
continent of Asia, to the interior in search of a king said
by coast natives—or so understood by Columbus—to be at
war with the great Khan. "These envoys found pleasant
villages with large houses surrounded with fields of such
unknown vegetables as maize, potatoes and tobacco;"
and upon the authority of Columbus's diary, "they met
on the road a great many people going to their villages,
men and women with brands in their hands, made of
herbs for taking their customary smoke," but such con-

vincing evidences of Asiatic splendor as cities and kings, as rich stuffs and the gold and spices of their desires in abundance were not divulged, and shortly after, perplexed and disappointed, the admiral continued on his way.

Barely more than the easterly north coast of the new territory occupied the attention of Columbus upon this voyage, but in subsequent venturings it is recorded that he familiarized himself with the greater part of the southern coast line from Cape Maisi on the east—named Alpha and Omega by Columbus as being the extremity of Asia*—as far as Batabano and the Isle of Pines to the West, but that Cuba was an island and not a part of the Asiatic mainland never dawned upon his mind. There is no reason to believe that those portions of Cuba lying beyond the westerly boundary of the present Province of Matanzas, and comprising the rich and fertile fields of the provinces now known as Havana and Pinar Del Rio were ever explored by him. That the new land was rich and promised well for the pockets of his king and the king's men who would venture here however, was soon sufficiently obvious, for even the most cursory examination of its products disclosed the existence of pearls, mastic, aloes, a soil fertile beyond the ordinary, and in its rivers indications of gold. Surely here was a tempting morsel for the Spanish maw and the admiral lost no time in returning to Spain with

* "The Discovery of America." Vol I. p. 436 —John Fiske

6

THE PALACE, HAVANA,

*Residence of the Military-Governor*

the evidences of his glorious treasure-trove, leaving behind him a small band of his followers at a convenient
point on the Island of Hispaniola, later known as San
Domingo and to-day as Haiti. This body of men, forty
in number, remained of their own volition, not alone because there was not room for all upon the one ship which
the desertion of Pinzon and the wreck of the Santa Maria
on Christmas Day had left the admiral, but for the further
reason that they found the " life upon the island lazy, and
the natives, especially the women, seemed well disposed
toward them. A blockhouse was built of the wrecked
ship's timbers and armed with her guns and in commemo-
ration of that eventful Christmas it was called Fort Na-
tivity (La Navidad)." * This was the first white settlement of the new world, and in its immediate influence
upon the situation it was of so baneful a nature that it
seems almost a pity that its members could not have gone
to the bottom of those unknown waters with the wreck
of the Santa Maria. Theirs would have been a happier
and a more glorious ending had this been the case.

Three times after its discovery Columbus returned to
Cuba, but until 1511, when its permanent occupation
began, it appears to have been avoided by other conspicuous explorers. It was not until 1508 that its definite
classification as an island was made upon the report of
one Sebastian Ocampo, who, at the instance of Nicolas

* " The Discovery of America."—Fiske.

7

# UNCLE SAM TRUSTEE

de Ovando, Governor of San Domingo, undertook the thorough exploration of the rich waters of the neighboring seas.*

In 1511, five years after the death of the discoverer,

* There is much interesting discussion as to this point none of which appears to be conclusive. One Juan de la Cosa who accompanied Columbus upon his voyage of 1494 and who subscribed under oath, on penalty of having his tongue slit if this was violated in later statements, to the belief that Cuba was part of the continent of Asia, in 1500 made himself responsible for a map upon which Cuba is represented as an island. There is no evidence however that La Cosa's change of mind was based upon observation or upon any real conviction. Another map made two years later by Alberto Cantino indicates the detection of the insularity of Cuba in 1502, but as to the certainty of its conclusions there seems to have been much confusion. The cartographers of those days worked as often upon hearsay and rumor as upon conviction and observation. "Because Florida (yet without a name) purported to be a piece of the Continent and because until after 1508 most people believed Cuba to be a piece of the Continent, the old maps used to mix them together without rhyme or reason; and the perplexity was increased by the fact that the true Cuba was often called Isabella. Sometimes the island appeared under the latter designation, while the name Cuba was placed upon the Florida peninsular: sometimes the two were fused in one, because while geographers found both countries mentioned or drawn upon maps they knew only of the one as being actually visited, and hence tried to correct the apparent error." (Fiske.) It is quite clear that from the first Cuba has been an inspiration to the imagination, and that it was as easy to write mendaciously of it then as now, when so much that is palpably false has been sent from that unfortunate island for the "information" of the curious, is sufficiently obvious.

8

# DIEGO COLUMBUS

Cuba's permanent troubles began with the arrival of an expedition fitted out by Diego Columbus, son of the admiral, for the purpose of colonization. This expedition consisting of about 300 men was under the control of Diego Velasquez, who became lieutenant-governor of the Island of Cuba, by virtue of his command, and subject to the orders of Don Diego Columbus, now Admiral of the Indies, and since 1509, when he succeeded Nicolas de Ovando, Governor of San Domingo. These colonists and their leader took their cue for the treatment of the native population from the notorious predecessor of Diego Columbus, the suave but unscrupulous Nicolas de Ovando, of whose problems, administration, character and methods a word or two may not come amiss in showing the precise nature of the woes which now beset the unhappy red-men of Cuba.

Upon his second voyage to these waters in 1493 Columbus brought with him a fleet of seventeen ships and 1,500 men ready to try their fortunes in these rich islands of the West. In the night of the 27th of November, 1493, this imposing force reached the harbor of La Navidad, where a year before the settlement of the original forty had been left behind. A salute was fired to apprise the settlers of its arrival but there was no response and the following morning the admiral landed. His welcome is best described in the words of John Fiske in his incomparable work on "The Discovery of America" as

follows: * "On going ashore next morning and exploring the neighborhood, the Spaniards came upon sights of
dismal significance. The fortress was pulled to pieces and
partly burnt, the chests of provisions were broken open
and emptied; tools and fragments of European clothing
were found in the houses of the natives, and finally
eleven corpses, identifiable as those of white men were
found buried near the fort. Not one of the forty men
who had been left behind in that place ever turned up
to tell the tale. The little colony of La Navidad had
been wiped out of existence. From the Indians, however, Columbus gathered bits of information that made
a sufficiently probable story. It was a typical instance
of the beginnings of colonization in wild countries. In
such instances human nature has shown considerable
uniformity. Insubordination and deadly feuds among
themselves had combined with reckless outrages upon
the natives to imperil the existence of this little party of
rough sailors. The cause to which Horace ascribes so
many direful wars, both before and since the days of
fairest Helen, seems to have been the principal cause on
this occasion. At length a fierce chieftain named Caonabo, from the region of Xaragua, had attacked the Spaniards in overwhelming force, knocked their blockhouse
about their heads, and butchered all that were left of them.

* "The Discovery of America."—Copyright 1892, by John
Fiske. Houghton, Mifflin & Company, Boston, Mass.

"This was a gloomy welcome to the land of promise. There was nothing to be done but to build new fortifications and found a town. The site chosen for this new settlement, which was named Isabella, was at a good harbor about thirty miles east of Monte Christi. It was chosen because Columbus understood from the natives that it was not far from there to the goldbearing mountains of Cibao, a name which still seemed to signify Cipango. Quite a neat little town was presently built, with church, market-place, public granary, and dwelling-houses, the whole encompassed with a stone wall. An exploring party led by Ojeda into the mountains of Cibao found gold dust and pieces of gold ore in the beds of the brooks, and returned elated with this discovery. Twelve of the ships were now sent back to Spain for further supplies and reinforcements, and specimens of the gold were sent as an earnest of what was likely to be found."

The hostility between the red-man and the settler as thus indicated forced Columbus to expedients. Landing on shores that he had expected to find friendly and finding only a condition of warfare confronting him, foraging expeditions for food had to be undertaken which served only to make matters worse. "This state of things," Mr. Fiske continues, "led Columbus to devise a notable expedient yet one which was attended by deplorable results. In some of the neighboring islands lived the voracious Caribs. In fleets of canoes they would swoop upon the coasts of Hispaniola, capture men and women by the score, and carry them off to be cooked and eaten. Now Columbus wished to win the friendship of the Indians about him by defending them against these enemies, and so he made raids against the Caribs, took some of them captive, and sent them as slaves to Spain, to be taught Spanish and converted to Christianity, so that they might come back to the islands as interpreters, and thus be useful aids in missionary work. It was really, said Columbus, a kindness to these cannibals to enslave them, and send them where they could be baptized and rescued from everlasting perdition; and then again they could be received in payment for the cargoes of cattle, seeds, wine, and other provisions which must be sent from Spain for the support of the colony. Thus quaintly did the great discoverer, like so many other good men before and since, mingle considerations of religion with those of domestic economy. It is apt to prove an unwholesome mixture. Columbus proposed such an arrangement to Ferdinand and Isabella, and it is to their credit that, straitened as they were for money, they for some time refused to accept it. Slavery, however, sprang up in Hispaniola before anyone could have fully realized the meaning of what was going on. As the Indians were unfriendly and food must be had, while foraging expeditions were apt to end in plunder and bloodshed, Columbus tried to regulate matters by prohibiting such expeditions and in lieu thereof imposing a light tribute or tax upon the entire population of Hispaniola above fourteen years of age. As this population was dense, a little from each person meant a good deal in the lump. The tribute might be a small piece of gold or of cotton, and was to be paid four times a year. Every time that an Indian paid this tax, a small brass token duly stamped was to be given him to hang about his neck as a voucher. If there were Indians who felt unable to pay the tribute, they might as an alternative render a certain amount of personal service in helping to plant seeds or tend cattle for the Spaniards.

" No doubt these regulations were well meant, and if the two races had been more evenly matched, perhaps they might not so speedily have developed into tyranny. As it was, they were like rules for regulating the depredations of wolves upon sheep. Two years had not elapsed before the alternative of personal service was demanded from whole villages of Indians at once. By 1499 the island had begun to be divided into *repartimientos,* or shares. One or more villages would be ordered, under the direction of their native chiefs, to till the soil for the benefit of some specified Spaniard or partnership of Spaniards ; and such a village or villages constituted the *repartimiento* of the person or persons to whom it was assigned. This arrangement put the Indians into a state somewhat resembling that of feudal villenage; and this

13

was as far as things had gone when the administration of Columbus came abruptly to an end. . . . In 1502 the Spanish sovereigns sent to Hispaniola a governor selected with especial care, a knight of the religious order of Alcantara, named Nicolas de Ovando. He was a small, fairhaired man of mild and courteous manners, and had an excellent reputation for ability and integrity. We are assured on the most unimpeachable authority that he was a good governor for white men. As to what was most needed in that turbulent colony, he was a strict disciplinarian, and had his own summary way of dealing with insubordinate characters. When he wished to dispose of some such incipient Roldan he would choose a time to invite him to dinner, and then, after some polite and interesting talk, whereby the guest was apt to feel highly flattered, Ovando would all at once point down to the harbor and blandly inquire, ' In which of those ships, now ready to weigh anchor, would you like to go back to Spain?' Then the dumbfoundered man would stammer, ' My Lord, my Lord,' and would perhaps plead that he had not money to pay his passage. ' Pray do not let that trouble you,' said this well-bred little governor, ' it shall be my care to provide for that.' And so without further ceremony the guest was escorted straight from dinner-table to ship.

" But this mild-spoken Ovando was capable of strange deeds, and the seven years of his administration in His-

MAJOR GENERAL JOHN R. BROOKE, U. S. A.

paniola were full of horror. . . . His methods with Indians may be illustrated by his treatment of Anacaona, wife of the chieftain Caonabo who had been sent to Spain. Ovando heard that the tribe, in which this woman exercised great authority, was meditating another attack upon the Spaniards, and he believed that an ounce of prevention was worth a pound of cure. His seat of government was at the town of San Domingo, and Anacaona's territory at Xaragua was 200 miles distant. Ovando started at once with 300 foot soldiers and seventy horse. On reaching Xaragua he was received in a friendly manner by the Indians, who probably had no wish to offend so strong a force. Games were played, and Ovando proposed to show the Indians a tournament, at which they were much pleased, as their intense fear of the horse* was beginning to wear off. All the chieftains of the neighborhood were invited to assemble in a large wooden house, while Ovando explained to them the nature of the tournament that was about to take place. Meanwhile the Spanish soldiers surrounded the house. Ovando wore upon his breast the badge of his order, a small image of God the Father, and as he stood talking with the chiefs, when he knew the preparations to be complete, he raised his hand and touched the image. At

---

* Horses had but recently been imported by the Spanish into the Indies and were at first regarded with great manifestations of fear by the natives, who looked upon them as a species of wild beast.

this concerted signal the soldiers rushed in and seized the chiefs, and bound them hand and foot. Then they went out and set fire to the house, and the chiefs were all burnt alive. Anacaona was hanged to a tree, several hundred Indians were put to the sword, and their country was laid waste. Ovando then founded a town in Xaragua, and called it the City of Peace, and gave it a seal on which was a dove with an olive-branch." . . . Continuing in a later paragraph Mr. Fiske says: " We have seen how by the year 1499 communities of Indians were assigned in *repartimiento* to sundry Spaniards, and were thus reduced to a kind of villenage. Queen Isabella had disapproved of this, but she was persuaded to sanction it, and presently in 1503 she and Ferdinand issued a most disastrous order. They gave discretionary power to Ovando to compel Indians to work, but it must be for wages. They ordered him, moreover, to see that Indians were duly instructed in the Christian faith, provided that they must come to mass, ' as free persons, for so they are.' It was further allowed that the cannibal Caribs, if taken in actual warfare, might be sold into slavery. Little did the sovereigns know what a legion of devils they were letting loose. Of course the doings in Hispaniola always went the full length of the authority granted from Spain, and generally went far beyond. Of course the Indians were compelled to work, and it was not for wages; and of course, so long as there was no legal machinery for protecting the natives, any Indian might be called a cannibal and sold into slavery. The way in which Ovando carried out the order about missionary work was characteristic. As a member of a religious order of Knights, he was familiar with the practice of *encomienda,* by which groups of novices were assigned to certain preceptors to be disciplined and instructed in the mysteries of the order. The word *encomienda* means 'commandery' or 'preceptory,' and so it came to be a nice euphemism for a hateful thing. Ovando distributed Indians among the Spaniards in lots of 50 or 100 or 500, with a deed worded thus: 'To you, such a one, is given an *encomienda* of so many Indians, and you are to teach them the things of our holy Catholic Faith.' In practice the last clause was disregarded as a mere formality, and the effect of the deed was simply to consign a parcel of Indians to the tender mercies of some Spaniard to do as he pleased with them. If the system of *repartimientos* was in effect serfdom or villenage, the system of *encomiendas* was unmitigated slavery.

"Such a cruel and destructive slavery has seldom if ever, been known."

With so strenuous and effective an example as that of Ovando before his eyes Lieut.-Gov. Velasquez began his work in Cuba. The policies of Ovando had become the recognized policies for the Indies of the home government, and it was hardly to be expected that the more humane ideas of the subordinate should prevail against those of his superiors even granting that he had any such, which is not at all clear.  The enslavement of the peaceful native soon became a fact.  The systems of *repartimiento* and *encomienda* accomplished this wherever the inevitable combat between opposing forces and wanton massacre of the weaker was not sufficient.  The compulsion of the native to follow unaccustomed occupation, privations and disease, completed the work of ruin. The administration of Ovando in San Domingo reduced the number of natives from about a million and a half in 1492 [estimated] to 40,000 in 1509, and in 1537 the Contador of the Island of Cuba reported to the Queen of Spain that in twenty farms visited by him only 130 Indians were to be found, including those which had been imported !

Thus was the civilization of Spain introduced into these " Fortunate Islands."

# Chapter II

THE Velasquez expedition landed near Cape Maisi and its first permanent settlement was made in 1512 at the point now known as Baracoa, about one hundred miles to the northeast of Santiago, which thus enjoys the distinction of being the oldest city of Cuba. The first cathedral in Cuba was erected at Baracoa by Pope Leo X, in 1518. The avowed object of the expedition was that of colonization and subjugation. It was sufficiently successful from the Spanish point of view in this first effort at Baracoa, for two years later Velasquez was able to move further without endangering his base. The settlements of Trinidad and Santiago de Cuba the latter for a while being designated the capital, followed that of Baracoa in 1514, together with the establishment of points of communication with the Spanish Colonists at Jamaica, and the mainland, at Sancti Spiritus, Bayamo, Puerto Principe, and

19

San Cristobal de la Habana, now known as Batabano. Here, several centuries later, a conference having something to do with the relations of the Republic of Cuba after many years of strife and suffering beyond belief a tangible reality, and Cuba's Trustee, Uncle Sam. represented by Gen. Leonard Wood, took place. The name of the then Batabano was in 1519 transferred to a settlement on the site of the present city of Havana, which in 1552 became the capital of the Island. From the first in spite of her vicissitudes Cuba has managed to retain her original name, that by which it was known to its aboriginal owners and pronounced Koo-bah, although various attempts to change it were made from time to time. As we have seen, on some of the early and unveracious maps it was known as Isabella and Columbus had chosen to call it Juana. On the death of Ferdinand in 1516, Velasquez renamed it Fernandina. In later years its name was twice changed, once to Santiago after the patron Saint of Spain, St. Jago; and once Ave Maria in honor of the Virgin. Cuba seems however to have been destined to remain the fixed designation of this down-trodden region until a happier time should come.

The Government of all Spanish Colonies at this period was conducted upon the theory that all newly discovered territory belonged to the crown and the Viceroy, Governor, or Captain-General was the personal representative of the throne. He was clothed with despotic power, meting out punishment at his own sovereign will, and holding the lives of all beneath him completely in his hands. At the time of Velasquez's appointment his powers came to him through the medium of the servants of the crown at San Domingo, so that technically the Island was at once placed in a condition of double vassalage, and what the consequent drain upon her resources became it is not difficult to surmise. Velasquez continued to rule as Lieut.-Governor, or as Adelantado, under the eye of the Governor and Audiencia of San Domingo until 1524, when he died. Of his rule it has been said that it was energetic and efficient, characterized by vigor and intelligence. That he was harsh and cruel to the natives appears to be beyond all question, and it is recorded that one of the native chiefs, burned at the stake, by order of Velasquez, while undergoing his ordeal observed that he preferred " hell to heaven if there are Spaniards in heaven." Since the death of Velasquez in 1524, Cuba has had 135 rulers, of whom history records that, with few exceptions, " they did nothing toward the development of the Island or the welfare of the people," although clothed with despotic power almost from the beginning.

In judging them perhaps we should remember that like masters breed like servants, and an official whose mission it is to enrich the pockets of his King through the manipulation of powers granted to him as a prize, is not expected to be overnice in the methods he employs to extract revenue from the people beneath his sway. In some peculiar fashion which history does not explain at least two honest men appear to have obtained the Cuban appointment, Don Luis de Las Casas, and Don Francisco de Arrango, a native of Havana. The former attempted to break up the institution of slavery, while the latter as a native born Cuban was possessed of constructive ideas of Statesmanship which for a time bade fair to relieve the oppressive conditions by which his people were kept in grinding poverty. "Arguing before his home government in behalf of certain reforms Arrango told them that serious dissent permeated every class of the community, and was bid in return to employ a still more stringent system of rule. To this Arrango replied that force was not remedy, and that to effectually reform the rebellious they must first reform the laws. His earnest reason carried conviction, and finally won concession. By his exertions the staple productions of the island were so much increased that the revenue, in place of falling short of the expenses of the government as his enemies had predicted, soon yielded a large surplus. He early raised his voice against the iniquitous slave trade, and suggested the introduction of white labor, though he admitted that the immediate and wholesale abolition of slavery was impracticable. This was the rock on which he split, as it regarded his influence with the Spaniards in Cuba, that

22

MAJOR EUGENE F. LADD, U. S. V.
*Treasurer of the Island*

is, with the planters and rich property holders. Slavery with them was a sine qua non. Many of them owned a thousand Africans each, and the institution, as an arbitrary power as well as the means of wealth, was ever dear to the Spanish heart. Former and subsequent Captains-General not only secretly encouraged the clandestine importation of slaves, after issuing an edict prohibiting it, but profited pecuniarily by the business. It was owing to his exertions that the duty on coffee, spirits, and cotton was remitted for a period of ten years, and that machinery for the sugar plantations was allowed to be imported into Cuba from the United States free of all duty." *

It was this rare person among the Governors of Cuba who upon being offered a patent of nobility declined it, saying that "the King could make noblemen, but God only could make gentlemen." It is a vast pity that Arrango appears to have been the only exception in this connection to prove the rule.

In the interesting report of the United States Census Bureau accompanying the results of the Cuban Census of 1899, made under the direction of Lieut.-Col. J. P. Sanger, U. S. A., is a comprehensive statement of the workings of the Spanish theory of Colonial Administration as it affected Cuba, from which I quote. I quote at some length for the reason that in no better way can I hope to

* Due South.—Ballou

convey to the minds of those who read this story an adequate idea of how persistently and wickedly this struggling island has been oppressed by those who should have been most mindful of her interests. The economic sins of Spain are by no means the least with which she stands indicted.

"That, in the administration of her colonies, Spain was a bad exception to a general rule of liberal and generous government on the part of other countries toward their colonial dependencies is by no means the case. In fact, much the same ideas appear to have influenced all of them at the outset, although the results were different, as might be expected of governments having different origins, forms, and theories. The prevailing idea appears to have been that the political and economic interests of colonies were always to be subordinated to those of the home country, no matter how injurious the consequences, and, while in some instances this course was modified with most beneficial results, it was followed unremittingly by Spain to the end of her supremacy over Cuba. Aside from the fact that during the early history of Cuba Spain had little surplus population to dispose of, and that through the expulsion of the Jews and Moors she lost a large and valuable part of it, her trade restrictions, established at the beginning of the colonial period in her history and continued without essential modification for nearly three hundred years, would account, in some measure, for the slow increase in the population and industries of Cuba. These restrictions appear to have originated in the royal cedula of May 6, 1497, granting to the port of Seville the exclusive privilege of trade with the colonies. At the same time the *Casa de Contratacion,* or Council of Trade, was established, upon which was conferred the exclusive regulation of trade and commerce, although later the Council exercised its functions under the general control of the Council of the Indies. San Domingo, and later Vera Cruz, were the only colonial ports authorized to trade with Seville. In 1717 the trade monopoly of Seville was transferred, by royal order, to the port of Cadiz, in Spain. While Santiago was the capital of Cuba, trade between the island and the home ports mentioned was restricted to that place, and when, in 1552, the capital was transferred to Havana, that city became the sole port of entry until 1778, except during the English occupation of the island, 1762-63, when Havana was opened to free trade. By the royal decree of October 12, 1778, trade between Santiago, Trinidad, Batabano, and other Spanish ports was authorized. This privilege was extended to Nuevitas in 1784, to Matanzas 1793, Caibarien 1794, and Manzanillo and Baracoa in 1803. Prior to this, Cuban ports were practically under an embargo of the strictest kind. Even between the ports of Havana and Seville or Cadiz, there was no free communication, but all trading vessels were gathered into fleets, or *flotas,* from time to time, and made the voyage accompanied by Spanish war ships, partly for protection against freebooters and pirates, but chiefly to prevent trade with other ports. In 1765 this restriction was removed. The maritime laws regulating trade and commerce forbade trade even between the colonies, and as early as 1592 trade with foreigners was only permitted by special authority, and in 1614 and 1680 trade with foreigners was prohibited under pain of death and confiscation of the property concerned. The treaties of the period appear to have recognized these prohibitions as entirely justifiable under the rules of international intercourse as they existed at that time. Thus by the treaties of 1648 and 1714 between Spain and the Dutch provinces it was agreed by the contracting parties to abstain from trading in the ports and along the coast of the Indies belonging to each of the treaty nations. Again, by the treaty of Madrid between England and Spain, similar engagements were made, although article 10 provided that in case vessels arrived at the prohibited ports under stress or shipwreck they should be kindly received and permitted to purchase provisions and repair damages. This privilege was subsequently withdrawn by royal orders of January 20 and April 15, 1784, which prescribed that no vessel belonging to a foreign nation should be permitted to enter, even under the pretext of seeking shelter. The severity of these restrictions was modified later on and, by a royal order of January 8, 1801, Cuban ports were thrown open to the commerce of friendly and neutral nations. Other commercial privileges were granted in 1805, 1809, 1810, and 1812, due, in great measure, if not entirely, to the French invasion of the Peninsular and its effect on Spanish possessions in the West Indies and America. But these concessions to trade with Spanish colonies were but temporary, as by royal orders of January 10, November 17, and July 10, 1809, foreign commerce with Spanish-American ports was prohibited. Against these last restrictions of trade the various Spanish colonial Governors, and especially the Captain-General of Cuba, protested on the ground of the necessities of the colonies and the inability of Spain to meet them. These objections having been favorably considered by the Council for the Indies, foreign trade with Havana was extended for six months. Many other decrees and royal orders affecting trade with Cuba and the other Spanish colonies were promulgated during the period between 1775 and 1812, but they throw no additional light on this subject. It is plain that Spain was always averse to granting trade facilities to her colonies, and only did so for a time when forced by her necessities; but having once opened Cuban ports and to that extent established the privilege of foreign trade, which it was difficult to recall, the next step was to restrict it as far as possible by duties, tonnage, and port dues, and arbitrary tariffs imposed from time to time in such a way as to render foreign commerce unprofitable. Without going into details it may be said that up to 1824 duties on foreign commerce were much greater than on Spanish merchandise, and while from that year they were generally less restrictive, still they were always high enough to compel Cubans to purchase from Spanish merchants, who, as Spain did not herself produce what was needed, bought from French, German, American, or other sources, thereby raising prices far above what they would have been under a system less hampering. In fact, up to 1818 Cuba does not appear to have had a tariff system. In that year a tariff was promulgated making the duties twenty-six and one-half per cent on agricultural implements and forty-three per cent *ad valorem* on other foreign merchandise. This was modified in 1820 and 1822 and the duties reduced to twenty per cent on agricultural implements and thirty-seven per cent *ad valorem* on foreign industrial products. On all Spanish importations under this classification the duties were two-thirds less. The tariff of 1824 was less prohibitive. Not satisfied, apparently, with this arrangement for excluding foreign trade or with the amount of customs revenue, an export tariff was established in 1828 on sugar and coffee, which had by that time become important products. On sugar the duty was four-fifths of a cent per pound, and on coffee two-fifths of a cent per pound. If exported in foreign vessels, the duty on sugar was doubled and on coffee was increased to one cent per pound. With slight modifications these duties continued to August 1, 1891, when, under the McKinley tariff law, a reciprocal commercial agreement was proclaimed by President Harrison between Spain and the United States, which enabled Cuba to seek its nearest and most natural market. In a short time nearly the entire trade of Cuba was transferred to the United States, and Cuba enjoyed a degree of prosperity never before attained. But with the termination of this agreement by the tariff law of 1894, the old practice of differential, special, and discriminating duties against foreign trade was re-established, thus forcing upon the Cubans compulsory trade with Spain. There seems to be no question among impartial and intelligent judges as to the injurious effect of this system on the growth of Cuba's population and material progress, both largely dependent on commercial advantages. Another evil born of the system and given a certain amount of immunity through the reverses and disasters of the Spanish navy, in consequence of which Spain was unable to protect her commerce or fully enforce trade regulations, was smuggling, which began with trade restrictions and monopolies and has continued to this day, the amount of merchandise smuggled being, for many years, nearly equal to that regularly imported and exported. From smuggling on a large scale and privateering to buccaneering and piracy is not a long step, and under the name of privateers French, Dutch, English, and American smugglers and buccaneers swarmed the Caribbean Sea and Gulf of Mexico for more than two centuries, plundering Spanish *flotas* and attacking colonial settlements. Among the latter, Cuba was the chief sufferer. Sallying forth from Santo Domingo, Jamaica, the Tortugas, and other islands and keys, these marauders raided the island throughout the whole extent of its northern, eastern, and southern coast line, levying tribute, kidnapping individuals, and carrying off whatever was needed. In 1538 they attacked and burned Havana. In 1544 they attacked Baracoa, Matanzas, and Havana, which they again sacked and burned. In 1604 Giron, a French buccaneer, landed twice in Santiago, capturing the Morro, and in 1679 French buccaneers again raided the province. Incursions on a smaller scale were frequent, causing the Captain-General to issue an order requiring all men to go armed and all persons to retire to their homes after nightfall. By the terror they excited these raids retarded somewhat the development of agriculture by compelling the people to concentrate in the towns for protection. On the other hand, they stimulated the construction of fortifications in the harbor of Havana and other ports, which, a few years later, made them safe

BRIG. GEN. ADNA R. CHAFFEE, U. S. A.

against such incursions. Coupled with trade restrictions and extending throughout the entire life of Cuba as a dependency of Spain, excessive taxation has always prevailed. Apart from imports and exports, taxes were levied on real and personal property and on industries and commerce of all kinds. Every profession, art, or manual occupation contributed its quota, while, as far back as 1638, seal and stamp taxes were established on all judicial business and on all kinds of petitions and claims made to official corporations, and subsequently on all bills and accounts. These taxes were in the form of stamps on official paper, and at the date of American occupation the paper cost from 35 cents to $3 a sheet. On deeds, wills, and other similar documents the paper cost from 35 cents to $37.50 per sheet, according to the value of the property concerned. Failure to use even the lowest-priced paper involved a fine of $50. There was also a municipal tax on the slaughter of cattle for the market. This privilege was sold by the municipal council to the highest bidder, with the result that taxes were assessed on all animals slaughtered, whether for the market or for private consumption, with a corresponding increase in the price of meat. Another tax established in 1528, called the *derecho de averia,* required the payment of 20 ducats ($16) by every person, bond or free, arriving in the island. In 1665 this tax was increased to $22, and continued in force to 1765, thus

31

retarding immigration, and, to that extent, the increase of population, especially of the laboring class.
An examination of these taxes will show their excessive, arbitrary, and unscientific character, and how
they operated to discourage Cubans from owning property or engaging in many industrial pursuits tending to
benefit them and to promote the material improvement
of the island.

" Taxes on real estate were estimated by the tax inspector on the basis of its rental or productive capacity,
and varied from four to twelve per cent. Similarly, a
nominal municipal tax of twenty-five per cent was levied
on the estimated profits of all industries and commerce,
and on the income derived from all professions, manual
occupations, or agencies, the collector receiving six per
cent of all taxes assessed. Much unjust discrimination
was made against Cubans in determining assessable
values and in collecting the taxes, and it is said that
bribery in some form was the only effective defence
against the most flagrant impositions. Up to the year
1638 the taxes were collected by royal officers appointed
by the King, and their accounts were passed on by the
*audiencia* of Santo Domingo. In that year *contadores*
(auditors) were appointed who exercised fiscal supervision over the tax collectors, until, by royal *cedula* of
October 31, 1764, the intendancy of Havana was created,
the administration of taxes being conducted as in Spain.

# A GOVERNMENT MONOPOLY

Since 1892 the taxes have been collected by the Spanish Bank under a ten years' contract, the bank receiving a commission of five per cent. About eighteen per cent of the assessed taxes remained uncollected between 1886 and 1897, and the deficits thus caused were added to the Cuban debt, ever a subject of universal discontent. If to high taxes, high tariffs, and utter indifference, apparently, to the needs of the island be added a lack of banking facilities of all kinds, and a system of currency dependent entirely on the Spanish Government and affected by all its financial difficulties, we have some of the reasons why the economic development of Cuba has been slow. 'All her industrial profits were absorbed by Spain, leaving no surplus to provide for the accumulation of capital and the material progress of the island,' which was apparently regarded as a government monopoly, whose productive capacity was in no wise connected with its economic interests. Accordingly, such interests were invariably subordinated to those of Spain—with which they rarely accorded—no matter how injurious the result. That this course should have been followed in the early period of Spanish colonization is not strange. All sorts of economic experiments, based on what are now considered absurd economic theories, were tried about that time by European countries in vain efforts to promote national prosperity by entirely unnatural methods. Thus, for many years Cuba was prohibited, in common with other colonies, from the cultivation of raw products raised in Spain, thus reversing the theory and practice under which England subsequently developed her manufacturing industries at home, successfully colonized all parts of the habitable globe, and established her enormous colonial trade, by the very natural process of paying for the raw products of her colonies in manufactured articles. No nation in Europe during the sixteenth century was in a better condition than Spain to establish such a system, as she was essentially a manufacturing country. But with the expulsion of the Moors her manufactures were practically ruined; the wealth which for many years had poured in from the colonies in exchange for the supplies shipped them now passed through her to other countries in consequence of her extinguished industries, and she became little more than a clearing house for foreign products. Five-sixths of the manufactured articles used in Spain were imported, and foreigners, in direct violation of Spanish laws, soon carried on nine-tenths of the trade with her colonies. It may be said that results equally unfortunate appear to have attended all other branches of Spanish colonial government. Under a policy so shortsighted that it was blind to the most ordinary precautions, and long after repeated warnings should have suggested a greater measure of economic and political independence for Cuba, the entire system of Cuban government and administration was retained in the hands of Spanish officials to the exclusion of native Cubans, thus substituting for home rule a government which, however necessary in the earlier history of the island, became, with the lapse of centuries, an object of suspicion and hatred to a large majority of Cubans, as the medium through which Spain exercised despotic power over them and appropriated to herself the wealth of the island. That these feelings would have yielded to greater economic and political freedom, there can be no question. Political independence was not generally advocated at first. Autonomy under the protection of Spain was as far as the industrial classes cared to go, and had this been granted ten years earlier Cuba might and probably would have remained a Spanish colony. It was the economic rather than the political aspect of the island that concerned the greater part of its population. But in Cuba political and economic conditions were inseparable under the theory of colonial government which prevailed, and economic concessions were not to be thought of if the practice of stripping Cuba by the various means described without giving Cubans the least opportunity to prevent it in a peaceful way was to continue. That they would ever resort to force was not believed, or if believed, not feared, in the face of a despotic Governor-General with a local army and navy to enforce his authority and the whole power of Spain in reserve. Besides, the Cubans had given ample proof of their loyalty. But the rulers of Cuba, usually blind to its interests, were to test the loyalty of her people beyond the limits of endurance, and, as a result, to lose for Spain her 'ever faithful island.' A large number of the Governors of Cuba have been Spanish politicians, appointed without special reference to their fitness, but as a reward for services, personal or political, rendered to the Spanish Government. The resources of Cuba were always available to the home party in control for this purpose, which accounts in some measure for the unanimity of Spanish opinion respecting political concessions to the island. It was necessary that its control should remain absolutely in the hands of the Captains-General representing the home government; but there is very little question that had all of them exercised their authority with moderation, lightened the burden of taxation, removed or modified many trade restrictions, promoted public works, and used their authority to extend the influence of the Cubans in the administration of the island, the dominion of Spain might have been continued for years to come, as much of the political agitation would have been avoided; the gulf between Spaniards and Cubans would have been bridged over, until, through these and other influences, an adjustment of the economic situation would have brought peace and prosperity to the people."

But the peace and prosperity of the people of Cuba

have not been the object of the Spaniard from the beginning. In dealing with native or with settler, the object of the authorities at home has been that of plunder. Politicians of wrecked fortunes were sent here to recoup their fallen estate, by whatsoever means they might deem best and they have almost invariably made the most of their opportunity. In other words the " ever faithful island " has been a prey to the rapacious and the mercenary from the first moment of her appearance among the known lands of the earth, up to the moment when, as the Ward of the United States, she and her interests became the care of the authorities at Washington through the representatives of the latter chosen from the ranks of the Army establishment.

# Chapter III

INSTITUTION OF SLAVERY—HISTORY OF CUBAN SLAVE
TRADE—A PORTUGUESE DESCRIPTION—PRIVATEERS
—ATTACKS UPON HAVANA—FERNANDO DE SOTO—
FORTIFICATIONS—LA FUERZA—MORRO CASTLE—LA
PUNTA—TWO CENTURIES OF UNREST—SIR HENRY
MORGAN—TRIES TO ESTABLISH HEADQUARTERS IN
CUBAN WATERS—ESQUEMELING'S DESCRIPTION OF
CUBA, AND THE SACKING OF PUERTO PRINCIPE.

*B*UT it was not alone the rapacious rulers sent by
Spain to wring blood money from the veins
of the natives and settlers that constituted the
greatest of Cuba's woes. The gradual extinction
of the aboriginal, and the prime necessity of the
Spanish pioneer to have someone else do his work for
him—for these sons of Castille were not of that strenuous cast that settled upon the forbidding coasts of rock-
bound New England—resulted in the importation of
negro slaves into Cuba. In a letter from Ferdinand to
Ovando, Governor of San Domingo, in 1501, it was prohibited to admit Jews, Moors and new converts into the
Indies " but an exception was made in the case of the
negro slaves, who were allowed to pass, the officers of
the royal revenue to receive the money paid for their
permits." The negro was known already by the Spaniard
as a good worker and when the latter found that his systems of *repartimiento* and *encomienda* were working the

extinction of the red-man who tilled his fields, and delved in his mines, and in otherwise released him from the necessity for individual toil, face to face with a proposition which required a personal physical exertion he naturally turned to the consideration of available labor. Negro slavery solved this difficult problem for him and in 1517 the first license to import negroes into the West Indies was given by Charles V. This provided for the importation of 8,000 slaves in eight years, 1,000 of which were to go to Cuba. Quoting from the United States Census report on this subject we find that "a second monopoly on the same terms and for the same number was granted in 1523, but this grant was revoked and a license given to import 750 men and 750 women, 300 to go to Cuba. In 1527, 1,000 negroes were imported into Cuba; and again in 1528 a license was given to import 4,000 negroes into the Indies. The number of slaves imported between 1521 and 1763 is estimated by Humboldt at 60,000, and by 1790 the number had reached a total of 90,875. From 1790 to 1820 the importation of slaves into Havana, as shown by the returns of the custom-house, was 225,575, to which should be added one-fourth for those smuggled, making the total importation from 1521 to 1820, 372,449. Between this date and 1853 it is estimated that there were 271,659 importations, lawful and contraband, a total of 644,108, about one-third being females. From 1853 to 1880, when the slave trade was finally suppressed, over

200,000 slaves were smuggled into the island, making a grand total of between 950,000 and 1,000,000.

"It is not proposed to give here a detailed account of the Cuban slave trade or of negro slavery in the island. While it was fraught with all the horrors of this nefarious business elsewhere, the laws for the protection of slaves were unusually humane. Almost from the beginning slaves had a right to purchase their freedom or change their masters, and long before slavery was abolished they could own property and contract marriage. As a result the proportion of free colored to slaves has always been large. Of the efforts to abolish the slave trade in Cuba much might be written; it is sufficient for our purposes to state the principal facts. By the treaty of Vienna, 1815, to which Spain was a party, slavery was abolished. By a treaty with England signed September 24, 1817, Spain agreed to stop the slave trade May 30, 1820, in consideration of the sum of £400,000. Again, on June 28, 1835, another treaty was made with England abolishing the slave trade. In addition to these treaties the Spanish Government promulgated several decrees and laws after 1835 for the suppression of the slave trade and the abolition of slavery. Despite these measures, however, and the active cooperation of the native Cubans, who were zealously opposed to the slave trade, and the repeated protests of the British Government, it continued to 1880 with but little interruption. The correspondence between England and Spain fully explains the failure of Spain to enforce her laws and treaty engagements. Under what is now known as the Moret law, enacted by the Spanish Cortes July 4, 1870, the gradual abolition of slavery was commenced. The civil war in the United States and the Cuban insurrection of 1868-78 hastened it, as did the law of February 13, 1880, which abolished slavery. Nevertheless, it continued in remote parts of the island for several years thereafter, although generally abolished by the year 1887.

"The condition of the negro in Cuba for many years appears to have been far better than that of the colored population of our Southern States, or of any of the West India Islands under foreign control, and their personal privileges much greater. No hard and fast 'color line' has separated the colored and white Cuban population, although outside of the Cuban army there has not been much of what may be called social intercourse; but in respect to all public benefits, whether ecclesiastical, civil, or military, they have had about the same consideration from the Spanish Government as the white Cubans. No doubt the free association of colored and white Cubans resulted largely from the common struggle in which they were engaged against Spain, and the fact that the laws made no discrimination between them.

Colored men made up a large proportion of the Cuban army of 1895-98, some of them, like Antonio Maceo, holding high rank.

"While the statistics of Cuba show a larger proportion of colored than white criminals, the colored population are in some respects superior to the colored population of our Southern States, being more self-reliant, temperate, frugal, and intelligent, and since the abolition of slavery showing a strong desire to own their homes, to educate their children, and to improve their condition. In certain kinds of agriculture they are preferred to any other race, and in every discussion of the labor question in Cuba they must be seriously considered."

The slave-trade however has ever cursed those among whom it has been countenanced, and in the modern world the institution has owed its growth and maintenance to that perverted section of the European peninsular which held the Indies in its grip. It was one of the leading "industries" of the Portuguese, and a great boon to the shiftless and lazy Spaniard. For a generation too far removed from a period when it existed in the United States genuinely to comprehend its horrors, the picture drawn of the condition of the unfortunate black-man, after falling into the hands of his captors, quoted from Sir Arthur Helps's Spanish Conquest, by John Fiske, may not lack pertinence:

"A graphic description of the arrival of a company of

LIEUT. FRANK ROSS McCOY, U. S. A.

these poor creatures, brought by Lancarote in the year 1444, is given by an eye-witness, the kind-hearted Portuguese chronicler, Azurara. The other day, he says, which was the eighth of August, very early in the morning by reason of the heat, the mariners began to bring to their vessels, and to draw forth those captives whom, placed together on that plain, it was a marvellous sight to behold, for amongst them there were some of a reasonable degree of whiteness, handsome and well made; others less white, resembling leopards in their color; others as black as Ethiopians, and so ill-formed, as well in their faces as in their bodies, that it seemed to the beholders as if they saw the forms of the lower world. But what heart was that, how hard soever, which was not pierced with sorrow, seeing that company; for some had sunken cheeks, and their faces bathed in tears, looking at each other; others were groaning very dolorously, looking at the heights of the heavens—and crying out loudly, as if asking succor from the Father of nature; others struck their faces with their hands, throwing themselves on the earth; others made their lamentations in songs, according to the customs of their country, which, although we could not understand their language, we saw corresponded well to the height of their sorrow. But now—came those who had the charge of the distribution, and they began to put them apart one from the other, in order to equalize the portions; wherefore it was necessary to part children and parents, husbands and wives, and brethren from each other. Neither in the partition of friends and relations was any law kept, only each fell where the lot took him. And while they were placing in one part the children that saw their parents in another, the children sprang up perseveringly and fled unto them; the mothers enclosed their children in their arms and threw themselves with them upon the ground, receiving wounds with little pity for their own flesh, so that their offspring might not be torn from them! And so, with labor and difficulty, they concluded the partition, for, besides the trouble they had with the captives, the plain was full of people, as well of the town as of the villages and neighborhood around, who on that day gave rest to their hands, the mainstay of their livelihood, only to see this novelty."

In a foot-note to this quotation Mr. Fiske observes that " Azurara goes on to give another side to the picture, for being much interested in the poor creatures, he made careful inquiries and found that in general they were treated with marked kindness. They became christians, and were taught trades or engaged in domestic service; they were also allowed to acquire property, and were often set free. This however was in the early days of modern slavery. At a later date, when Portuguese cruisers caught negroes by the hundred and sold them at Seville, whence they were shipped to Hispaniola to work in the mines, there was very little to relieve the blackness of the transaction."*

Such were the industrial conditions for which Cuba had to thank the Spaniard. Natives annihilated, an exotic slavery was brought in to suffer and to toil, and to form the stock of a hybrid posterity which has not in anywise served to mitigate the woes of the long suffering island.

Additional trials now began for Cuba from the depredations of the soldiers and sailors of fortune all the world over. Adventurers, pirates, buccaneers, cast envious eyes upon this rich Pearl of the Antilles. In 1538 a French privateer, whose Commander naturally coveted a country so rich as to warrant the rapacity of the Spaniard to such a degree as has been indicated, attacked Havana and reduced it to ashes. and in consequence thereof the marvellous system of fortifications which at the close of Spanish supremacy existed in Cuba was instituted. Fernando de Soto, best known to us of to-day as the discoverer of the Mississippi River, was the Governor of Cuba at this time. He was a far more active and constructively useful person than the general run of Spanish Governors, for noting the ease with which his charge was a prey to the chance buccaneers of the Caribbean waters, he caused to be built at Havana—

* "The Discovery of America." Copyright, 1892, by John Fiske. Houghton, Mifflin & Co., Boston, Mass.

after the event—the Castillo de la Fuerza, a fortress of magnitude which is still one of the most instructive points of interest in Cuba. This was the first of those fortifications which modern warfare has rendered useless, but which, none the less, must inspire with wonder the twentieth century mind, which has yet to solve the problem of fire-proof construction, even in its armories. De Soto was the first independent Governor of Cuba, the Crown having realized in time that so valuable an island should not be doubly tribute to Spain, the " rake-off " to use a modern expression, being the perquisite of the Governor of San Domingo. It cost the Cubans no less, but the " unearned increment " of San Domingo was saved to the Spanish pocket.

La Fuerza apparently did not sufficiently impress the chance enemy, and of course Cuba had many at that time. The reason for this as it occurs to the modern mind, was that La Fuerza was built within the beautiful, and easily defendable, harbor, and not upon one of the two more obviously available points of defence at the mouth thereof —the very neck of a bottle. In 1554 the French again successfully attacked Havana, since 1552 the Capital of Cuba, and destroyed it. La Fuerza at the rear was unable successfully to destroy an enemy to the fore, or to defend the city against him. The second destruction of Havana resulted in the building of two more fortresses, that now known as Morro Castle, of horrific reputation to the

Easterly, and La Punta, a merely supplementary fortification, on the Westerly side of the narrow entrance to the harbor. Both these fortifications still remain, the one La Punta, with its sea wall, a healthful adjunct to the City of Havana. thanks to American modifications of its purposes, as will be seen later ; the other Morro Castle, a massive and enduring monument to Mediaeval Spain in Cuba. The past and the present find no more instructive contrast than is to be seen in Havana to-day by those who will observe the engineering efforts of Spain in the Morro on the one side of the harbor, and those of the United States at the point of La Punta on the other.

In the two centuries following the Island of Cuba hardly knew the meaning of the word rest. The country was kept in a constant state of turmoil and fear of invasion from the self-seeking interests of the old world, authorized and unauthorized. The colonizing fever of the age sent French, English and Dutch expeditions against them in the name of authority, and in addition to these were the raids of the buccaneers who were quite as alive to the riches of Cuba, and to the value of its harbors and rivers as a *rendezvous,* as their more legitimate, but no less rapacious competitors, preying authoritatively upon the unfortunate denizens of the island. As a fair example of what Cuba had to suffer in the days of which I write, I venture to include here a portion of the writings of one John Esquemeling, one of the followers of the famous Buccaneer Sir Henry Morgan, a hero who " sacked Porto Bello " and " burnt Panama ; " the leading pirate of his age who not infrequently descended upon Cuba for purposes of profit and convenience. As the testimony of an eye-witness it is interesting. Writing in 1684, Esquemeling says :

" Captain Morgan, seeing his predecessor and Admiral Mansvelt was dead, endeavored as much as he could, and used all the means that were possible, to preserve and keep in perpetual possession the Isle of St. Catharine, seated near that of Cuba. His principal intent was to consecrate it as a refuge and sanctuary to the Pirates of those parts, putting it in a sufficient condition of being a convenient receptacle or storehouse of their preys and robberies. To this effect he left no stone unmoved whereby to compass his designs, writing for the same purpose to several merchants that lived in Virginia and New England, and persuading them to send him provisions and other necessary things towards the putting the said island in such a posture of defence as it might neither fear any external dangers, nor be moved at any suspicions of invasion from any side that might attempt to disquiet it. At last all his thoughts and cares proved ineffectual by the Spaniards retaking the said island. Yet, notwithstanding, Captain Morgan retained his ancient courage, which instantly put him upon new designs. Thus he equipped at first a ship, with intention

48

to gather an entire fleet, both as great and as strong as he could compass. By degrees he put the whole matter in execution and gave order to every member of his fleet that they should meet at a certain port of Cuba. Here he determined to call a council and deliberate concerning what were best to be done, and what place first they should fall upon. Leaving these new preparations in this condition, I shall here give my reader some small account of the aforementioned Isle of Cuba, in whose ports this expedition was hatched, seeing I omitted to do it in its proper place.

" The Island of Cuba lies from East to West, in the latitude and situation of twenty to three and twenty degrees North, being in length one hundred and fifty German leagues and about forty in breadth. Its fertility is equal to that of the Island of Hispaniola. Besides which, it affords many things proper for trading and commerce, such as are hides of several beasts, particularly those that in Europe are called Hides of Havana. On all sides it is surrounded with a great number of small islands, which go altogether under the name of Cayos. Of these little islands the Pirates make great use, as of their own proper ports of refuge. Here most commonly they make their meetings and hold their councils, how to assault more easily the Spaniards. It is thoroughly irrigated on all sides with the streams of plentiful and pleasant rivers, whose entries form both secure and spacious ports, besides many other harbors for ships, which along the calm shores and coasts adorn many parts of this rich and beautiful island; all which contribute very much to its happiness, by facilitating the exercise of trade, whereunto they invite both natives and aliens. The chief of these ports are Santiago, Bayame, Santa Maria, Espiritu Santo, Trinidad, Xagoa, Cabo de Corrientes and others, all which are seated on the south side of the island. On the northern side hereof are found the following: La Havana, Puerto Mariano, Santa Cruz, Mata Ricos and Barracoa.

"This island has two principal cities, by which the whole country is governed, and to which all the towns and villages thereof give obedience. The first of these is named Santiago, or St. James, being seated on the south side, and having under its jurisdiction one-half of the island. The chief magistrates hereof are a Bishop and a Governor, who command over the villages and towns belonging to the half above-mentioned. The chief of these are, on the southern side, Espiritu Santo, Puerto del Principe and Bayame; on the north side it has Barracoa and the town called De los Cayos. The greatest part of the commerce driven at the aforementioned city of Santiago comes from the Canary Islands, whither they transport great quantity of tobacco, sugar, and hides; which sort of merchandize are drawn to the head city from the subordinate towns and villages. In former times the city of Santiago was miserably sacked by the Pirates of Jamaica and Tortuga, notwithstanding that it is defended by a considerable castle.

" The city and port De la Havana lies between the north and west side of the island. This is one of the most renowned and strongest places of all the West Indies. Its jurisdiction extends over the other half of the island, the chief places under it being Santa Cruz on the northern side and La Trinidad on the south. Hence is transported huge quantity of tobacco, which is sent in great plenty to New Spain and Costa Rica, even as far as the South Sea; besides many ships laden with this commodity that are consigned to Spain and other parts of Europe, not only in the leaf but also in rolls. This city is defended by three castles, very great and strong; two of which lie towards the port, and the other is seated upon a hill that commands the town. 'Tis esteemed to contain ten thousand families, more or less; among which number of people the merchants of this place trade in New Spain, Campeche, Honduras and Florida. All the ships that come from the parts aforementioned as also from Caracas, Cartagena and Costa Rica, are necessitated to take their provisions in at Havana, wherewith to make their voyage for Spain; this being the necessary and straight course they ought to steer for the South of Europe and other parts. The plate-fleet of Spain, which the Spaniards call Flôta, being homeward bound, touches here yearly, to take in the rest of their full cargo, as hides, tobacco and Campeche-wood.

"Captain Morgan had been no longer than two months in the above-mentioned ports of the South of Cuba, when he had got together a fleet of twelve sail, between ships and great boats; wherein he had seven hundred fighting men, part of which were English and part French. They called a council, and some were of opinion 'twere convenient to assault the city of Havana, under the obscurity of the night. Which enterprize, they said, might easily be performed, especially if they could but take a few of the ecclesiastics, and make them prisoners. Yea, that the city might be sacked, before the castles could put themselves in a posture of defence. Others propounded, according to their several opinions, other attempts. Notwithstanding, the former proposal was rejected because many of the Pirates had been prisoners at other times in the said city; and these affirmed nothing of consequence could be done, unless with fifteen hundred men. Moreover, that with all this number of people they ought first to go to the island De los Pinos, (the Isle of Pines), and land them in small boats about Matamano (Batabano), fourteen leagues distant from the aforesaid city, whereby to accomplish by these means and order their designs.

"Finally, they saw no possibility of gathering so great a fleet; and hereupon, with that they had, they concluded

OFFICERS' QUARTERS, CAMP COLUMBIA
*Showing Military Road constructed by Americans*

MILITARY ROAD OF AMERICAN CONSTRUCTION

to attempt some other place. Among the rest was found, at last, one who propounded they should go and assault the town El Puerto del Principe. This proposition he endeavored to persuade, by saying he knew that place very well, and that, being at a distance from the sea, it never was sacked by any Pirates; whereby the inhabitants were rich, as exercising their trade for ready money with those of Havana, who kept here an established commerce which consisted chiefly in hides. This proposal was presently admitted by Captain Morgan and the chief of his companions. And hereupon they gave order to every captain to weigh anchor and set sail, steering their course towards that coast that lies nearest to El Puerto del Principe. Hereabouts is to be seen a bay, named by the Spaniards El Puerto de Santa Maria. Being arrived at this bay, a certain Spaniard, who was prisoner on board the fleet, swam ashore by night, and came to the town of Puerto del Principe, giving account to the inhabitants of the design the Pirates had against them. This he affirmed to have overheard in their discourse, while they thought he did not understand the English tongue. The Spaniards, as soon as they received this fortunate advice, began instantly to hide their riches, and carry away what movables they could. The Governor also immediately raised all the people of the town, both freemen and slaves; and with part of them took a post by which of necessity the

Pirates were to pass. He commanded likewise many trees to be cut down and laid amidst the ways to hinder their passage. In like manner he placed several ambuscades, which were strengthened with some pieces of cannon, to play upon them on their march. He gathered in all about eight hundred men, of which he distributed several into the aforementioned ambuscades, and with the rest he begirt the town, displaying them upon the plain of a spacious field, whence they could see the coming of the Pirates at length.

"Captain Morgan, with his men, being now upon the march, found the avenues and passages to the town impenetrable. Hereupon they took their way through the wood, traversing it with great difficulty, whereby they escaped divers ambuscades. Thus at last they came into the plain aforementioned, which, from its figure, is called by the Spaniards, La Savana, or the Sheet. The Governor, seeing them come, made a detachment of a troop of horse, which he sent to charge them in the front, thinking to disperse them and by putting them to flight, pursue them with his main body. But this design succeeded not as it was intended. For the Pirates marched in very good rank and file, at the sound of their drums, and with flying colors. When they came near the horse, they drew into the form of a semi-circle, and thus advanced towards the Spaniards, who charged them like valiant and courageous soldiers for some while. But seeing that the Pirates were very dextrous at their arms, and their Governor, with many of their companions killed, they began to retreat towards the wood. Here they designed to save themselves with more advantage; but, before they could reach it, the greatest part of them were unfortunately killed by the hands of the Pirates. Thus they left the victory to these new-come enemies, who had no considerable loss of men in this battle, and but very few wounded, howbeit the skirmish continued for the space of four hours. They entered the town, though not without great resistance of such as were within; who defended themselves as long as was possible, thinking by their defence to hinder the pillage. Hereupon many, seeing the enemy within the town, shut themselves up in their own houses, and thence made several shots against the Pirates, who, perceiving the mischief of this disadvantage, presently began to threaten them, saying: If you surrender not voluntarily, you shall soon see the town in a flame, and your wives and children torn in pieces before your faces. With these menaces the Spaniards submitted entirely to the discretion of the Pirates, believing they could not continue there long, and would soon be forced to dislodge.

"As soon as the Pirates had possessed themselves of the town, they enclosed all the Spaniards, both men, women, children and slaves, in several churches; and gathered all the goods they could find by way of pillage. Afterwards they searched the whole country round about the town, bringing in day by day many goods and prisoners, with much provision. With this they fell to banqueting among themselves and making great cheer after their customary way, without remembering the poor prisoners, whom they permitted to starve in the churches. In the meanwhile they ceased not to torment them daily after an inhuman manner, thereby to make them confess where they had hid their goods, moneys and other things, though little or nothing was left them. To this effect they punished also the women and little children, giving them nothing to eat; whereby the greatest part perished.

" When they could find no more to rob, and that provisions began to grow scarce, they thought it convenient to depart and seek new fortunes in other places. Hence they intimated to the prisoners: They should find moneys to ransom themselves, else they should be all transported to Jamaica. Which being done, if they did not pay a second ransom for the town, they would turn every house into ashes. The Spaniards, hearing these severe menaces, nominated among themselves four fellow prisoners to go and seek for the above mentioned contributions. But the Pirates, to the intent they should return speedily with the ransoms prescribed, tormented several in their presence, before they departed,

with all rigor imaginable. After few days the Spaniards returned from the fatigue of their unreasonable
commissions, telling Captain Morgan: We have run up
and down, and searched all the neighboring woods and
places we most suspected, and yet have not been able
to find any of our own party, nor consequently any fruit
of our embassy. But if you are pleased to have a little
longer patience with us, we shall certainly cause all that
you demand to be paid within the space of fifteen days.
Captain Morgan was contented, as it should seem, to
grant them this petition. But, not long after, there came
into the town seven or eight Pirates, who had been rang-
ing in the woods and fields, and got thereabouts some
considerable booty. These brought among other prisoners a certain negro, whom they had taken with letters
about him. Captain Morgan having perused them,
found they were from the Governor of Santiago, being
written to some of the prisoners; wherein he told them:
They should not make too much haste to pay any ransom for their town or persons, or any other pretext.
But, on the contrary, they should put off the Pirates as
well as they could with excuses and delays; expecting
to be relieved by him within a short while, when he
would certainly come to their aid. This intelligence
being heard by Captain Morgan, he immediately gave
orders that all they had robbed should be carried on
board the ships. And withal, he intimated to the

Spaniards that the very next day they should pay their ransoms, forasmuch as he would not wait one moment longer, but reduce the whole town to ashes in case they failed to perform the sum he demanded.

" With this intimation Captain Morgan made no mention to the Spaniards of the letters he had intercepted. Whereupon they made him answer; that it was totally impossible for them to give such a sum of money in so short a space of time; seeing their fellow-townsmen were not to be found in all the country thereabouts. Captain Morgan knew full well their intentions, and, withal, thought it not convenient to remain there any longer time. Hence he demanded of them only five hundred oxen or cows, together with sufficient salt wherewith to salt them. Hereunto he added only this condition, that they should carry them on board his ships, which they promised to do. Thus he departed with all his men, taking with him only six of the principal prisoners, as pledges of what he intended. The next day the Spaniards brought the cattle and salt to the ships, and required the prisoners. But Captain Morgan refused to deliver them till such time as they had helped his men kill and salt the beeves. This was likewise performed in great haste, he not caring to stay there any longer, lest he should be surprised by the forces that were gathering against him. Having received all on board his vessels, he set at liberty the prisoners he had kept as hostages of his demands." *

So we have Cuba in the first two hundred and fifty years of her existence with, first her native population enslaved and annihilated by the invader, who because of his own love of thrift, and lack of shift, introduces the vile institution of slavery into her borders, and then is seemingly unable to defend that which he has wrested from its rightful owners, and wrought with iniquity, from other disreputable elements that have embarked upon enterprises of piratical intent. Despoiled by Spain, the island becomes the quest of the adventurer and the Buccaneer, and through the incompetence of the Conqueror is prey to the cupidity of all mankind.

How have the settlers of Cuba met these dreadful conditions?

* " The Buccaneers of America," by John Esquemeling. Edited by Henry Powell. London: Swan, Sonnenschein & Co. New York: Charles Scribner's Sons.

# Chapter IV

CUBAN INSURRECTIONS—THE FIRST IN 1717—THE CONSPIRACY OF 1823—THE UPRISING OF 1826—CONGRESS OF AMERICAN REPUBLICS—BOLIVAR—THE BLACK EAGLE—SPECIAL LAWS FOR CUBA—LOPEZ—HIS FILIBUSTERING EXPEDITION — THE CONSPIRACY OF VUELTA ABAJO—SPANISH REFORM COMMISSION—THE TEN YEARS' WAR—CAPITULATION OF ZANJON—REPRESENTATION IN THE CORTES—GOMEZ—WEYLER—RECONCENTRATION — INCIDENTAL NOTES — CAPTURE OF HAVANA BY LORD ALBEMARLE—LAS CASAS—SPANISH TROOPS IN CUBA—MOTIVES OF UNITED STATES.

*I*T would be impossible to suppose that Cuba so constantly harassed from without should remain always tranquil from within. Downtrodden, robbed, humiliated as they were, these people at last turned upon their incompetent rulers and demanded reforms, by which they might be guaranteed life and happiness at least, if indeed liberty were an unknown quantity in their days. It is therefore proper that we should narrate briefly the history of Cuban insurrection.

The turning of the Antillean worm was long in coming, and it was not until 1717 that any serious opposition to the insular government manifested itself. The effort was futile in results, although for a time it seemed to be marked by elements of success. The Governor of Cuba, Captain-General Vicente Roja, was compelled to withdraw from the island in the face of riots accompanied by much bloodshed. The principal cause of this outbreak was not, however, due to a lack of protection from outside enemies, but to the tyrannical imposts of those within Cuba's borders. Indeed the internal trouble has been the besetting vexation of Cuba. She has from this first beginning resented the impositions of her rulers more than she has feared the depredations of her exterior foes—and properly so. Cuba's sufferings, deep as these have been, have been greatest at the hands of those sent to protect her interests, not from the depredations of the stranger outside her gates. She has been robbed not so much by her avowed enemies as by the guardians of her peace. The cause of the insurrection in Roja's administration was his attempt to enforce the Government monopoly in tobacco. The trouble was of short duration, though of seeming proportions at first. Roja fled, but returned and nothing was gained by the outbreak, save ultimate effect in that it bred in the people of Cuba a feeling that with concerted action something might be done to relieve intolerable conditions. The future insurrections in the island are adequately summed up in Colonel Sanger's report on the Census of Cuba, to the War Department at Washington, from which I quote as follows: " Apart from uprisings among the negroes, stimulated no doubt by the success of their race over the French in the neighboring island of San Domingo there were no other attempts at insurrection

on the part of Cubans until after the conspiracy of
1823, planned by a secret society known as the ' Soles de
Bolivar.' This conspiracy resulted from the attempt of
Captain-General Vives to carry out the instructions of
Ferdinand VII, after the abrogation of the Spanish liberal
constitution of 1812, and was intended as a protest against
a return to absolutism in Cuba; but, apparently,' it failed
of effect, and there was no relaxation of efforts to establish the old order.   The conspiracy was of a serious character and extended over the entire island, but centered
in Matanzas, where among the revolutionists was Jose
Maria Heredia, the Cuban poet.   The effort failed,
and the leader, Jose Francisco Lemus, and a large number of conspirators were arrested and deported.   A feeling of bitter resentment against the Government was the
result, and a period of agitation and public demonstration followed.   Frequent uprisings were attempted in
1824, but failed.

" It would have been well for Spain had Ferdinand VII
been warned by these events and endeavored, by concilia-
tory measures, to allay such manifest feelings of discontent.   But neither he nor his advisers would see the
' handwriting on the wall.'   The political agitation continued, and in 1826 a small uprising took place in Puerto
Principe, directed by the Sociedad de la Cadena, and
aimed against the abuses of the regiment Leon quartered
there.   The same year (June 22) the Congress of Ameri-

CLASS ROOM FOR BOYS

A SMALL CUBAN FAMILY

can Republics assembled at Panama, to which the Presi·
dent of the United States appointed Mr. John Sergeant, of
Pennsylvania, and Mr. Richard Anderson, of Kentucky,
as envoys extraordinary and ministers plenipotentiary.
Mr. Anderson was United States minister to Colombia
and died en route to the congress, which had adjourned
before Mr. Sergeant arrived, to meet at Tacabaya. But
it did not meet again, and consequently the United States
delegates took no part in its deliberations.

" The objects of this congress, as set forth in the correspondence, were to urge the establishment of liberal principles of commercial intercourse, in peace and war, the
advancement of religious liberty, and the abolition of slavery, to discuss the relations of Hayti, the affairs of Cuba
and Porto Rico, the continuation of the war of Spain on
her Spanish colonies, and the Monroe doctrine which announced as a principle, ' that the United States could not
view any interposition for the purpose of oppressing them
(governments in this hemisphere whose independence had
been declared and acknowledged by the United States),
or controlling in any other manner their destiny, by any
European power in any other light than as a manifestation of an unfriendly disposition toward the United
States.'

" While the United States no doubt sympathized with
the objects of the congress, the debates in the Senate and
House of Representatives indicated a desire to avoid inter-

ference with Spain, a pseudo friendly nation, or the slavery question, and that it was not prudent to discuss questions which might prove embarrassing to the United States if called on to consider them at a future time. As a result, the American delegates were given limited powers, and this, coupled with the conservative attitude of the United States, resulted in the failure of the congress to achieve any result.

" The year before Francisco Agüero and Manuel Andres Sanches, a second lieutenant in the Colombian army, had been sent from Cuba to the United States and to Colombia to urge their interference and assistance. An expedition was organized in Colombia to be led by the famous Colombian patriot, Simon Bolivar, but the failure of the Panama congress caused the abandonment of the expedition. On the return of the emissaries to Cuba they were arrested, tried and executed. Following this effort, in 1830, a revolution was planned by the society of the 'Black Eagle,' a Masonic fraternity having its base of operations in Mexico, with secondary bases in Havana and at various points throughout the island. The attempt failed, and several of the conspirators received sentence of death, afterwards commuted by Captain-General Vives to life imprisonment. The object of the conspiracy was the independence of Cuba, the pretext a report that the island was to be ceded to Great Britain.

" In 1836 the constitution of 1812 was reestablished in

Spain, but proved of no benefit to Cuba. On the contrary, the deputies sent from Cuba to the constitutional convention in Madrid were excluded, and, by a royal decree of 1837, the representation in the Cortes which had been given Cuba in 1834 was taken away, and it was announced that Cuba would be governed by special laws. These, the Cubans claim, were never published. From this time to 1847 several uprisings or insurrections occurred throughout Cuba, followed in that year by a revolutionary conspiracy organized by Narciso Lopez, and having in view the liberation of the island or its annexation to the United States. It had been arranged to make the first demonstration on the 4th of July, in the city of Cienfuegos, but the plot was made known to the Spanish Governor, and Lopez and his companions fled to the United States, where, in 1849, they organized a filibustering expedition, which was prevented from leaving by the vigilance of the Government. In 1850 Lopez organized a second expedition, which sailed from New Orleans May 10 and landed with 600 men at Cardenas, attacking its small garrison. A portion surrendered with Governor Ceniti and the remainder went over to the insurgents. As the uprising upon which Lopez depended did not take place, he reembarked the same day and made his escape to Key West.

"Undeterred by these failures, he organized a third expedition of 480 men in 1851, which sailed from New

Orleans and landed, August 12, at Playitas, near Bahia Honda, 55 miles west of Havana. Colonel Crittenden, of Kentucky, with 150 men, formed part of the force. On landing Lopez advanced on Las Pozas, leaving Colonel Crittenden in El Morillo. Meeting a Spanish force under General Enna, Lopez was defeated after a gallant fight, his force dispersed and he with some 50 of his men was captured and taken to Havana, where he was garroted. In attempting to escape by sea Crittenden and his party were overtaken and on the 16th of September were shot at the castle of Atares.

"In the same year an uprising took place in Puerto Principe, led by Juaquin de Agüero, but the movement came to naught and he and several of his companions were executed. Following the attempt of Agüero came the conspiracy of Vuelta Abajo, organized in 1852 by Juan Gonzalez Alvara, a wealthy planter of the province of Pinar del Rio. Associated with him were several other prominent Cubans, and among them Francisco de Fras, Count of Pozos Dulces. This attempt at revolution was discovered and the leading conspirators arrested. They were tried and sentenced to death, but were finally transported under sentence of life imprisonment. Meantime the Liberal Club of Havana and the Cuban Junta in New York were raising money and organizing expeditions destined for Cuba. Some of them sailed, and in 1859 an attempt was made to land at Nuevas Grandes. But these expeditions accomplished little, except to keep alive the spirit of revolution.

"From this time to the outbreak of the revolution of 1868 the condition of Cuban affairs does not appear to have improved. Taxes continued excessive and duties exorbitant, reaching at times an average of 40 per cent *ad valorem* on all imports, and so distributed as practically to prohibit trade with any country except Spain. Small uprisings and insurrections were frequent and there were many executions. Meanwhile the results of the civil war in the United States, and more particularly the abolition of slavery, encouraged the Cubans to hope for liberal reforms, especially in the trade and industries of the island, but no concessions appear to have been made until the year 1865, when, by a royal decree of November 25, a commission was appointed by Isabella II to consider the question of reforms in the administration of Cuba. Nothing came of it, however, although it afforded an opportunity to the few Cuban delegates who were present to formulate their views. They demanded greater political and economic liberty, a constitutional insular government, freedom of the press, the right of petition and assembly, the privilege of holding office, and representation in the Cortes. It would have been well for Spain had she listened to these complaints and made some effort to satisfy them, but nothing was done and as a result the revolution of 1868 generally known as the 'Ten Years'

War,' was commenced at Yara in the province of
Puerto Principe. It was ended by the capitulation of
Zanjon, February 10, 1878, and in its more serious phases
was confined to the provinces of Santiago and Puerto
Principe. No battles or serious engagements were
fought, although a guerrilla warfare of great cruelty and
intensity was carried on. While the casualties of the
fighting were comparatively few for a war of such duration, there were many deaths from disease, executions,
and massacres, and the Spanish troops suffered severely
from yellow fever, which prevailed at all times in the
sea-coast cities.

" The effect of the ten years' war on the material condition of Cuba cannot be stated with accuracy. The
population had increased in the ten years previous to the
outbreak at the rate of 17 per cent; during the war, and
for ten years after, the increase was but 6 per cent. A
great number of lives and a large amount of property
were destroyed, and an enormous debt was incurred,
while taxes of all kinds increased threefold. The war
is said to have cost the contestants $300,000,000, which
was charged to the debt of Cuba. By the capitulation
of Zanjon Spain agreed to redress the grievances of Cuba
by giving greater civil, political, and administrative privileges to the people, with forgetfulness of the past and
amnesty for all then under sentence for political of-
fenses. It has been claimed by Cubans that these

promises were never fulfilled, and this and the failure of the Cortes to pass the bill reforming the government of Cuba, introduced in 1894 by Señor Maura, minister for the colonies, are generally given as the causes of the last rebellion. On the other hand, Spain has always insisted that every promise was observed, and that even more was granted than was asked for or stipulated in the articles of capitulation. Thus, by the decree of March 1, 1878, Cuba and Porto Rico were given representation in the Spanish Cortes, upon the basis of their respective populations, and the provincial and municipal laws of 1877 promulgated in Spain were made applicable to Cuba. By proclamation of March 24, 1878, full amnesty was given to all, even to Spanish deserters who had served in the insurgent army; on May 23, 1879, the penal code of Spain and the rules for its application were given effect in Cuba; on April 7, 1881, the Spanish constitution, full and unrestricted, as in force in Spain, was extended to Cuba by law; in 1885 the Spanish law of civil procedure was given to Cuba, and on July 31, 1889, the Spanish civil code, promulgated in 1888, was put in operation in Cuba and Porto Rico.

"After examining all the evidence, however, the student of Cuban history will probably conclude that while the Spanish government was technically correct in claiming to have enacted all laws necessary to make good her promises, there was a failure usually to execute them, and that, as a matter of fact, political conditions in Cuba remained practically as before the war, although very much improved on the surface." The promised reforms and the general amnesty to insurgents were granted only in consideration of the latter abandoning the revolution and laying down their arms, which requirement the insurgents complied with. But "Spain unhesitatingly violated the agreement with a cynical disregard of good faith, her promise of amnesty was only partially kept, and she imprisoned or executed many who had been engaged in the insurgent cause, while the promised reforms were either totally neglected or carried out by some mockery which had neither reality nor value." *

"A serious permanent fall in the price of sugar in 1884 and the final abolition of slavery in 1887 added to the economic troubles of the people, and in conjunction with continued political oppression, kept alive the feelings which had brought on the war. The Cubans believed that notwithstanding the capitulation of Zanjon they were still mere hewers of wood and drawers of water, with but little voice in the government of the island, and that Spain was the chief beneficiary of its wealth. And such would appear to have been the fact if the following figures, taken from official sources, can be relied upon: From 1893 to 1898 the revenues of Cuba,

* The War With Spain, by Henry Cabot Lodge. Copyright, 18,9, by Harper & Bros.

under excessive taxation, high duties, and the Havana lottery, averaged about $25,000,000 per annum, although very much larger in previous years, depending on the financial exigencies of the Spanish Government." In 1860 they contributed $29,610,779; in 1880. $40,000,000 and in 1882, $35,860,246.77. "Cuba was expected to contribute *whatever was demanded.* Of this amount, the statement continues, $10,500,000 went to Spain to pay the interest on the Cuban debt, $12,000,000 were allotted for the support of the Spanish-Cuban army and navy and the maintenance of the Cuban government in all its branches, including the church, and the remainder, less than $2,500,000, was allowed for public works, education, and the general improvement of Cuba, independent of municipal expenditures. As the amounts appropriated annually in the Cuban budget were not sufficient to cover the expenditures and there was a failure to collect the taxes, deficits were inevitable. These were charged to the Cuban debt, until, by 1897, through this and other causes, it aggregated about $400,000,000, or an amount per capita of $283.54—*more than three times as large as the per capita debt of Spain and much larger than the per capita debt of any other European country.*

"Under such perverted economic management," Colonel Sanger concludes, "it is not surprising that another rebellion was planned, and that the war of 1895-1898 followed." The result of Spain's "treachery and of the bloodshed which accompanied it, and of the increased abuses in government which followed it was that the Cubans again prepared for revolt, and in February 1895, another revolution broke out."

The detailed story of the revolution of 1895-98 is too long to be narrated here. One who desires a full and vivid picture of all that Cuba endured at that time cannot do better than to read the opening chapters of Mr. Charles M. Pepper's work *Tomorrow in Cuba*. For our immediate purpose it suffices to say that under the leadership of men like José Marti, Maximo Gomez and Generals Garcia and Maceo the insurgents formed a government, and carried on a vigorous guerrilla warfare which soon set the whole island aflame, drove Martinez Campos into a confession of failure and brought the unspeakable Weyler with his horrors and atrocities into action. " The real head and front of this Rebellion was Maximo Gomez, a man of marked ability and singular tenacity of purpose. His plan was to refuse all compromises, to distribute his followers in detached bands, to ravage the country, destroy the possibility of revenue and win in the end either through the financial exhaustion of Spain or by the intervention of the United States, one of which results he believed "—and as the event showed, rightly— " must come if he could only hold on long enough."*

* "The War With Spain," by Henry Cabot Lodge. Copyright, 1899, by Harper & Bros.

# ENTER WEYLER

The sufferings of Cuba under the rule of Weyler form one of the most abhorrent pages in all history. General Weyler entered the Cuban capital in February 1896. He was already known as the Butcher thanks to his reputation for corrupt and cruel practices in previous public capacities, notably in the Philippines and in the suppression of riots at Barcelona. " His military movements were farcical, consisting in marching columns out here and there from garrisoned posts, having an ineffective brush with the Cubans, and then and there withdrawing the troops, with as little effect as the proverbial King of France who marched up the hill. The insurgents continued their operations without serious check; they broke through the trochas, swarmed into Pinar del Rio, wandered at will about the country, and carried their raids even into the suburbs of Havana. Weyler, who seems never to have exposed himself to fire, but to have confined his operations in the field to building more trochas, made his few military progresses by sea, and preferred to stay in Havana, where he could amass a fortune by blackmailing the business interests, and levying heavy tribute on all the money appropriated to public uses by the bankrupt and broken treasury of Spain. If, however, Weyler was ineffective as a commander in the field and no lover of battle, he showed that he was energy itself in carrying out a campaign of another kind, which was intended to destroy the people of the island, and

73

which had the great merit of being attended with no risk
to the person of the Captain-General. A large portion of
the Cuban population in the country were peasants taking
no part in the war, and known as 'pacificos.' They were
quiet people, as a rule, and gave no cause for offence,
but it was well known that their sympathies were with
the insurgents, and it was believed that they furnished
both supplies and recruits to the rebel forces. Unable
to suppress or defeat the armed insurgents, the Spanish
government characteristically determined to destroy these
helpless 'pacificos.' Accordingly an edict, suggested apparently by Weyler, was issued on October 21, 1896,
which applied to Pinar del Rio, and was afterwards extended to all the island, and which ordered the army to
concentrate all the pacificos, practically all the rural population, in the garrisoned towns. These wretched people
were to be driven in this way from their little farms,
which were their only means of support, and herded in
the towns and in the suburbs of Havana, where they
had nothing before them but starvation, or massacre at
the hands of Spanish soldiers and guerrillas. Whether
the idea of this infamous order originated in Havana or
Madrid is not of much consequence. The Queen-Regent,
for whom some persons feel great sympathy, because
she is an intelligent woman and the mother of a little
boy, set her hand to the decree which sent thousands
of women and children to a lingering death, and the

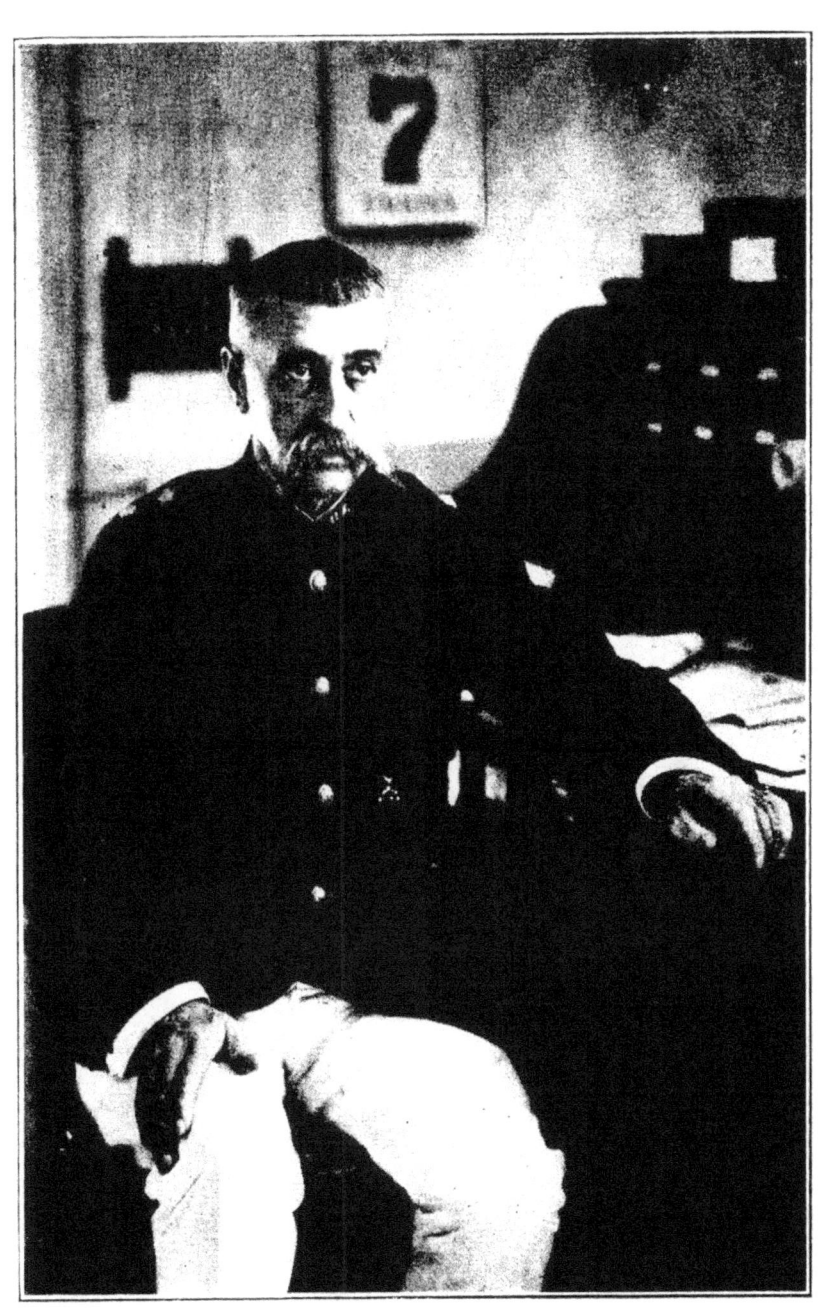

BRIG. GEN. WILLIAM LUDLOW, U. S. A.

whole government of Spain is just as responsible for all the ensuing atrocities as Weyler, who issued the concentration edict and carried it out with pitiless thoroughness and genuine pleasure in the task.

" By March, 1896, Spain had sent 121,000 soldiers to the island, which gave her, at that time with the forces already in Cuba, 150,000 men. Her debt was piling up with frightful rapidity; the insurgent policy of preventing the grinding of the sugar-cane was largely successful, had paralyzed business, and wellnigh extinguished the revenues. It was apparent to all but the most prejudiced that even if the insurgents could not drive the Spaniards from Cuba, the island was lost to Spain. With 200,000 soldiers in 1897 Spain had utterly and miserably failed to put down the rebels, who never had in arms, in all parts of the island, over 35,000 men. The Spanish government could give protection neither to its own citizens nor to those of foreign nations, nor could it even offer security to business, agriculture, or property. So Spain, impotent and broken, but as savage and cruel as she had ever been in her most prosperous days, turned deliberately from the armed men she could not overcome to the work of starving to death the unarmed people, old and young, men and women, whom she could surely reach." *

* " The War With Spain," by Henry Cabot Lodge. Copyright, 1899, by Harper & Bros.

Incidentally Cuba's history has amounted in general, outside of the details we have specified, to this: in 1762 the Capital, Havana, was captured by an English fleet and army under the command of Lord Albemarle, the fleet consisting of 200 vessels of all classes and the army of 14,041 men. These were opposed in an obstinate defence, largely due to the fortifications, by a Spanish force of 27,610 men. The siege lasted from the 6th of June until the 14th of August when the city capitulated. There was then a " Treaty of Paris " under the provisions of which the spoils of the invader amounted to £735,185 and this paid " Cuba was returned to the Spaniards." And then according to the authority who writes the article on Cuba for the *Encyclopaedia Brittanica* " the true era whence its importance and prosperity are to be dated " began. He continues:" The administration of Las Casas, who arrived as captain-general in 1790, is represented by all Spanish writers as a brilliant epoch in Cuban history. He promoted with indefatigable perseverance a series of public works of the first utility, introduced the culture of indigo, extended the commercial importance of the island by removing as far as his authority extended the trammels imposed upon it by the old system of privilege and restriction, and made noble efforts to effect the emancipation of the enslaved native Indians. By his judicious administration the tranquillity of the island was maintained uninterrupted at the time of the revolution in San Domingo; although, as is generally believed, a conspiracy was formed at the instigation of the French among the free people of color in Cuba. In 1795 a number of French emigrants arrived from San Domingo. In 1802 Jesu Maria, a populous suburb of Havana, was destroyed by a fire, which deprived 11,400 people of their habitations. On the deposition of the royal family in Spain by Napoleon (the news of which arrived in July, 1808) every member of the Cabildo took oath to preserve the island for the deposed sovereign, and declared war against Napoleon. Since that time the island has been ruled over by a succession of governor-captain-generals from Spain, armed with almost absolute authority, some of whom have conducted themselves honorably, while the names of others are loaded with infamy, the office having been frequently sought and bestowed only as the means of acquiring a fortune. The deprivation of political, civil, and religious liberty, and exclusion from all public stations, combined with a heavy taxation to maintain the standing army and navy, have resulted in a deadly hatred between the native Cubans and the mass of officials sent from Spain. This has manifested itself in frequent risings for greater privileges and freedom."

These uprisings have been amply covered in the preceding paragraphs of this chapter, but it is interesting to note in connection with these the authoritative statement of this observer that "in a debate on Cuban affairs in the

Cortes of Madrid in November, 1876, it was stated that, during the past eight years, in attempting to crush the insurgents, Spain had sent to Cuba 145,000 soldiers and her most favored commanders, but with little or no results. On the other hand, Cuba under the perpetual apprehension of the rebellion, has seen her trade decreased, her crops reduced, and her creoles deserting to the United States and Spanish republics; and her taxes have been trebled in vain to meet the ever-increasing expenses and floating debts."

Now what has Uncle Sam's attitude been toward these people for so long a time as he has himself been a person of independent circumstances? He had had this sick neighbor for over a century—from 1776 until 1898. What have been the relations between himself and his Cuban cousin—since 1898 his ward? He has been accused of cherishing notions of conquest in connection with Cuba. Selfishness has been his alleged motive in all his dealings with the Cuban question.

What are the facts of history to prove this assumption one way or the other? Could he have acquired possession of Cuba long ago, properly and quietly, or not? It is worth while in considering the United States as a Trustee of Cuban interests to look into this question somewhat. We shall deal with the question frankly and leave the reader to form his own conclusions.

# Chapter V

*T*HE wail of Cuba first reached the ears of the United States—which had troubles of its own —during the Administration of James Monroe, President in 1823, which established in Spanish American matters at least a policy of "reserve and caution." *   The receptivity of our National ear is not to be attributed to American philanthropy, but to the conditions brought up by the question involved in the Monroe Doctrine, invented by John Quincy Adams and still a blessing.   Should Cuba pass into the control of any other power—and incidentally should the principles of the slave territory of the United States, be menaced by the existence of free negroes upon an adjacent island? Adams as Secretary of State in April, 1823, wrote to the American Minister at Madrid: "It is scarcely possible to resist the conviction that the annexation of Cuba to our Federal Republic will be indispensable to the continuance and integrity of the Union."   Prior to this— in 1820—in response to a proposition from the Portuguese Minister that the United States and Portugal as "the two great powers of the Western hemisphere should concert together a grand American system," Mr. Adams

* Morse's "Life of John Quincy Adams."

79

made reply, "as to an American system, we have it; we constitute the whole of it; there is no community of interests or of principles between North and South America." "This sound doctrine," says Mr. Morse, the biographer of Adams, "was put forth in 1820; and it was only modified during a brief period in 1823, in face of the alarming vision not only of Spain and Portugal restored to authority, but of Russia in possession of California and more, France in possession of Mexico, and perhaps Great Britain becoming mistress of Cuba." Adams deemed the supposition that England or Spain could long retain their possessions on this side of the Atlantic a physical, moral and political absurdity. Yet while Secretary of State, and later as President, he did not reach out the long arm of Uncle Sam for the acquisition of a territory richer than Florida, and in point of fact the stronghold of Spanish power in the Western hemisphere. He was in favor of acquiring Louisiana, Canada and Cuba—an Imperialist of the first order—and even "encroachments never seemed distasteful to him." Cuba however remained where it was and the man who through the medium of another defied the rest of the known world to enter into the sphere of Uncle Sam's influence, left the Cuban in the thrall of Spain without an uplifting of his finger to make it otherwise. Doubtless there was policy in this but the fact remains. Cuba might then and there have become the property of Uncle Sam, and Uncle Sam turned his back upon the bargain.

All the more remarkable was this failure to seize upon opportunity because of the inevitable and irrepressible conflict which had for sometime been raging between the United States and the powers of the old world, for territorial supremacy in the Western hemisphere. As Mr. Henry Cabot Lodge points out in his brief history of the War with Spain, " the irrepressible conflict between Spain on the one side and England and Holland on the other, after the former had been crippled in Europe, was transferred from the Old World to the New. They seemed at first very remote from each other in the vast regions of the American continents, but nevertheless the two opposing forces, the two irrevocably hostile systems, were always drawing steadily together, with the certainty that when they met one of them must go down before the other. The Seven Years' War drove France from eastern North America, and fixed forever the fate of that region. It was to be English, not French:

The lilies withered where the lion trod.

The expulsion of France not only removed the long-standing northern peril to the English colonies, but swept away the last barrier between them and Spain. In the American Revolution, France, seeking her revenge for the conquests of Pitt, forced Spain to become her ally against England: but Spain had no love for the rebellious colonists. A treacherous nominal friend, she tried to wrest advantage from their weakness, and to secure to herself in final possession the Mississippi valley and the great Northwest. Failing in this, she sought, after American independence had been won, by false and insolent diplomacy, and by corrupting intrigues among the Western settlers, to check the American advance across the continent. It was all in vain. Through woodland and savanna, over mountain and stream, came the steady tramp of the American pioneer. He was an adventurer, but he was also a settler, and what he took he held. He carried a rifle in one hand, he bore an axe in the other, and where he camped he made a clearing and built a home. The two inevitable antagonists were nearing each other at last, for they were face to face now all along the western and southern borders of the United States. The time had come for one to stop, or for the other to give way. But there was no stopping possible in the Americans, and through the medium of French ownership the Louisiana purchase was made, the Mississippi became a river of the United States, and their possessions were stretched across the continent even to the slopes of the Rocky Mountains. Still not content, the Americans pressed upon the southern boundary until, in 1819, they forced Spain, in order to avoid war, to sell them Florida and the northern coast of the Gulf of Mexico as far as Louisiana. Meantime, inspired by the example of the United States in rejecting foreign dominion, and borne forward by the great democratic movement which, originating in America, had swept over Europe, the Spanish colonies rose in arms and drove Spain from Central and South America.

"A few years passed by, and then the restless American advance pressed on into Texas, took it from Mexico, and a territory larger than any European state except Russia was added to the United States. Still the American march went on, and then war came with Mexico, and another vast region, stretching from Oregon to Arizona, became an American possession. All the lands of North America which had once called Spain master, which Cortez and De Soto, Ponce de Leon and Coronado, had bestowed upon the Spanish crown, had passed from the hands of the men who could not use them into those of the men who could. The expulsion of Spain from the Antilles is merely the last and final step of the inexorable movement in which the United States has been engaged for nearly a century. By influence and example, or more directly by arms and by the pressure of ever-advancing settlements, the United States drove Spain from all her continental possessions in the Western hemisphere, until nothing was left to the successors of Charles and Philip but Cuba and Puerto Rico.

"How did it happen that this great movement, at once

racial, political, and economic, governed as it was by forces which rule men even in their own despite—how did it happen to stop when it came to the ocean's edge? The movement against Spain was at once natural and organic, while the pause on the sea-coast was artificial and in contravention of the laws of political evolution in the Americas. The conditions in Cuba and Puerto Rico did not differ from those which had gone down in ruin wherever the flag of Spain waved upon the mainland. The Cubans desired freedom, and Bolivar would fain have gone to their aid. Mexico and Colombia, in 1825, planned to invade the island, and at that time invasion was sure to be successful. What power stayed the on-coming tide which had swept over a continent? Not Cuban loyalty, for the expression ' Faithful Cuba ' was a lie from the beginning, like many other Spanish statements. The power which prevented the liberation of Cuba was the United States; and more than seventy years later this republic has had to fight a war because at the appointed time she set herself against her own teachings, and brought to a halt the movement she had herself started to free the New World from the oppression of the Old. The United States held back Mexico and Colombia and Bolivar, used her influence at home and abroad to that end, and, in the opinion of contemporary mankind, succeeded, according to her desires, in keeping Cuba under the dominion of Spain."

# AN ILLOGICAL POLICY

The reasons which Mr. Lodge advances for the attitude of the United States with reference to Cuba Libre, or Cuba annexed, are by no means creditable to the Union, but they seem to be justified by the facts of history. Up to the outbreak of the Civil War we do not find much upon which to flatter ourselves in our attitude toward the Cuban question. "The Latin mind" the historian contends, "is severely logical in politics, which accounts in a measure for its many failures in establishing and managing free governments. Being of this cast of mind, the Spanish-American states, when they rose to free themselves from Spain, also freed their own slaves, and in this instance they were not only logical, but right. The people of the United States, on the other hand, were at once illogical and wrong, for they held just then that white men should be free and black men slaves. So they regarded with great disfavor this highly logical outcome of South-American independence, and from this cause Southern hostility brought the Panama Congress, fraught with many high hopes of American solidarity, to naught. The sinister influence of slavery led the United States to hold Cuba under the yoke of Spain, because free negroes were not to be permitted to exist upon an island so near their Atlantic seaboard. It was a cruel policy which fastened upon Cuba slavery to Spain as well as the slavery of black men to white, when both might have been swept away without

85

cost to America. Those who are curious in the doctrine of compensations can find here a fresh example. Lincoln, in the second inaugural, declared once for all that our awful Civil War was the price we paid for the sin of slavery; and the war of 1898 was the price paid at last, as such debts always are paid by nations, for having kept Cuba in bondage at the dictates of our own slave power.

"The United States had thus undertaken to stop the movement for the liberation of Spanish colonies at the point selected by itself, and had deliberately entered upon the policy of maintaining Spanish rule in its own neighborhood. This policy meant the assumption of a heavy responsibility, as well as a continuous effort to put to rest an unsettled question, by asserting stoutly, and in defiance of facts, that it really was settled if people would only agree pleasantly to think so. But in this, as in all like cases, the effort was vain. Cuba was held under Spanish rule, and the question which had received the wrong answer began almost at once to make itself heard, after the awkward fashion of questions which men pretend to have disposed of, but which are still restlessly seeking the right and final answer, and, without respect for policies or vested interests, keep knocking and crying at the door. Some American statesmen saw that there was a real question in Cuba demanding a real settlement, and declared, like John Quincy Adams and Henry Clay, that Cuba must be annexed, and that it would become indispensable to the integrity of the Union. Even then did Adams also assert that the transfer of Cuba to some other power was a danger obtruding itself upon our councils. But the plan of leaving the island with Spain prevailed. Cuba had come near to both independence and annexation, but both gave way before the slave power, and for twenty years the policy of 1825 had sway. As late as 1843, indeed, Webster said that negro emancipation in Cuba would strike a death-blow to slavery in the United States, thus giving cynically and frankly the bad and true reason for the policy steadily pressed since 1825. Never at rest, however, the slave power itself a few years after Webster's lucid definition of its Cuba policy, changed its own attitude completely. From desiring to keep Cuba in the hands of Spain, in order that Cuban negroes might remain slaves, it passed, as dangers thickened round it at home, to the determination to secure Cuba, in order that more slave territory might be added to the United States. Hence a continuous effort to get the island by annexation, and various projects, all fallen into more or less oblivion now, to bring that result about, were devised by American slaveholders and their allies. Their schemes ranged from Buchanan's offer to purchase, rejected with deep scorn by Spain the intelligent, to the Ostend Manifesto—a barefaced argument for conquest—and included attempts to bring about Cuban independence by exciting insurrections and landing filibustering expeditions. But the time was fast drawing near, even while the American slaveholders were thus seeking new territory, when the slave power would be thinking not of extension, but of existence."

Thus we see that the Cuban question from the time of its beginning as a thorn in the American side, was not precisely a straight question, but one with ramifications which bore in upon the American mind at every point of issue the inconsistency of a free people maintaining the institution of slavery. Prating of a certain preamble in an instrument of great historic influence which asserted the rights of all men to an equal chance in the pursuit of life, liberty and happiness, we arrogated to ourselves nevertheless the privilege of holding in our hands the lives of countless scores of human beings, of meting out to or withholding from them the happiness which our charter of rights accorded to "all men," and within the shadow of the temple of liberty stood the cabin of the slave. The blot of slavery upon our own escutcheon kept the hands of Uncle Sam pretty securely tied and all he could do in meeting the vexed question of Cuba and her wrongs, or Cuba and her riches, was to blow now hot, now cold, according to the temper of the statesmen who at the time worked the bellows of policy or of "eloquence" at the National forge. The inevitable trend of events, however, now began to remedy the complication. Cuba and her free negroes, Cuba and her slaves were forgotten and the question of expansion became less pressing upon the mind of Uncle Sam than that of contraction. He soon had to fight within his own borders to keep what he had, without vexing his mind over further territorial acquisitions.

The Civil War in the United States put the Cuban question to sleep for a brief period as far as any American cognizance of its complications was concerned, and there were not wanting those who, believing that its interest was bound up wholly in the slave power, now destroyed on the mainland, comforted themselves with the thought that never again could Cuba vex the soul of the American statesman. The slate was wiped clean and in the list of future troubles of the American people Cuba had gone the way of negro slavery in the United States, and secession. But there was soon to be a rude awakening for these comfortable souls. They had reckoned without a real knowledge of the habits of unsolved problems, or of the homing qualities of a National obligation. There is no National or International Bankruptcy law by which a moral debt can be evaded or even scaled down for the " benefit " of creditors and the deluded sons of Uncle Sam who fancied themselves discharged from all further responsibility in the matter of Cuba soon had cause to perceive the error of their ways. The revolution of 1868 sounded the bugle blast which brought the sleeping American up standing from his sweet dreams of peace and it was seen at once that there was still a Cuban question, and a mightier one than ever. It was relieved of some of those clouds of self interest which had hitherto served to blur over the barefaced iniquity of it and the active efforts of Carlos Manuel de Cespedes the leader of the insurgent forces to cripple the power of the Spaniard were not long in arousing an admiring sympathy for his cause among the people of the great Republic. Slavery of any kind was now become intolerable to the American mind and there was no differentiation between the two kinds, one of which held the negro in a material bondage and that other which kept his Cuban master in political chains. As the revolution progressed it seemed as if the psychological moment had arrived for Uncle Sam to take a hand in the quarrel and settle it once and for all. The idea of fighting was abhorrent to him of course, for he had had a stomach full of it in settling his own family troubles, but his Executive officer was a soldier who was never dismayed by the prospect of shot and shell, and it seemed as if such a one as he must cry a halt in commanding tones to the disturbers of his peace and the offenders of his principles. It became quite evident that Spain was not equal to the task of managing the island; murder, arson and pillage were going on at our very doors and the Grant Administration was compelled to take notice of it. With the smell of blood in the air, with the smoke of war rising from the ruins of ravaged plan-

tations within range of eye and nostril, with the raucous
noises of conflict dinning in the ear of the neighborhood
it would have been futile to say that life at last had become sweet and settled and that the millennium was at
hand. Then and there might the American people have
stepped in forcibly and saved themselves and Cuba many
hours of anxiety, much loss of life and war. Secretary
Fish, whose grandson's veins a quarter of a century later
shed almost the first American blood on Cuban soil in the
war of 1898, endeavored to meet the problem by the
peaceful method. "Let us purchase this bloody acreage,"
said he, "from those who cannot redeem it and substitute
Uncle Sam who can for St. Jago who has failed." The
idea was an excellent one and was so considered by the
ruling powers of Spain at the time, but the pride of the
Hidalgo, that beautiful abstraction which appears to be
the only real asset these peninsularities have left, and
which they never use to any good purpose, prevented the
consummation of the project. General Primm, the leading spirit of the Spanish government at that period, in-
wardly applauding the suggestion, outwardly denounced
it, and the question drifted on into an outrage, which
would have justified the forcible acquisition of Spain's
territorial remnants in this hemisphere. In 1873 an
American vessel, *The Virginius,* was captured on the high
seas and taken to Santiago, where fifty of her officers and
crew, American citizens, were blind-folded, stood up

against a dead wall and shot to death. The act set the country aflame and the President of the United States, the grim, dogged, silent soldier had his war cut out for him with a foundation of righteousness upon which to base it. But the dogs were held in leash, for slavery was not yet extinct in the United States—it was changed in kind but it was potent. Master Dollar cracked his whip and said, " No! War is an unholy thing for it disturbs me. Sheathe your swords gentlemen, I will settle this Cuban matter at so much per head. Fifty American lives are worth how much? We'll rest on a gold basis leaving lead to savages." The suggestion prevailed. The coffers of Uncle Sam were enriched and Spain got a receipt in full for her little diversion of treating American citizens as if they were Cuban chattels. What is a human life indeed that it should rise superior to the sweet serenity of an unruffled Stock-market!

The ten years' war continued and became daily more and more a source of discomfort to the American patriot and pocket. There were many who found little to plume themselves upon in the diplomacy which bartered lives for lucre. These of course were the so-called Jingoes who had not waked up to the fact that National honor might under circumstances of a certain kind become a purchaseable commodity. There were then as there are still persons of sufficiently obscure perceptions to believe that outrage and insult cannot be wiped out by a cash pay-

ment and who deny that the gold-cure is the long sought
for panacea for human ills. Despite the deep resentment
of these persons however against a policy which appeared to them to be an ignoble one two years passed by
without any outward manifestation of sufficient magnitude to warrant the authorities in changing their attitude.
But in 1875 Master Dollar's nerves again became sensitive. He found any kind of War anywhere disturbing to
his equilibrium and unless the conflict in Cuba was
brought to a speeedy close he was afraid his circulation
might be impaired. Hence it was that a polite intimation
was forwarded from Washington to Madrid that unless
Spain settled her squabbles with the Cubans Uncle Sam
might find it necessary to intervene. The intimation
was not without its effect. Spain recognized that while
she might be able to settle on moderate terms for the
destruction of American lives, she could hardly hope to
compensate us for injury to our business interests, and
this realization coupled with the imminent exhaustion of
her resources led her, after two years of deliberation, to
make peace, bound up with many beautiful promises, to
her rebellious colony. We have already seen what were
the provisions of the Treaty of Zanjon; how Cuba was
granted reforms, privileges and amnesty. We have also
learned how wantonly every one of these provisions was
violated. But at the moment the Cuban question again
appeared to be settled and the United States breathed

freely once more. Cuba was on her feet. The wicked Spaniard had reformed and we could now go about our business with that complacent satisfaction which characterizes the man who always does the right thing at the right moment. Thanks to ourselves, conditions of peace had been permanently restored and by that threat of intervention our debt to humanity had been paid.

Unfortunately the Cuban was looking at the situation close at hand, not through the large end of Uncle Sam's long distance telescope and he saw what Uncle Sam seemed not to see. The smiling face of the Spaniard which we fondly believed was the face of a benign father glad of his reforms and taking pleasure in a contemplation of the happiness of his children, was really but a mask which concealed the frowning of a sullen despot acting under a compulsion that he found detestable; what sincerity there was in the smile was that of derision that the compelling power on the continent was so easily fooled. Her sons who had been promised amnesty Cuba saw shot furtively to death; sequestered in the dungeons of Spanish fortresses; subjected to tortures worse than death, while the promised reforms never emerged from the land of promise into the realm of reality. So the insurgent, after eight years of vain endeavor to persuade the crafty Castilian to keep the faith, again aroused himself into action and set Uncle Sam once more agog. The revolution of Gomez, and Maceo and Garcia shifted the scene once more from peace to warfare. At this point we were disposed to regard the situation with indifference tinged with a slight irritation that the Cuban could not be content with that ease of circumstance which we had secured for him, and, as the conflict proceeded, for a year it assumed hardly more dignity in American eyes than as if it were a South American revolution. But the desperate earnestness of the leaders of the new-born revolution and the absolute unity which prevailed among their followers soon made themselves felt and changed all that, so that in 1896, when the insurgents began to show some signs of crowding the Spaniards into the sea, irritated indifference became positive and sympathetic interest. The brave fight the insurgents were making, Mr. Lodge states "aroused the sympathy of the American people, which showed itself in the newspaper press and in public meetings, always with gathering strength. When Congress met, the popular sentiment sought expression in both branches. A minority desired the immediate recognition of Cuban independence, a large number wished to recognize belligerency, an overwhelming majority wanted to do something, while the naturally conservative elements were led by a few determined men who were opposed to any interference of the remotest kind, and a few of whom, even if they did not openly avow it, were bent on leaving Spain a free hand in the island. Out of this confusion came, as might have been expected, a compromise, in which the men in the small minority, who knew just what they wanted, got the substance, and the large, divided, and undecided majority, who vaguely desired ' to do something for Cuba,' obtained nothing but a collection of sympathetic words. The compromise took the form of a concurrent resolution, which, after much debate, delay, and conference, finally passed both Houses. This resolution merely declared that a state of war existed in Cuba, that the United States would observe strict neutrality, and that the President should offer the good offices of the United States with the Spanish government to secure the recognition of the independence of the island. As the resolution was concurrent, it did not require the President's assent, and was nothing but an expression of the opinion of Congress. It therefore had little weight with Mr. Cleveland, and none at all with Spain. Whatever was done by the administration in offering our good offices to secure the recognition of Cuban independence, there was no result and the only part of the resolution which was scrupulously carried out was in observing neutrality, which was done by the President with a severity that bore heavily upon the Cuban side alone. The administration was in fact opposed to any interference in Cuba, and the action of Congress left it free to hold itself aloof."

With their customary astigmatic method of looking at things, the Spanish authorities undoubtedly read into the comfortable attitude of the Cleveland administration toward the Cuban question an indication that the real sympathies of the American people lay with them rather than with the insurgents—due largely to the American habit of permitting authority to go to great lengths before venturing either protest or active opposition. Taking this attitude, it was perhaps natural that the government at Madrid should have ventured on its crowning act of infamy in the substitution of General Weyler, as Captain-General of the unhappy island, for the more humane and statesmanlike Campos.

We have already told the story of the atrocious administration of Cuban affairs, both civil and military, under the direction of this medieval figure misplaced in a century of enlightenment. The general effect of Gen. Weyler's administration—outside of the large number of widows and orphans which it interjected into the immediate situation in Cuba—was to arouse to a degree which the American authorities could not afford to ignore, not alone the keen sympathy of the American people for their oppressed neighbors, but their active resentment of methods which they considered unspeakable and without warrant in an age presumed to be civilized.

The feeling in this country took concrete form in a resolution presented by a majority of the Senate Committee on Foreign Relations, recognizing the republic of Cuba, and presented for the consideration of the Senators on December 21, 1896. Naturally this resolution caused great excitement throughout the country, and Master Dollar rose up in wrathful opposition to what he considered the unwarranted disturbance of his comfort. The stock market became uneasy to a degree, and the contingent " unsettlement of values " which was heralded far and wide in certain quarters sufficed to make the venturesome Senators, who had presented the resolution, appear in the light of enemies to their country.

Nevertheless the movement antagonistic to Spain had now attained to such proportions that the question made forcible entrance into the politics of the land. The financial interests of the country might say what they pleased; the Secretary of State might announce—as he did in an interview in a Washington newspaper—that no attention would be paid to the joint resolution, even if it passed both Houses over the President's veto; the President himself might resolutely set his face against active participation in the conflict—yet the hour was surely at hand when the pressing necessities of the Cuban could no longer be ignored, in behalf of merely business interests.

Strenuous efforts were made to send the Cuban question once more into that state of somnolence which had characterized its condition during the period of the Civil War; but, like Banquo's ghost, it would not down. The newspapers would not remain silent upon the subject—could not remain silent upon the subject; that which their editorial columns might exclude, their news columns were bound to present to the public eye. And once presented to the public eye, the doings of Gen. Weyler were such that no " power in heaven, on earth or in the waters under the earth " could have hoped successfully to make the Cuban question less than a paramount issue.

It gradually dawned upon the minds of the American public that the enforcement of neutrality meant nothing more or less than that the United States had become the ally of Spain and was assisting a grinding tyranny in its effort to suppress that which, in our own charter of rights, was allowed to be the privilege of all men, irrespective of station.

It was not alone the feeling among Americans, however, that a neighbor was being ill-treated by a harsh master, but it soon became evident, even upon the most cursory examination, that American citizens, deserving of our protection—not only deserving it but guaranteed it—were suffering wrong. A naturalization paper proving citizenship in the United States appeared to have no more effect upon the ruling powers at the palace at Havana, than as if it were so much blank paper. And, encouraged by Washington's seeming indifference to the rights and protection of suffering American citizens, the Spaniard soon went to the extreme length of oppression, regardless of the citizenship of the oppressed.

It so happened that at this juncture, the United States was represented at Havana in the Consul-General's office by Gen. Fitzhugh Lee, who, in his reports to the home government, laid bare the intolerable condition into which matters had been allowed to drift. But even this did not seem to awaken the administration to the necessity for immediate action; and it was not until a series of concrete cases in the imprisonment of Scott, the murder of Dr. Ruiz, and the outrageous treatment of the prisoners captured on board of the filibustering schooner *Competitor* were actually brought before the American public that the situation became so acute that the United States government was bound in honor to take action.

What President Cleveland would have done in this emergency is, of course, merely a matter of conjecture. The fact, however, that at this point there was a change in Washington, and that Mr. McKinley succeeded to the office of President of the United States, makes any surmise on this point of comparative unimportance. The Republican party in its platform in the campaign of 1896 had taken a strong ground in regard to Cuba, and had pledged itself to compel Spain to make a final settlement of the long unsettled question. Mr. McKinley was in full sympathy with this declaration of his party; and, through his sincere desire to see the whole world at peace, could be counted upon actively to meet the exigencies of the situation. Immediately upon assuming control, the McKinley administration, finding the crux of the situation in the American prisoners, who were still deprived of their

CAPTAIN HUGH L. SCOTT, U. S A.

liberty and their rights, made immediate demand upon Spain for their prompt release, and for a suitable indemnity for their losses.

There was no mistaking the import of this demand, and the Spaniard at once emerged from his dream of an alliance with the United States in the oppression of the Cuban, and by the end of April, 1897, every American prisoner in the island of Cuba had been released.

Relieved of the complications which made the subject of immediate and imminent interest to the American people, the question now resolved itself into the point, whether or not the Cubans should be granted by our recognition of their existence as a recognized body, the privilege of belligerent rights; and on May 20, 1897, the Senate, without division, passed a joint resolution recognizing Cuban belligerancy. The lower house, however, did not think it wise to keep the question in so live a form before the American people, and were disposed to permit it to sink into the obscurity with which a house committee alone can surround any great issue. But at that precise moment President McKinley again took the question in hand, and by a most timely message, called the attention of the House to the indubitable fact that wrongs were still being perpetrated in Cuba, that war was still a material fact, and that under the system of reconcentration instituted by Gen. Weyler, not only the natives of the island, but American citizens were being starved to death. He therefore requested an appropriation of $50-000 for the purchase of supplies to be sent to those of our fellow-citizens who were being slowly tortured to death by the unspeakable methods of the Spaniard.

The money was voted at once, and the act received presidential approval on the 24th day of May, 1897. We demanded from Spain, and she immediately acquiesced, her assent to send ships and food to our American consuls for the relief of starving Americans. These were fed, with plenty to spare for those who were not Americans; and by this act, the United States at last had practically interfered in Cuban matters. As Senator Lodge puts it: " No more complete act of intervention than this, which tended to cripple the military measures and check the starvation campaign of the Spaniard, could be imagined." Conditions were such that the most potent ammunition which could be provided for the embarrassment of the Spanish plan of campaign, was the plain, ordinary staples of food, which should prolong the existence of those whom Weyler was trying to kill.

The first material step toward the acceptance of his trust had at last been made by Uncle Sam. The next step, which indicated that we had at last waked up to our real duty in the premises, was taken in the autumn of 1897, when we asked for the recall of Gen. Weyler, "above all, for the revocation of the reconcentration edict," the inhumanity of which as it was applied in practice—whatever may have been its value as a theory—had been sufficiently demonstrated to justify the act.

The Spanish ministry complied instantly with our requests, asking, however, in return that we should give them the opportunity to try autonomy in Cuba. With probably full knowledge of the futility of yielding to any such request as this, the United States government found it advisable to give Spain one more chance; but it was not many weeks before it became evident that the crafty Castilian was up to his old tricks. With the exception of the recall of Gen. Weyler in October, 1897, in which Mr. Lodge says, "no deception or postponement was possible"—not one of the Spanish promises was kept, nor is there any reason to believe that Spain thought seriously at any time of keeping them. Spanish diplomacy was again trying to place Uncle Sam in his usual ridiculous position as party of the second part in an international game of confidence.

Agitation in the United States, however, was somewhat quieted, because of the American love of fair play. Certain concessions had been made to Spain, in return for concessions Spain had made to Cuba at our instigation, and a reasonable period of time in which to permit the trying of new experiments of government under the captain-generalcy of Gen. Blanco—a much milder man than the brutal Weyler—was considered only just and proper. But week after week passed, and to the intelligent observer, it became clear that Spanish autonomy could be neither practical nor, in the nature of things, general ; and before many days the Cuban question reached again that stage of acuteness which seemed to demand immediate and drastic action.

Then dawned the vital year of 1898, in which the inexorable trend of events forced Uncle Sam into the position of trustee for the demoralized people of Cuba. So important in its relation to our story are the events and complications of this year of 1898 that I shall treat of it in a separate chapter.

# Chapter VI

*W*HATEVER the disposition of the authorities of the United States to suppress the Cuban question, the progress of events, beginning almost with the dawn of January, 1898, was such as to keep the subject conspicuously in the public eye. In the first place it became increasingly evident as days passed that the autonomy which the Spanish government had prepared for Cuba, and in view of which we had practically promised to hold ourselves aloof from the situation, was nothing like as full as that which had been promised.

Even granting the different point of view of the Spaniard and the Anglo-Saxon, there was not in evidence a sufficiently full degree of autonomy for the Cubans to satisfy even a Spanish standard. It was, of course, true that if Spain had granted to Cuba such a government as Great Britain has granted to Canada, the Cubans would be much better off than the Spaniards at home; and that, naturally, was a condition not likely to prove tolerable or acceptable to the Spanish government. The captain-general was to have control over the legislative bodies proposed for Cuba, complete supervision of the courts of justice, entire control of the regulations affecting the financial relations between Cuba and Spain, and the autonomous Cuban government was not allowed to do

105

anything which in any wise conflicted with any one of the minor policies of the home government, to say nothing of the large.

The situation was duly pointed out by the pro-Cuban American newspapers day after day; and, even if the public had been willing to forget the frightful condition of affairs which existed at our very doors at that time, it would not have been allowed to do so. More material incidents, however, soon came into being, which awakened even the most somnolent dreamer to a realization of the extreme importance of the Cuban question, and the relation of the United States thereto.

The President of the United States was grossly insulted by the Spanish minister at Washington. Señor Dupuy de Lome had chosen to write a letter—under cover of confidence, no doubt—to a friend, in which he alluded in terms of much coarseness to the Executive, attributing to him, in a most offensive manner, traits of character which even Mr. McKinley's enemies never claimed were to his discredit. The propriety of its publication by American newspapers was, of course, questionable. Nevertheless, it reached the public eye; and, as a result, the ill-feeling which existed between the United States and Spain was gravely accentuated; and the necessity which arose of sending Mr. de Lome his passports and requesting him to return to Madrid, served as no amelioration of the conditions.

The situation had become most grave; and that the war clouds which now began to appear upon the horizon might be dissipated, seemed the forlornest of forlorn hopes. Nevertheless there were not a few who believed that a natural disinclination to plunge the country into a war of magnitude, for which it was by no means prepared, would deter the President and the Congress from taking the last irremediable step.

The insulting letter of minister de Lome, concerning the President appeared on the ninth of February, 1898; and on the morning of February sixteenth, just one week later, came the news that on the night before in the harbor of Havana, the battle-ship *Maine* had been blown up and totally destroyed, with two hundred sixty-four men and two officers killed.

The question seemed settled. At first glance, it appeared as if war must be declared on the instant. The United States had been very vitally injured, and this time in such a fashion that further toleration of the conditions which made the attack a possible one could no longer be regarded with our usual equanimity. The whole country was outraged, and in a mood for fierce and prompt retaliation; but the hour had not yet arrived. An immediate reaction—largely the result of the calm message of Captain Sigsbee, the commander of the *Maine,* who asked that, even in the face of the awful slaughter at Havana, the people should suspend their judgment until

the truth were known—set in. The calm which precedes
the storm took the place of the great wave of wrath
which had swept from one end of the country to the
other; and the American people wishing to be right before going ahead, sat back and awaited the verdict of a
commission appointed to investigate and to report on the
question of how the *Maine* came to her destruction.
" To those who understood the people," says Mr. Lodge,
" this grim silence, this stern self-control were more
threatening than any words of sorrow or of anger could
possibly have been." But Spain was too far gone in her
orgy of arrogance to take heed; and, instead of appre-
ciating the calm self-control of the American public, and
offering to make whatever reparation was in her power
for a disaster, with which she might not have had much
to do, thereby showing an appreciation of the attitude
which the American people had taken toward her in a
stressful moment, she added insult to injury. With crass
stupidity, Spain announced to the world, without any investigation of the causes of the explosion, and before
anyone had even looked at the wreck, that the *Maine*
was blown up from the inside, and that the disaster was
the natural result of the well-known carelessness of the
American naval officers. This statement was proclaimed
by the Spanish and their sympathizers at every point; and
the more the story was told, the greater was the fanning
of the flame of indignation in the breasts of the American

people. Still the American people held their peace. A
long and anxious period of waiting followed, and as
days passed the feeling throughout the country grew more
and more intense. The people were marvelously patient
however and barring one or two outbursts in legislative
halls in the various parts of the land, and the ebullient
attitude of certain sensational newspapers, there was no
overstepping of the bounds of caution and temperate use
of speech. But when the report finally came from the
commission appointed to investigate the *Maine* disaster,
and it was clear beyond a reasonable doubt that the war-
ship had been blown up from the outside, it became
equally clear that the end had arrived and a new beginning
had to be made. Spain's persistence in the insulting lie
which placed responsibility for the disaster upon the
officers and men of the destroyed vessel might now have
been moderated without avail. The American people
after seventy years of shilly shallying with a corrupt and
vicious neighbor had made up their minds that he should
move out and if he declined to act upon a hint should be
thrown out. The President sent messages to Congress
reciting conditions and laying the question at its doors,
whereupon Congress after much scratching of its political
head finally took the plunge. On April 20th, 1898, the
following joint resolution for the recognition of the independence of the people of Cuba, demanding that the
Government of Spain should relinquish its authority and

government in the island of Cuba, and withdraw its land and naval forces from Cuba and Cuban waters, and directing the President of the United States to use the land and naval forces of the United States to carry these resolutions into effect, was approved:

*Whereas the abhorrent conditions which have existed for more than three years in the island of Cuba, so near our own borders, have shocked the moral sense of the people of the United States, have been a disgrace to Christian civilization, culminating as they have, in the destruction of a United States battle ship, with two hundred and sixty-six of its officers and crew, while on a friendly visit in the harbor of Havana, and cannot longer be endured, as has been set forth by the President of the United States in his message to Congress of April eleventh, eighteen hundred and ninety-eight, upon which the action of Congress was invited: Therefore,*

*Resolved by the Senate and House of Representatives of the United States of America in Congress assembled,*

FIRST. *That the people of the island of Cuba are, and of right ought to be, free and independent.*

SECOND. *That it is the duty of the United States to demand, and the Government of the United States does hereby demand, that the Government of Spain at once relinquish its authority and government in the island of Cuba and withdraw its land and naval forces from Cuba and Cuban waters.*

THIRD. *That the President of the United States be, and he hereby is, directed and empowered to use the entire land and naval forces of the United States, and to call into the actual service of the United States the militia of the several States, to such extent as may be necessary to carry these resolutions into effect.*

FOURTH. *That the United States hereby disclaims any disposition or intention to exercise sovereignty, jurisdiction or control over said island except for the pacification thereof, and asserts its determination, when that is accomplished, to leave the government and control of the island to its people.*

Five days later war was declared by an Act of Congress in the following terms:

*Be it enacted by the Senate and House of Representatives of the United States of America in Congress assembled,* FIRST. *That war be, and the same is hereby, declared to exist, and that war has existed since the twenty-first day of April, Anno Domini eighteen hundred and ninety-eight, including said day, between the United States of America and Kingdom of Spain.*

SECOND. *That the President of the United States be, and he hereby is directed and empowered to use the entire land and naval forces of the United States, and to call into actual service of the United States the militia of the several States, to such extent as may be necessary to carry this act into effect.*

111

The final step had been taken and two powers that had stood face to face for three quarters of a century in a mutual relation which had been a constant menace to the peace of both had now directly joined the issue. The arts of Dollars, and Diplomacy had failed. Arms were the last resource and were resorted to.

It is not my purpose here to give any account of the hostilities that followed. It is of Uncle Sam as a Trustee in times of Peace when his real achievements have been accomplished that I prefer to speak. Of Dewey and of Sampson at Manila and at Santiago, of the campaigns of the Army in the Phillipines, Cuba and Porto Rico, others may write. The no less renowned victories of the period of Peace, harder won because won only through long days and nights of toil and embarrassments incredible and without the stimulating plaudits of the populace to cheer the leaders on, are the portion of this story. Suffice it to say that the recalcitrant Spaniard was finally ejected and by the terms of a Protocol signed at Washington August 12th, 1898, hostilities were suspended. The wording of the Protocol was as follows:

### PROTOCOL

*William R. Day, Secretary of State of the United States, and His Excellency Jules Cambon, ambassador extraordinary and plenipotentiary of the Republic of France at Washington, respectively possessing for this purpose full authority from the Government of the United States and the Government of Spain, have concluded and signed the following articles, embodying the terms on which the two Governments have agreed in respect to the matters hereinafter set forth, having in view the establishment of peace between the two countries, that is to say:*

*Article 1. Spain will relinquish all claim or sovereignty over or title to Cuba.*

*Article 2. Spain will cede to the United States the island of Porto Rico and other islands now under Spanish sovereignty in the West Indies, and also an island in the Ladrones, to be selected by the United States.*

*Article 3. The United States will occupy and hold the city, bay, and harbor of Manila pending the conclusion of a treaty of peace which shall determine the control, disposition, and government of the Philippines.*

*Article 4. Spain will immediately evacuate Cuba, Porto Rico, and other islands under Spanish sovereignty in the West Indies; and to this end each Government will, within ten days after the signing of this protocol, appoint commissioners, and the commissioners so appointed shall, within thirty days after the signing of this protocol, meet at Havana for the purpose of arranging and carrying out the details of the aforesaid evacuation of Cuba and the adjacent Spanish islands; and each Government will, within ten days after the signing of this protocol, also ap-*

*point other commissioners, who shall, within thirty days after the signing of this protocol, meet at San Juan, in Porto Rico, for the purpose of arranging and carrying out the details of the aforesaid evacuation of Porto Rico and other islands under Spanish sovereignty in the West Indies.*

*Article 5. The United States and Spain will each appoint not more than five commissioners to treat of peace, and the commissioners so appointed shall meet at Paris not later than October 1, 1898, and proceed to the negotiation and conclusion of a treaty of peace, which treaty shall be subject to ratification according to the respective constitutional forms of the two countries.*

*Article 6. Upon the conclusion and signing of this protocol hostilities between the two countries shall be suspended, and notice to that effect shall be given as soon as possible by each Government to the commanders of its military and naval forces.*

In the treaty of peace signed at Paris on December tenth, 1898, the following article was given precedence over all others:

### ARTICLE I.

*Spain relinquishes all claim of sovereignty over and title to Cuba.*

*And as the island is, upon its evacuation by Spain, to be occupied by the United States, the United States will, so long as such occupation shall last, assume and discharge the obligations that may under international law result from the fact of its occupation for the protection of life and property.*

Uncle Sam had at last performed his first duty in the premises. Another equally important remained. He had rescued a helpless child from the hands of a brutal father. It now became his office to nurse the sickly infant back to health again, to start him along the road to prosperity, to administer his property until such a time as he should be able to care for his own.

Uncle Sam Neighbor had been transformed into Uncle Sam Trustee. As to his intentions in the Administration of his trust he had already made indirectly and then directly to the citizens of Cuba a statement in the instructions of the President, through the Secretary of War to the Military Commander of the United States forces in the captured Province of Santiago, bearing date of July 18th, 1898, as follows:

To the SECRETARY OF WAR.

SIR: The capitulation of the Spanish forces in Santiago de Cuba and in the eastern part of the Province of Santiago, and the occupation of the territory by the forces of the United States, render it necessary to instruct the military commander of the United States as to the conduct which he is to observe during the military occupation.

"The first effect of the military occupation of the

enemy's territory is the severance of the former political relations of the inhabitants and the establishment of a new political power. Under this changed condition of things the inhabitants, so long as they perform their duties, are entitled to security in their persons and property and in all their private rights and relations. It is my desire that the inhabitants of Cuba should be acquainted with the purpose of the United States to discharge to the fullest extent its obligations in this regard. It will therefore be the duty of the commander of the army of occupation to announce and proclaim in the most public manner that we come not to make war upon the inhabitants of Cuba, nor upon any party or faction among them, but to protect them in their homes, in their employments, and in their personal and religious rights. All persons who, either by active aid or by honest submission, co-operate with the United States in its efforts to give effect to this beneficent purpose will receive the reward of its support and protection. Our occupation should be as free from severity as possible.

" Though the powers of the military occupant are absolute and supreme and immediately operate upon the political condition of the inhabitants, the municipal laws of the conquered territory, such as affect private rights of person and property and provide for the punishment of crime, are considered as continuing in force, so far as they are compatible with the new order of things, until they are suspended or superseded by the occupying belligerent, and in practice they are not usually abrogated, but are allowed to remain in force and to be administered by the ordinary tribunals, substantially as they were before the occupation. This enlightened practice is, so far as possible to be adhered to on the present occasion. The judges and the other officials connected with the administration of justice may, if they accept the supremacy of the United States, continue to administer the ordinary law of the land, as between man and man, under the supervision of the American Commander-in-Chief. The native constabulary will, so far as may be practicable, be preserved. The freedom of the people to pursue their accustomed occupations will be abridged only when it may be necessary to do so.

" While the rule of conduct of the American Commander-in-Chief will be such as has just been defined, it will be his duty to adopt measures of a different kind, if, unfortunately, the course of the people should render such measures indispensable to the maintenance of law and order. He will then possess the power to replace or expel the native officials in part or altogether, to substitute new courts of his own constitution for those that now exist. or to create such new or supplementary tribunals as may be necessary. In the exercise of these high powers the commander must be guided by his judgment and his experience and a high sense of justice.

" One of the most important and most practical problems with which it will be necessary to deal is that of the treatment of property and the collection and administration of the revenues. It is conceded that all public funds and securities belonging to the government of the country in its own right, and all arms and supplies and other movable property of such government, may be seized by the military occupant and converted to his own use. The real property of the state he may hold and administer, at the same time enjoying the revenues thereof, but he is not to destroy it save in the case of military necessity. All public means of transportation, such as telegraph lines, cables, railways and boats belonging to the state, may be appropriated to his use, but unless in case of military necessity they are not to be destroyed. All churches and buildings devoted to religious worship and to the arts and sciences, all schoolhouses, are, so far as possible, to be protected, and all destruction or intentional defacement of such places, of historical monuments or archives, or of works of science or art, is prohibited, save when required by urgent military necessity.

Private property, whether belonging to individuals or corporations, is to be respected, and can be confiscated only for cause. Means of transportation, such as telegraph lines and cables, railways and boats, may although they belong to private individuals or corporations, be seized by the military occupant, but unless destroyed under military necessity are not to be retained.

While it is held to be the right of the conqueror to levy contributions upon the enemy in their seaports, towns, or provinces which may be in his military possession by conquest and to apply the proceeds to defray the expenses of the war, this right is to be exercised within such limitations that it may not savor of confiscation. As the result of military occupation the taxes and duties payable by the inhabitants to the former government become payable to the military occupant, unless he sees fit to substitute for them other rates or modes of contribution to the expenses of the government. The moneys so collected are to be used for the purpose of paying the expenses of government under the military occupation, such as the salaries of the judges and the police, and for the payment of the expenses of the Army.

# THE PROMISE

Private property taken for the use of the Army is to be paid for when possible, in cash at a fair valuation, and when payment in cash is not possible, receipts are to be given.

All ports and places in Cuba which may be in the actual possession of our land and naval forces will be opened to the commerce of all neutral nations, as well as our own, in articles not contraband of war, upon payment of the prescribed rates of duty which may be in force at the time of the importation.

WILLIAM McKINLEY.

Such in general were our promises to the people of Cuba. To what extent has Uncle Sam kept faith with his ward?

# PART II
## THE TRUST

# THE TRUST

## Chapter I

### BRIGADIER-GENERAL LEONARD WOOD AT SANTIAGO.

*T*HE key-note of the American administration of Cuban affairs was struck within a fortnight of the great naval battle of Santiago, by Brigadier-General Leonard Wood, who, upon the 20th of July, 1898, was ordered by Gen. Shafter " to take command of the city of Santiago, to clean it up, maintain order, feed the people, and start them at work."

By virtue of the victory of July 4, 1898, the city of Santiago and the province as well, fell naturally into the hands of the United States. It was not until a period of nearly six months had elapsed that the further negotiations between Spain and Uncle Sam resulted in our taking possession in trust of the whole island of Cuba. The experiment, therefore. in which the United States had embarked—that of administering the affairs of a colony, which, while not its own, had yet become its charge—began at this point ; and upon the officer immediately placed in control fell the responsibility of formulating the proposition which was to be demonstrated.

It was fortunate for the United States that it had at its command at this precise moment a man of a kind peculiarly fitted for the special work in hand. Leonard Wood was not only a soldier but a physician; and, whatever the justice of the criticism which has been passed upon the Washington administration for its appointment of Gen. Wood to this singularly delicate commission, and to my mind there has been no justice in it, the immediate complications in Cuba showed that if a hopeful issue were to be expected, the guiding mind should be that of the soldier, with the sympathetic touch of the man who cures us of our ills. The material situation was such that it demanded the firm grasp of the military man, of course; but equally necessary was the sympathetic touch of the physician.

General Wood had gone to Cuba as colonel of the now famous regiment of Rough Riders; and, because of his efficient work in the organization of this troop, and later of his gallantry in action, he had risen by degrees to the rank of Major-General of Volunteers. To those who had known him, his appointment as military governor of the province of Santiago came as no surprise, for to them he had repeatedly shown himself a man of great force of character, undoubted courage, of excellent executive ability, and, above all, the possessor of sound common sense. He was not long in establishing a reputation as a fighter, but it was not until he undertook work of a semi-civil nature that the full measure of the man began to dawn not only upon his friends but upon the country. Mr. Matthews has well said that in this capacity Gen.

BENEFICENTIA, AT HAVANA

MATERNITY ROOM AT BENEFICENTIA

# SETTING THE PACE

Wood did his greatest work in Cuba, and set a standard which will not only be a monument to him, but a lasting credit to the United States; and which will be the model, so far as efficiency and results go, for the government by the United States of extra territorial regions· which may come under their jurisdiction. It was Gen. Wood's great privilege to have set the pace in honest, efficient, economical government of the island of Cuba, which became the standard by which the earlier military governors of the island were guided, and to which he himself, during his occupancy of the military governorship at Havana, consistently adhered.

The complications which beset Gen. Wood upon assuming command of the city of Santiago, of which for the time being he became practically the mayor or "alcalde," were unusually difficult. It is estimated that there were about 120,000 people, of one kind and another, in Santiago at the time of his assuming control. There were the victorious American troops to be cared for, and, it must be confessed, to be held in a state of strictest discipline at a time, when, flushed with the wine of victory, they were inclined to overstep the bounds of modesty. There were the vanquished Spanish troops, some 100,000 of whom had surrendered with the city, and had laid down their arms. There were as many more in various parts of the province who had to be cared for. In addition to these, were the citizens of Santiago the city, and the denizens

125

of Santiago the province,—Cubans, to whom the coming of the victorious American army was welcome in the sense that this American army was the harbinger of their own liberty. And to such an extent were they carried away by this beautiful realization of their dream of centuries that it is not surprising that more often than not, they confounded liberty with license.

The health of the city was bad. There was starvation on every side, and pestilence was in the air. Abject poverty was met with at every corner, and cleanliness was a virtue which for generations had been almost unknown. The houses were filled with dying or dead, and even upon the highways, by the hundreds, were men, women and children in the last stages of starvation, and not a few who had passed beyond the vale.

Everything susceptible of demoralization was demoralized. There were no schools. The hospitals had become mere refuges for the suffering, whether their maladies were of mind or of the body. And, owing to the conditions which war always interjects into the life of a country, all commercial enterprises had stopped. The streets were filled with the idle, and the industrious of the vicinity were those only who were engaged in enterprises of a questionable kind.

It was not a matter of weeks but merely of days before it was evident that this army surgeon, who was sneered at as being the doctor merely of the illustrious individual, was of that greater type of physician who can administer to the diseases of the body politic. His wonderful personal force, his unusual sanity of mind, his unflinching courage allied to his instinctive ability as an organizer, soon made Gen. Wood's influence felt in this small, though very significant field of activity. Tender as a woman in such relations of his official life as required the softer manner, there was still vividly in the recollection of those who might have been disposed to regard tenderness as weakness, his injunction to his soldiers in action, when he uttered his famous order, " Don't swear—shoot." In a modification of this utterance, seemed to lie the guiding principle of his civil administration. The import was the same, but the phraseology altered; and " Don't swear—work " became the motto not only of the General himself but of those who helped him in those early days.

Gen. Wood labored at this time under the advantage which is always that of a man vested with unlimited powers, and who is, for a time, allowed to go about his work upon his own initiative without interference from a higher officialism. Strong of purpose, and with that same self-reliance which has caused so many heart-burnings among those who would bend him to their own purposes in his later administration of Cuban affairs, Gen. Wood mapped out his own course of procedure; and, within a week, the convalescence of the sick city of Santiago began.

The streets were cleaned; the dead were buried; the poor were fed; the idle were set at work; the initial steps of the wonderful work in sanitation, which has shown such marvelous results in the later administration of Cuba, were taken; schools were established; order was restored; the citizenship which lurked within dark recesses and lived upon unscrupulous devices—whether Cuban, Spanish or American—was warned to employ itself in useful directions, or to relieve the community of its presence; the Custom House was placed upon a basis at least of honesty, if not of immediate efficiency; a police force was organized; useless offices were abolished; the militant side of American control was made subordinate to the civil: and where there had been a community demoralized by war, there was within a month established a city enjoying the blessed privileges of peace.

Gen. Wood's first official act was the issuance of a charter of civil rights, which announced to those who had come under his jurisdiction just what were their privileges under the form of government which had been established. There was little in this proclamation which indicated a government by martial law, but the anomalous condition was presented of a soldier standing sponsor for such a state of affairs as might rightly have been looked for under conditions of peace.

This bill of rights, which was formulated after proper consideration of the matter, provided for the freedom of

THE BENEFICENTIA LAUNDRY, 1900

THE BENEFICENTIA LAUNDRY, 1902

the press, the right of peaceable assembly, the right of habeas corpus, and the right to give bail for all offences not capital. In this was the most significant part of Gen. Wood's scheme of reconstruction. It was his intent that the idea should be impressed upon the people of Cuba, in so far as he had anything to do with their affairs that the civil law was supreme, and that unless there should be a proper respect for the laws, the Cubans could not hope to establish anything in the nature of self-government. The militaristic idea was to be avoided in every possible way that the citizens over whom he had been set for the time, would permit it to be avoided. Whenever and wherever they were willing to show themselves amenable to a discipline which was of a purely civil nature, the strong arm of the soldier would not be exerted against them; but, at the same time, he gave these people clearly to understand that at no time would he tolerate infringements of his proclaimed ordinances, even if it required the full power of his military strength to restrain the offender.

The effect was immediate and healthy. At first the plain, every-day people had treated every American in the city with a "cringing courtesy" that seemed born of a fear of an over-bearing and an ill-used power, while the attitude of the so-called better classes was one of indifferent apathy. These conditions were soon changed: where "cringing courtesy" had been was now respectful grati-

tude; and where there had been apathy there arose a condition of confident interest. There were so many evidences on every side of lofty ideals combined with practical effort for the alleviation of their miseries, that the
people could not fail to see that those now in authority
had come not to rob or to oppress them, but to help them
to get upon their feet again.

Among these obvious indications of a helpful purpose
was the establishment at Santiago of a Sanitary Department, at the head of which Gen. Wood placed Maj. George
M. Barber. This Department began its work within
twenty-four hours of Gen. Wood's assumption of the
functions of his office. Of course, it was difficult to secure labor for the various unpleasant duties of a department of this nature, and it was here that possibly, for the
moment, the military hand of the newly appointed governor bore most heavily upon the people. It was not
pleasant for idle men to be awakened from their dream
of leisure, to enter the deserted houses, of which there
were many in Santiago, to remove from them the bodies
of men, women and children, who had been dead for a
longer time than one likes to think of; it was not pleasant for these men to go into the work of cleaning out
the breeding places of the germs of pestilence: and
naturally few who were willing to volunteer for any
such service could be found. But that they should be

found, and that the work should be done, was a matter of pressing importance.

At first, before it was possible to make the appeal courteous to these people, labor was obtained by the sheer exercise of force; but when the natives, who had long been without sufficient food and the common necessities of life, found that the United States did not propose to place burdens upon their shoulders which should be without compensation, and that, in return for the work which they were asked to do, they were actually to be paid, either in money, or in what they needed more than that, food supplies—the task became less difficult.

In sixty-eight days, the records of the department show that Major Barber removed 1,161 dead persons and animals from houses which were broken into for the purpose of discovering why it was that they had become a noisome menace to the community. These bodies, for the most part, were burned, for the purpose of obliterating the possibility of pestilence; and it was no uncommon sight to see the bodies of men and beasts, and heaps of garbage being destroyed by fire, because, for the lack of time or other reasons, they could not be got rid of in a more seemly or a more practical manner. It is said that on one day, when there were 216 deaths in the city of Santiago, the sanitary board burned more than one hundred bodies, and buried the rest. Still further to assure the public safety, it was ordered that those who failed to report deaths, should be considered criminals in the eyes of the law, and should be punished accordingly.

The immediate necessities having been thus met, the four hundred years' accumulation of filth in the city of Santiago was next taken in charge by the street cleaning branch of this department. Every available cart in the city, and such additional labor as was required, were impressed into the service, with the result that within a period of eight months, the health of the city of Santiago became quite as salubrious as that of any city of its class and size in the United States—except perhaps, as Gen. Wood says, for the constant presence of malaria.

Mr. Franklin Matthews, in showing the results of the first ten months of Gen. Wood's administration of affairs at Santiago, gives interesting comparisons of the death rate for a number of years, quoting from a letter of Major Barber's, who said that for the month of April, 1899, there were nine days with but one death, whereas in previous years, taking the 12th of April as a basis for comparison, the reported deaths had been as follows:

April 12, 1893.................... 11 deaths.
April 12, 1894.................... 17 deaths.
April 12, 1897.................... 32 deaths.
April 12, 1898.................... 41 deaths.
April 12, 1899, the first period under American control, no deaths.

THE KITCHEN, BENEFICENTIA, 1900

THE KITCHEN, BENEFICENTIA, 1902

The department of street cleaning reached its highest stage of efficiency in June, 1899, when Major Barber employed about thirty-five teams a day throughout the city, removing with these, two hundred loads of refuse each day. Two of these carts were kept constantly busy disinfecting the sections of the city which had been cleansed, and starting them afresh. The entire force at Major Barber's command consisted of himself, two assistants, and about six hundred men—the latter, all of them, Cubans.

Starting in with an unorganized body of this size, the force was soon, by the application of strict military ideas, reduced to the plane of an orderly and efficient following, who not only placed the city of Santiago in a condition of cleanliness which almost any American city might well envy, but who also, by their efforts, earned the resources by which they were enabled to keep body and soul together, and to provide for those dependent upon them. Not only was the work of vast benefit to the municipality as such, but to its citizens as individuals, many of whom, undoubtedly, were kept alive and started afresh on the path to prosperity by the wise forethought of those who, at a moment's notice, took upon their shoulders the burdens of their government.

The sanitary work thus begun and given a sufficient impetus to carry it along, and placed under such control that this impetus daily received such augmentations as rendered it more and more efficient as time passed, Gen. Wood turned his attention to the condition of affairs in other departments. He discovered that which was nothing new to those familiar with Spanish methods of administration, that there had been an appalling laxity in the management of these various bureaus. There were no official records of any value in existence; or, at least, if they existed, there were none to be found. There was no money in the treasury; and there was no evidence anywhere, in fact, that there had been any semblance of a government in the city or province of Santiago.

Bearing in mind the delicate sensibilities of these unfortunate people with whom he was now thrown into official contact, Gen. Wood endeavored, in so far as possible, to abide by the ideas of government, to which they had been most accustomed. Materially, there may have been no suggestion of an orderly management of public affairs, but it was found that there were ideals, after all. The Spaniard has never been lacking in these; it is only in his practices that he has been a person really to be complained of. His ideals have been beautiful, and his dreams have been iridescent: his practices are the only things that have been unspeakable.

The machinery of administration was thoroughly reorganized; and where there were to be found officials who, in the past, had served tolerably well in minor positions, these men were given a chance to show their metal, and were promoted to positions of some responsibility, but under a constant surveillance. Salaries everywhere were reduced, and sinecures were abolished. The best test of the Spanish official was found in this somewhat drastic method of procedure. The man who had good stuff in him, realizing the conditions which existed, could not complain if his service was rewarded with less pay than formerly; and, of course, any official who objected to the full and proper fulfilment of the functions of his office, very soon made himself known, and his services were,—equally, of course—easily dispensed with, without arousing the animosity even of his friends and of his neighbors.

A Department of Public Works was established, to which the continued maintenance of street cleaning was assigned, and the work of repairing the water supply, and of the laying of new pavements in the streets, which had fallen into a wofully disreputable state,—was begun. The water supply of Santiago, like that of Havana, was of potentially good quality; but, through years of neglect and incredible mismanagement, it had fallen into a deplorable state. There were hardly a dozen yards of pipe without as many leaks; and, as a result, the streets had been materially damaged from beneath as well as upon the surface; and great quantities of water—which might well be used for other purposes—were going to waste. These conditions were rectified, and before long,

135

in every part of the city a moderate supply of water was available. The sanitary effect was of inestimable value, since the impurities of the soil no longer penetrated to the vehicles of the water supply, and the physical condition of those who consumed it was improved. In addition to this, a yellow fever hospital was established on one of the islands of the harbor, and several detention hospitals were placed at the water's edge, thoroughly equipped for the purpose of meeting the now sporadic cases of disease which might manifest themselves.

A more difficult, because less physical, complication arose in the condition of the courts of justice. These had practically been closed during the war, and the prison houses were filled with criminals and others awaiting trial, whose estate was, indeed, a deplorable one. Until he could get a properly organized force in this direction, so as adequately to meet the requirements of justice formally, Gen. Wood took it upon himself to go through all the prisons and personally to investigate every case of injustice he possibly could hope to remedy himself. He administered justice in his capacity of military ruler of the province; and upon the establishment of his bill of rights, and the opening of the courts, reforms in the prisons were soon in operation, which removed, in so far as it was possible to remove them, the injustices under which those who were incarcerated therein were suffering.

THE SHOE SHOP, BENEFICENTIA

THE TAILOR SHOP, BENEFICENTIA

The school question next occupied the attention of the military governor. Schools of one kind or another were established in all parts of the province, and were soon in operation, although, of course, without proper equipment. The main point was the inculcation of the idea of the desirability of education among the people, and the striking of the initial note of a reform which should be of the most potential value to the island in the future. In this agreeable work, Gen. Wood found a ready acquiescence among the people, who were only too anxious in some way to have their little ones taken, for a portion of the day at least, off their hands, and given some kind of occupation which should take their little minds off the miseries by which they were surrounded.

To the credit of the Cubans, it must be said that everywhere teachers were found willing to work for less money than they had ever received before; and the Governor, having at that time in his control the customs duties of the province to expend as his judgment assured him was for the best, supplied from the rather meagre funds of the custom house such deficiencies as the cities and towns of the province were unable to meet in the management of the school work. Thirty kindergartens were established in the city of Santiago, and such other schools as could be made available were started from time to time. The parents were pleased, the teachers were enthusiastic, and there is no lack of testimony to the fact

that the children themselves hailed the advent of the
schools with a real delight. This does not prove that
the Cuban child is radically different from the children
of other nations, who "plod their ways unwillingly to
school," so much as it indicates that school work of an
uplifting and ennobling kind in Cuba was such a novelty
that it impressed on their young minds the idea that they
were being entertained while being instructed.

The charitable work found its chief concern in
relief of the conditions of the helpless and the sick.
There were hundreds of needy persons, of course, who
had to be provided for instantly to keep them from starvation; but among them were many who were sufficiently
able-bodied to pay with service for that which was provided for them. The sick and helpless destitute were
provided with rations until such time as they should be
cured, or were able to work, while the able-bodied were
immediately cared for by the vast amount of labor which
had to be done in connection with the cleaning of the
city, the building of bridges, the construction of roads,
and the rehabilitation of the water supply.

Wages for public works were seventy-five cents, and
fifty cents a day, according to the class, and a ration of
food. Many of the workmen preferred taking all their
pay in rations. It was definitely understood at the beginning that where men were able to work and would not,
they must starve until they did. An easy attitude was

taken toward the most of them, however, because the general atmosphere of the city was one of sickness and of weakness; and, for a time, rations were issued to the extent of from 18,000 to 25,000 a day, sometimes running up to 40,000, and upon one occasion to 50,000. This continued up to 1899, but was not necessary in the large after October, 1898, when the province was practically in a position properly to care for itself.

The revenues from which all the expense of the maintenance of this reestablished government, the cost at which this efficiency was given to the great work which has since continued in Cuba, including salaries, the support of the schools, the maintenance of the lighthouses, the expenditures for sanitary and police measures, the repavement of the streets, and the reconstruction of the water-works,—were all provided without direct taxation of any sort, being appropriated from the funds taken in at the custom house; and so carefully were the revenues at Gen. Wood's disposal administered that at the beginning of 1899, when the province of Santiago became subject to the ruling powers at Havana, Gen. Brooke, having been appointed governor of the whole island, Gen. Wood was able to show a balance to the credit of the province of $250,000. As Mr. Matthews puts it, " The wholesome lesson of living within one's income was thus taught to the people of Cuba."

The chapters which follow in this book show in some

detail the great amount of uplifting work which the various departments of the insular government at Havana have been able to accomplish in three and one-half years of military occupation. Immeasurable credit is due to all the heads of departments, and to all the officers connected with the administration of Cuban affairs. Ideas which have been important, principles which have been guiding, methods which have been vital, have been suggested by many minds; and it has been my effort to give, wheresoever it is possible to do so, credit to those to whom it is due. To Gen. Brooke, to Gen. Ludlow, to Gen. Wood, and to the subordinates of all these officers, the Cuban, as well as the American, owes a deep debt of gratitude; the one for lifting him up from the mire of despair and ruin, the other for the performance of their functions in such a way as to reflect everlasting credit upon American enterprise, energy, good faith, and philanthropy. But in awarding this credit, it must not be forgotten that the very key-note of Cuban administration, the essence of American success in the unfortunate island, which has for so long a time been our trust, was struck by Brigadier-General Leonard Wood in those early days in Santiago, when that which has since become the successful administration of Cuba in the large, was in all its essentials that same American administration in miniature. To the constructive mind of the retiring Military-Governor of Cuba we owe our present enviable position in the eyes of the world as an unselfish upbuilder of a down-trodden people, and when we consider the difficulties of his labors, the discouragements that have met him at many a turn, the obstacles thrown across his path by the envious and the malicious, a warmth more than ordinary should characterize our cry of " Well done, good and faithful servant."

# Chapter II

A GENERAL SURVEY OF CUBA AT THE CLOSE OF THE
WAR—FIRST STEPS TOWARD REGENERATION—GEN-
ERAL LUDLOW.

*T*HE Hon. Juan Gualberto Gomez, a representative negro of Cuba, a member of the Constitutional Convention at Havana, and a possible
future President of the Cuban Republic, is reported
to have said that he preferred Spanish slavery to
American rule. I am somewhat loath to believe that
Señor Gomez has been correctly reported in this instance,
since the eminent statesman of Santiago impressed me
when I had the pleasure of meeting him in February
1901, as being a person of some intelligence and too well
fed to " die of grief," as it is said he threatened to do
unless *Cuba Libre* was immediately established without
any reference whatever to American rights in the premises, and without any guarantee of stability. True or not,
the ebullition lacked importance, since if Mr. Gomez did
speak the words imputed to him, it will not be long before
he will find himself repudiated by the real public sentiment of the island, and if he did not break forth as alleged,
the statement that he did so is a mere idle rumor which
may be dismissed into that limbo of forgotten things to
which all other perversions of fact that emanate from
Cuba are relegated by time.

MAJOR WILLIAM MURRAY BLACK, U. S. A.
*Chief of Department of Public Works*

I make use of Mr. Gomez's alleged remark only because it gives me a nail upon which to hang a few pictures of the before-and-after order, showing, as mere words could not possibly show, some of the things that the United States have done for these people whose friends have chosen to represent them as being wholly devoid of the sentiment of gratitude. Scourged by Spain for 400 years, Cuba has been scoured by the United States for four, and a glance at the photographs which are presented in these pages will show some of the transformations.

It is scarcely conceivable that one who visits Havana to-day can fail to observe the marvelous transformation that has been wrought in that city by the American authorities, under the successive Military Governors, guided by the engineering skill of Major William Murray Black, until the spring of 1901 chief of the Department of Public Works. There are few people who are at all familiar with Cuban affairs who do not know the Havana of old by reputation at least. Not alone politically, but physically, that this potentially beautiful little city was a plague-spot, and a constant menace to the health, one might almost say, of this hemisphere, is a matter of common knowledge. Its streets were narrow, ill-paved, and dirty. Its sewers were barely less than so many open rivers of refuse and disease-breeding streams of filth. One could almost find one's way about its dark and devious streets by following this odor or that, provided one had been there long enough to differentiate one smell from another, and know whither and whence each one led. Refuse that was not carried off into the harbor by these sewers was left to accumulate and to decay in the highways themselves. The decaying bodies of dead animals were no uncommon sight on the public thoroughfares, and when these were merely of cats or dogs they were left to time and the processes of nature to remove; large carcasses were carted away and dumped at any convenient point— were sometimes taken out to sea and thrown overboard; not so far out, however, that they did not frequently return to become an offence upon the shores of the gulf.

Persons who swept the floors of their houses cast their sweepings into the streets. Garbage was similarly treated, except at the governor's palace and in other public buildings, where for some inscrutable reason large quantities of it were retained in-doors. Nearly two score of cartloads of dirt were removed from the former when the Americans came into control, and it is related by a keen observer of conditions as they existed at the close of Spanish supremacy, Mr. Franklin Matthews, that in one of the rooms of La Fuerza Castle, occupied by the civil guard, and in the group of public buildings of which the Captain-General's palace was the chief, the bodies of no less than fifteen dead cats and dogs were found. " These animals had not died of starvation," Mr. Matthews adds.

" They had strayed into this room in their search for food, and had died of the foul atmosphere. *A candle would not burn in the place.*"

A further pleasing feature of life in Havana under the Spanish system, preferred, according to rumor, by Mr. Gomez, who must not be confounded with Gen. Gomez, was the delicious habit householders had of emptying the day's collection of dirty water from second-story windows into the streets, whence it might, or might not, find its way to the gutter, and thence to the sewer openings at the corner, to pass any one of which was to risk one's health, and unless one held one's breath, to draw into one's system a select assortment of germs which might prove pleasing bottled for a bacteriological museum, but which most individuals would prefer not to have roaming around inside of them. Other customs, which may better be left to the imagination than described here, became fixed habits in the comparatively more squalid sections of the city, and the utter neglect of the public highways, some indication of which the reader may derive from an inspection of the 1899 pictures in these pages resulted in the city's becoming hardly less than a sort of municipal cesspool.

In most communities afflicted with such intolerable conditions, it might be expected that relief could be found along the harbor-front, or somewhere along such stretches of coast-line as Nature has vouchsafed. Those for instance who sometimes find the atmosphere of New York too subtly suggestive of earth for their comfort, are not unused to spending an afternoon, or an evening hour or two, on one of the roomy recreation piers provided for the purpose which are so health-giving to the toilers of the city in summer days. But until American days in Cuba this was not feasible for the overpowered citizens of its cities not because there were no recreation piers, and not because there was no beautiful coast-line, but because the water's edge in most of them and in Havana especially was a reeking mass of sewage and decayed organic matter, which, in bays that have no visible movement of their waters except in times of storm, possesses few attractions to the lover of fresh air. "The moment we stepped upon the wharf at the landing," writes Mr. Matthews in describing the conditions as they existed in Havana in 1899, "we needed no visual proof to know that we were in Havana. An odor which only such a city could produce, and a description of which need not be given, reached our nostrils." It requires no stretch of the imagination to see how such a harbor-line could be no refuge for those who thirsted for a breath of pure sweet air. Along the coast line, from La Punta to the terminus of the Vedado, conditions were better, but if the testimony of disinterested persons may be believed, they were scarcely more tolerable than those which aroused such a furor of discontent among the dwellers along the Long Island coast

146

some years ago when the offal of the New York city streets, dumped too close to the shores, was strewn along the beach from Coney Island to Far Rockaway.

Viewing the situation in the general and not in the specific case, to appreciate the work of the American authorities in Cuba it will be necessary first to review somewhat the condition of affairs in Havana and the island at large at the end of 1898 when the Americans took possession. As is well known, excepting in a few of the larger cities, the ordinary pursuits of the island had been almost entirely abandoned. The greater part of the sugar estates had been devastated and the mills and machinery destroyed. Very little tobacco was under cultivation and the vast herds of cattle which had formed the principal wealth of the dwellers of the plains in the interior of the island, had completely disappeared. Ruins dotted the country on every side and the former laborers and their families had either been gathered into the cities, or in the ranks of the Cuban Army, or had perished miserably. It has been seriously estimated that had the war lasted six months longer the entire rural population of Cuba would have been wiped out. The railroads had been but little molested excepting for some bridges and stationhouses burned and a portion of the rolling stock destroyed. Public works throughout the island had been suspended, and in the cities even the necessary collection of garbage had been almost totally neglected for months.

All of these conditions, added to the customary neglect of
sanitation which had always prevailed to a great extent in
Cuba, bade fair to make the succeeding summer the
most unhealthy known in the annals of the island. For
months such of the garbage of Havana as had been removed from the streets had been piled within the city
limits, at the head of the bay, in a festering, ill-smelling
heap. The 112 miles of Havana streets were heaped with
filth of all kinds, and of these streets ninety-three miles
which had been either paved with macadam or left unpaved, were so worn by long travel that the water from
the rains, and from slops thrown from the street doors,
lay in puddles in which the accumulated filth putrefied
under the hot rays of the sun. The roughness of some of
these streets was such that nothing but a large cart or
Army wagon could traverse them safely. As stated by
General Ludlow in his first report:—

"The physical condition of the city could only be described as frightful. There were several thousands of
reconcentrados in and about who had been herded like
swine and perishing like flies. They were found dead
in the streets and in their noisome quarters where disease
and starvation were rampant. Other thousands were
lacking food, clothing and medicines. The regular service of the city was practically paralyzed; street cleaning
had stopped and the force was suspended, and the houses
of assistance and hospitals were destitute of resources,

even food. No sanitary measures or rules were in force and the starving population—natives and citizens, as well as reconcentrados—used the street or any open place for the deposit of refuse and filth of all kinds. A woman killed by a railroad train lay on a principal street (Carlos III) for eight hours because an ambulance and the proper officials could not be found to remove her. It was nearly the same with all other branches of the city administration ; officials, clerks and employees had been unpaid for many months and the public offices were practically abandoned."

In Havana the government was in the hands of Spanish sympathizers between whom and the now jubilant Cubans there was the bitterest enmity. The government of the island and of the cities under the Spanish laws was so arranged as to afford a maximum of funds for the office holders and a minimum of return to the people. The laws themselves were most cunningly and ably devised. To a reader of the various proclamations, orders and legislative acts, the laws seemed innocent enough, but a closer investigation showed that no measure involving an expenditure of money could be taken excepting with the independent approval of a number of high officials, all of whom were of Spanish appointment, and that the execution of these laws could be expedited, or postponed indefinitely, at the will of the various functionaries. No work of a public character, whether executed by private or State funds, could be carried on without a concession, and a careful examination made later by the American authorities of many of these concessions showed that whatever may have been the benefits conveyed, the rights of the people were but little cared for. Sometimes it would seem that no returns to the city whatever were made for important privileges and monopolies granted.

Judicial proceedings were simply farcical and the authority of the officials to place prisoners in the status known as incommunicado, in which they were not allowed to hold any communication whatever with any one excepting their jailers or judges, provided a fearful weapon of tyranny. In many cases prisoners were found to have been in jail without trial for terms far beyond the maximum limit of punishment allowed by the law for the offences of which they had been accused. Such offences as are punishable by police courts and justices of the peace in the United States were tried before what were known as courts of the first instance. In these courts the judge acted as judge, jury and prosecuting attorney; interrogatories were made in private and the accused was not allowed to confront either his own witnesses or the witnesses of the prosecution. Nor did the accused have any means for hastening his trial other than by a money payment. There were no courts of equity and even after the American occupation such was the working of the law that verdicts were found and sentences pronounced

VAPOR STREET, HAVANA, *in January,* 1900

VAPOR STREET, HAVANA, *in June,* 1900

in strict accordance with the law, in which there was not a shadow of justice.

Municipalities were governed by what were termed ayuntamientos of which the alcade, or mayor, was the presiding officer, and the members of which were elected for one year to serve without pay. These ayuntamientos were divided into committees of one, two or three persons, which had charge of the various public institutions and works of the city such as markets, slaughter-houses, street cleaning, street repairs, and others. Inasmuch as the greater portion of the working time of any counselor was required to carry out the executive functions thus vested in him, and as there was no salary attached, this form of government was fruitful of corruption and neglect of duty. The paid servants of the city were generally the relatives or friends of those in power, and as is usual in such cases what work was done was done by a very small part of the mass of officials.

In the city of Havana, with a population of 217,000 and covering an area of 5,240 acres, the engineer force consisted of two men known as municipal architects and four or five assistants, and of a director of water-works with two assistants, without instruments and without records worthy of the name. Throughout the island public office was looked upon, with a few honorable exceptions, as a place for repairing broken fortunes or for taking care of indigent relatives. Responsibility to the people was little thought of and it was a matter of common knowledge that men appointed to the higher positions were expected to remit definite sums of money to the appointing powers in Spain. Some of the most sought-after offices of the custom house had no salary nor legal fees attached to them. Men who were strictly honorable in their private dealings —and the Spanish merchant is proverbially honest in financial transactions with his brother merchants—thought it only right to defraud the government. The police force of Havana had consisted of the guardia civile, who were always posted in twos, but in spite of the large number of men so employed an assassination society known as "Nanigo" existed for many years in the city, the first essential of membership in which was the killing of some human being, and portions of the city were unsafe to enter or pass through by day or night.

Such were the conditions when General Castellanos at the head of the few remaining Spanish troops sorrowfully left the city of Havana at noon on January 1st, 1899. At twelve o'clock on that day an amateur photographer took two views in quick succession of the Morro Castle; in the first one the Spanish flag is flying, the sky is overcast and the picture is dark and gloomy; in the second the stars and stripes have just been run to the top of the pole, the sun has burst forth, and the brightness of the picture is, we hope, an augury of the future of Cuba.

When the evacuation of Havana began General Francis

V. Greene was in command of the American troops and he immediately took measures to clean the city roughly as the Spaniards left, placing in direct charge of the work Captain W. L. Geary of the 2d Volunteer Engineers, with a force of non-commissioned officers of the same regiment as inspectors, and employing Cuban labor. General William Ludlow succeeded General Greene in command on December 21st and continued the work, occupying, with American troops, the different districts of the city in succession as the Spaniards left them, so that by January 1st the whole of the city streets had been partially cleaned.

On January 1st the entire city was under American control and though a portion of the Spanish police force remained, the entire city was patrolled and guarded by regular troops of the American Army. General Brooke, the Military Governor of the island was at first, with his staff, at the Hotel Inglaterra in Havana, but soon removed to the Hotel Trotcha in Vedado which had, up to that time, been occupied by the American Evacuation Commission. General Ludlow and his staff were also at the Inglaterra until better quarters could be prepared for them. Two regiments of United States troops, the 8th and 10th Infantry, were camped within the city and furnished the necessary men for guard and patrol duty. In spite of the national enmity between the different classes of the inhabitants of Havana, due to the precautions taken, no collisions took place. It had been desired by the Cubans to set aside the first week in January for a grand fiesta in celebration of the departure of the Spaniards, during which the victorious Cuban Army, or such portion as was encamped near the city, was to join in a grand street parade. Such a procedure was justly looked upon as dangerous and, with the acquiescence of prominent Cubans, it was decided that it had best be postponed, much to the regret of the people, who, however, bore their disappointment well.

To swell the confusion the city was full of strangers, many of whom had come to Havana on legitimate business enterprises, but many more were of the crowd of adventurers who are always to be found on occasions of this kind.

General Ludlow had been appointed by the President the Military Governor of the city of Havana under the orders of the commanding officer of the Division of Cuba. He was " charged with all that relates to the collection and disbursement of the revenues of the port and city and its police, sanitation and general government, under such regulations as may be prescribed by the President." Later, these orders were modified by relieving him of the responsibility for the collection and disbursement of the customs revenues of the port.

The special fitness of General Ludlow for this task was recognized by all. He had proved his gallantry and ability as a soldier in two wars and as an engineer during the long period of peace, after the Civil War having been charged with many important public works, including the charge of the water department of the city of Philadelphia, by special permission of Congress, and the duties of Engineer Commissioner of the District of Columbia.

The work accomplished in Havana during the time when he was in charge there from January 1, 1899 to May 1, 1900, showed the wisdom of the choice, and a study of the annual reports presented by him discloses not only the vast amount of work accomplished, but also plans for further work of constructive value to the new Republic, shortly to take its place in the family of nations. It was always a matter of regret to General Ludlow during his entire term of office that he was unable to induce the Medical Department of the United States Army to begin the work which later, under Major Walter Reed, Surgeon, U. S. Army, has given to America the honor of having discovered the mode of propagation of yellow fever, and has permitted the American authorities practically to free Havana from that dread scourge. General Ludlow's work was confined to his duties in Havana. He had there to clean and render sanitary a city which for years had been a menace to the health of the southern ports of the United States and which was, at that time in a condition worse than had ever before been known; to keep the peace between the discordant classes of the population, the Cubans and Spaniards, in the capital city which

had, at the same time, been the hot-bed of the revolution
and the home of those most loyal to Spain; to organize
a city government which should be Cuban in its best sense
but which should protect the rights of property of the
Spanish minority; to provide for an honest administration
of the finances and restore the credit of a bankrupt city
whose resources were crippled by unwise, if not corrupt,
concessions; to care for the homeless and starving; to
fit the prisons, hospitals and asylums for the work for
which they were intended; to start schools; to make an
efficient and self-respecting police force; to see that justice
was duly administered, and last, but not least, do all this
without embittering a race alien in thought, feelings and
customs, proud of their descent, language and institutions,
sensitive to a degree, and already chafing over the delay
in the time when the Cuban flag should fly alone over the
island. The magnitude of the work was but a stimulus to
General Ludlow; the greater the difficulty the higher was
his courage. His staff officers always found in him wise
counsel and cheering words in their greatest trials. He
was loyal to his superiors and to his subordinates; ready to
correct where work was badly done but unstinting in
praise where praise was deserved; ready to assume responsibility not only for his own acts, but for those of his
staff when criticized by higher authority; able, honest and
just, he hated a lie and had small patience with those
whom he found to be working for private ends and

LUDLOW PLACE, 1898

LUDLOW PLACE, 1901

against the public interest. In person and manner he was the beau ideal of a soldier and a cultivated gentleman. This, too, went for much with the Cubans. He was the soul of hospitality, and understanding that phase of the Latin character which causes it to reason by the heart rather than by the head, he constantly strove to better the understanding between the Americans on duty in Havana and the natives, by bringing them together in social functions of various kinds. His sense of humor never deserted him and a ludicrous turn of events would relieve the tension of the severest stress.

His readiness to meet emergencies, also, can be shown by two instances: One was in the case of *El Reconcentrado,* a paper which made a large part of its income by blackmail and the publication of obscene and slanderous accusations against public and private persons. It soon became evident that severe measures had to be taken and the paper was suspended and the editors compelled to promise " not to publish a newspaper of any kind; not to " insult any authority nor the chief of police of Havana; " not to disturb the public order in any respect; nor to " publish the private life of any one; to live quietly and " honestly as good citizens." These editors went straightway to the United States where they endeavored to create trouble by proclaiming that General Ludlow had interfered with the liberty of the press. The matter was fully investigated by the United States authorities and the action of the General entirely sustained. How the matter was looked upon in Havana can be understood when it is known that a number of the leading ladies of the city had prepared themselves to call on the General and thank him for his action, in the name of the women of Havana, but were dissuaded on the ground that undue publicity would thus be given them.

Another example was the case of the strikes of September, 1899. One Sunday afternoon the minds of the working classes were inflamed by parties calling upon them to follow the example of the Chicago anarchists, and a manifesto was issued in which the following phrase occurred: " Since there were in Chicago seven martyrs " who offered their lives when they raised the red flag " that exalted all workers, we must hoist in this free coun- " try the same flag that caused the death of so many true " and noble comrades." The leaders ordered a general strike for a certain day, which was to include all the working people of the city. The situation was rendered the more grave by the fact that even the bread of Havana was obtained from the public bakeries, so that the execution of this strike order would have added the menace of famine to the ordinary dangers attending such turbulences. The workingmen of Havana had really no just cause for complaint and did not desire to strike. The many, however, were coerced by the few. Action had to be taken and that quickly, for already minor disturbances had occurred. General Ludlow went at once to the root of the matter. He arrested a dozen of the labor leaders, "selecting those who had publicly committed "themselves to incendiary proclamations and speeches, "etc. . . . They were informed that the strike would "not be permitted, and that they would be held respon- "sible for its abandonment; that all men found idle in "the street, without visible occupation or means of sup- "port would be held as vagrants; that there were ac- "commodations, such as they were, in the cárcel and "presidio for a thousand or two arrests, and in the "Morro and Cabaña casemates for as many more; that "they would be released and escape punishment if they "acted in good faith and stopped all agitation for a "strike; and that otherwise the full power of the gov- "ernment would be used to control the situation in every "sense." To this those whose comfort the order most vitally affected readily agreed, and were immediately discharged. At the same time General Ludlow issued a proclamation to the people of Havana in which, in well chosen words, the rights and limitations of liberty were fully described. The strike was over and no more trouble was had from this source.

Gen. Ludlow's staff learned to love him, and there was not one who would not willingly have worked night and day in executing his orders. As a good executive officer, he knew how to work through others and at once assigned his various duties, military and civil, to the different members of his staff, and during the entire period of his command there was not a time when each had not the feeling that he was in real charge of his particular work, and would not be overruled excepting for weighty reasons.

One of the first works was the appointment of an ayuntamiento to take the place of that left by the Spaniards, which, for many reasons, could not be left in office. After consultation with leading Cubans, a new ayuntamiento was selected from the best representatives of all classes of the city. This ayuntamiento remained in power until June, 1900, when it was replaced by one elected by popular vote. It was freely confessed, later, that up to date, it has been the only ayuntamiento that has performed its duties with anything like the right spirit. In his dealings with the ayuntamiento, General Ludlow showed a rare tact, and guiding, rather than directing them, never offended the sensitive Spanish pride.

Throughout he showed a thorough understanding of the best method of dealing with a race which had been long subjected to tyranny, and which, though aspiring to liberty, did not comprehend its limitations and responsibilities. He was firm and just, taking action only when necessary, but then promptly and without temporizing.

# Chapter III

*T*HE external transformation of Havana, thanks
to the application of American ideas and carried out with characteristic American energy,
has been little short of marvelous. It almost needs
to be seen to be believed. The photographs which
I am fortunately able to present with this story
tell a portion of the story, not all of it. They show
but a tithe of the herculean task which has been performed
by Generals Wood and Ludlow and by Major Black and
his well-organized department in the Augean Stable of
the Antilles. In the first place, a working system had to
be devised which in itself was enough to tax the energy
and resources of the most energetic and resourceful man
to the uttermost. When one considers the peculiar kind
of chaos which existed at the beginning of American control in Cuba, and realizes how utterly hopeless, how without beginning or end, was the tangled skein of ruin
wrought by Spanish incompetence, neglect, and corruption, the magnitude of the task which confronted these
American soldiers may be realized even by those who,
critically inclined, have viewed the situation from distant
armchairs and through the eyes of newspaper correspondents on the alert for sensational " scoops." The mere

161

organization of a department which might successfully hope to work the physical regeneration of a city fallen into such evil estate was in itself an achievement which not many men would care to undertake—a fact which General Ludlow appreciated to the full when in his report of 1899-1900 he wrote concerning Major Black's accomplished work even at that early date:

" The organization of the department, its gradual expansion, the training of its employees, the simplification of methods, the augmented efficiency, and the increased economy of service are enduring monuments to the energy, intelligence, and professional ability of the responsible officer, who has inaugurated and conducted a tremendous work with the most conspicuous success."

As organized, the Department consisted of the following subdivisions: Office of the City Engineer; including the chief clerk, stenographers, and record division; the Pay Department; Property Department; Department of Streets; Department of Street Cleaning and Parks; Department of Waters and Sewers; Department of Harbor Works; Department of Buildings; Department of Municipal Architect, and Department of Surveys.

As already stated, the work of cleaning the city of Havana had been begun by Captain Geary, assisted by a small force of non-commissioned officers of the 2d Volunteer Engineers, with Cuban workmen. The quarters of this force were in a shed on Zulueta street, in an enclosed piece of ground belonging to the city, which had formerly been the site of a part of the city wall. In this yard was found the stock which had belonged to the owner of a concession for paving the city streets. The regular street cleaning had been done, after a fashion, by machine sweepers, under a contract, which also included the removal of the garbage. Machine cleaning of the rough streets was simply impracticable, and that portion of the contract was discontinued at once. This was easily done since the contractor had not been paid for some time, and the contract time had expired. Temporary arrangements were made by means of which the removal of the garbage was continued. It had been the hope of the Chief Engineer that he would be able to form a modern department of municipal public works modeled on that of the District of Columbia Engineer Department, in which the employees should be Cubans. This was soon found to be impracticable inasmuch as, with but few exceptions, it had proved impossible to find on the island men capable of conducting the work, either clerical or out of doors. As soon as practicable, men were brought from the United States and, with the exceptions above noted, the responsible positions had to be filled with Americans. Whether through lack of training or through inherent defects, it seemed to be impossible for the Cubans at first to understand what was meant by a strict obedience to orders, and by accuracy in executing work.

This was exemplified in one case where one of the best Cubans was sent to count the number of sewer openings in a certain number of city blocks. He made three separate counts which all differed each from the others, until finally his chief in despair was compelled to send an American to do the work. This did not result from idleness or lack of desire to do, for many of the Cuban employees later became excellent public servants.

The volume of work confronting this Department at the outset was enormous. There were many public buildings in Havana which had been vacated by the Spaniards and which, when taken possession of by the Government of Intervention were found to have been looted, not only of their furniture but of all small movable articles they contained, such as gas fixtures, door knobs, Venetian blinds, etc., etc., and in general had been defiled with filth in the most disgusting manner. It was hard to believe that the palace of Segundo Cado, occupied by the officer second in command in the island, with his assistants, could have been the home of decent people. The fortifications, which had been garrisoned up to the last moment, were found to be in an equally filthy condition. This was particularly the case with the old Castillo de la Fuerza, the oldest fortification probably in the Western Hemisphere, built originally by Fernando de Soto, and first destroyed in 1538 by pirates, which had been promptly rebuilt and was in use successively

CALZADA DE JESUS DEL MONTE, 1899

CALZADA DE JESUS DEL MONTE, 1901

as the Governor-General's Palace, military prison, and barracks for the Guardia Civile, down to the date of occupation. It was a bastioned work of stone, with a tier of casemates on the ground floor, and with barracks built on the site of the barbette battery. On entering the fort in the early days it was necessary to hold the breath in passing the doors of these casemates, and when they were cleaned one of them was found to contain the bodies of about thirty cats and dogs, which had entered and perished by reason of the foul air. The building adjoining the palace of the admiral of the port, used as a post-office, was in an almost equally bad condition, and had been a deadly nest of yellow fever during the preceding summer. The shores of the bay were vile, and its waters polluted. The city abattoir, called the " Mataderos," was situated on the banks of a small stream flowing into the bay near its head. The stream through its whole course from the Mataderos to the bay was littered with the viscera of animals slaughtered, and its course lay directly across the streets which were the main thoroughfares of the suburbs, the Cerro and Jesus del Monte. Instances of this kind could be multiplied indefinitely. The condition of the streets has been described before.

All this had to be rectified and without delay. There were no tools nor implements of a proper kind to be had in Havana. There was nothing in the possession of the

city which could be used. In addition, the Cuban workmen employed were so suspicious of the good faith of
the Government, doubtless from long and doleful experience, that it was necessary to pay them every week, and
all this had to be done with vouchers similar to those
required in the United States, and without any adequate
force other than the men mentioned. Within the first
three months after, a very efficient department of municipal public works had been formed, and on the first of
March the organization of this department could compare favorably with any similar organization in the
United States.

Captain Geary was mustered out with his regiment
and returned to the United States in April. His work
had been of the utmost value and had been conducted
with fearlessness of danger and with the system of a
trained public servant. He was a graduate of the U. S.
Military Academy who had resigned and gone into the
civil service of the United States. When the war with
Spain broke out he volunteered and was made a Captain
in the 2d Volunteer Engineers; after the muster out of
his regiment he again volunteered and saw service in the
Philippines, and the country is now fortunate in having
him in the commissioned force of the Regular Army.

He was succeeded by Mr. P. D. Cunningham, civil
engineer, who later became chief engineer of the city of
Havana and remained such until his appointment as con-

sulting engineer of the Mexican Boundary Commission, a promotion thoroughly well deserved, but which afterwards led to the loss of his life by drowning while on survey work in the Rio Grande river. Mr. Cunningham was succeeded by Lieut. Wm. J. Barden, Corps of Engineers, U. S. Army, who still retains that position. The Chief Engineer of the Department was particularly fortunate in having the assistance of these gentlemen, both of whom showed the highest ability and devotion to duty. On their honesty, good judgment and business capacity, the fullest reliance could be placed. No small share of the success of the work in Havana is due to each.

In the Record Department the clerks had to be brought from the United States and trained in the card-index system. The magnitude of the work of this office is shown by the fact that 14,266 cases were placed on record up to December 31, 1900.

The Pay Department, until fully organized and finally developed under Messrs. W. F. Smith and Wm. C. Strong, was a source of anxiety. It was absolutely essential that no mistakes should be made in this Department, and that the Cubans should be shown that it was possible to handle public money without malfeasance of any kind. The accounts had to be so kept that, at all times, it could be shown at a moment's notice just what was the state of each specific allotment for each work, how much had been allotted, how much had been pledged, for materials or services rendered, and how much had been paid. What this means can only be appreciated by those who have had charge of large and complicated public works. Under the old régime, commissions had always to be paid to purchasing agents of the government, two bills being rendered, one showing the amount to be actually paid to the merchant and one the bill to be rendered on the government voucher. This system had to be absolutely broken up and it was long before the Cuban merchants found that no commissions were to be paid and that the government demanded the lowest market rates. On one occasion a bill having been rendered for certification to an assistant engineer, he said to the merchant presenting it: " I believe there is the usual commission; how much is it?" "Yes," said the merchant, " ten per cent." " Very well," said the engineer, " re-write your bill deducting ten per cent, and I will forward it for payment."

Another custom was that money in payment of labor was given in bulk to an official, who then allotted it to the foremen, who finally paid it to the laborers; each of these officials lowering the amount somewhat as it passed through his hands, as it was thoroughly recognized that each man having a government position had to render up a portion of his pay to the appointing officer. This custom was broken up with difficulty, for although from the first, the laborers were paid in person by the pay-master, it was some time before they discovered that they did not have to turn over a portion of their earnings to the foreman. Frauds of all kinds were attempted and the most elaborate system had to be devised to prevent them. The total amount disbursed up to December 31, 1900, was $4,374,498.10. This amount was fully accounted for and frequent inspections by the Inspectors-General, U. S. Army, and two inspections by skilled accountants, re-sulted in compliments to the Department. At the end of 1900 the number of vouchers was 615 per month. The force on the rolls was—laborers 3,440, and men of higher grade 446—total, 3,886. Payments were made from the first in United States currency. This was made neces-sary by the vagaries of the Spanish money used in the island, in which a five-dollar gold piece (centen) was worth $5.30 in gold (Spanish). Silver fluctuated in the neighborhood of from 65¢ to 85¢ on the dollar, in which $5.30 of Spanish gold was worth in the neighborhood of $4.50 American gold. Payments were made to the work-men, at first weekly; afterwards once in ten days, and later, as their confidence increased, semi-monthly.

The Property Department, in which materials were bought and cared for, was finally under the charge of Mr. Beauregard Weber, on whom fell the task of obtain-ing the materials called for by the assistant engineers in charge of the works, and of seeing that they reached their proper destination; caring for those that were not actually used at the time of purchase.

An incidental result of the clerical work of this and the other departments of the United States in Cuba, was the introduction of the typewriting machine and the enlargement of the sphere of women in Cuba by their employment as stenographers and typewriters, a thing unknown before the American intervention. One of the minor incidents in starting the office was the procurement of office furniture. This was mainly obtained from the pawnshops which had been thoroughly stocked with the finest office furniture, looted by the Spaniards before leaving. There is no doubt that a part of the furniture so bought was replaced in the very office from which it had been stolen a month earlier.

The Department of Streets was, in succession, under the charge of Captain Geary, Mr. Cunningham, and Mr. W. N. McDonald, who had as principal assistant for a portion of the time, Mr. José R. Villalon, who afterwards became Secretary of Public Works of the island. This department had charge of repairing the streets, made necessary, not only for traffic purposes, but also for sanitation. The difficulties overcome by this department in obtaining plant and materials for the repair of streets and training workmen, were enormous. By December, 1900, the entire 111 lineal miles of streets of Havana had been repaired, and most of the thoroughfares were in fine condition.

Preparatory to the work of sewering and paving Havana, which was from the start foremost in the mind of the Government of Intervention, it was necessary to make a detailed survey of the city to show the width, and length of the streets, positions of houses, and grades. Havana had been built up without any systematic arrangement of grades excepting on one or two streets. The result was that in the time of rains, the run off from a large district would be concentrated in a single street, and the sewers being inadequate, this street became a raging torrent with water up to the hubs of the wheels. It is credibly related that on one such occasion a mule which fell in Obispo street, the principal shopping street of the city, and which has about a three per cent grade, was drowned before it could be gotten on its feet.

Another interesting problem was the testing and selection of materials for the permanent paving of the city. Photographs of both paved and unpaved streets, published in the official reports, show better than words can express, some of the work of this Department. The cost of this work, after the Department had been organized, compares very favorably with the unit cost of similar work in the United States.

The Department of Street Cleaning and Parks was at an early date under the charge of Mr. A. C. Harper, who had been an assistant engineer in the Engineer Department of the U. S. Army. Under Mr. Harper, this department was thoroughly organized on a most improved modern basis. The streets were swept by hand, the men working in gangs, excepting towards the end of 1900, when it was found possible to secure a few responsible men who could be trusted to work singly during the entire day, in the streets of the business portion of the city. It was Mr. Harper's pride that the back alleys and streets of the slums were as clean as the business portion, and that the whole city, in spite of the bad pavements, should have its streets in better condition than those of Washington. Two million, five hundred and fifty thousand square meters were cleaned daily at an average cost of 26¢ per 1,000 square meters. In the last six months 4,645 cart loads of materials were removed per month, weighing in tons, 2,566 pounds. To bring about these results a plant had to be created, and laborers and foremen trained; and stables and repair shops established. The Department of Street Cleaning in Havana to-day, will bear comparison with that of any city of the world. The work of this Department included also the cleaning of the suburban towns in the Municipality of Havana, two of which, Regla and Casa Blanca, were in as bad condition as the worst parts of Havana.

As stated, at the time of the American occupation, garbage was being placed on some vacant ground at the

AGUILA STREET, HAVANA, 1900

AGUILA STREET, HAVANA, 1901

head of the bay. Prior to the war, it had been taken a few miles out into the country. Owing to the danger of sickness this disposal had to be changed. A crematory was erected, dumping platforms built, and a floating plant, consisting of lighters and tugs procured, and the material was burnt or taken to sea daily. Knowing the noisesomeness and discomfort in a community ordinarily caused by the presence of a garbage wharf, some difficulty was encountered in obtaining a site for it on the crowded shores of the Bay of Havana. The old San Ambrosia Hospital, otherwise known as the Hospital Militar, was a large building occupying a block of ground immediately to the north of the Navy Yard. Between it and the bay was a space, roughly, 130 meters square. A portion of it was occupied by some low stone buildings which formed adjuncts to the hospital. This hospital and its surroundings had probably the very worst reputation in the world as a yellow fever pest hole, with a mortality record of 60 per cent, and vessels which had discharged cargoes at the lumber wharves near it were subjected to extra quarantine on their arrival in the United States. The walls and the ground were supposed to be impregnated with yellow fever germs, and at first, in spite of the fine character of the building, there were serious thoughts of burning it to the ground for the purpose of removing it, and its accumulated filth and dangers. Incidentally, it may be stated, that after the building had been thoroughly repaired and cleaned up by the Engineer Department, its lower floors were and are now used as a storage warehouse, and the upper floor has been turned into a fine school, accommodating 1,300 pupils, and with all modern conveniences. It was rightly believed that no neighborhood which had stood the Hospital Militar, could be injured by establishing garbage wharves there, and the space between the hospital and the bay was set aside for this use. The small buildings previously spoken of were in such condition at the time of the American occupation, in one of them having been found a putrefying heap of human remains, that they had to be torn down and destroyed. A crematory was erected, and an office building for the inspector of the dumps, and platforms and other adjuncts were built. Under the energetic and able management of Mr. J. L. Mudge, the much feared Talipiédra Wharf, in spite of its use as a place for the collection of the city refuse, became actually a park to which on Sunday afternoons, the families of the neighborhood came to get a little pure air from the bay.

Havana is dotted with parks of greater or smaller extent, which contained many fine specimens of beautiful trees and plants. They were in awful condition at the time of the American occupation. Instead of grass spaces the ground was covered with flowering plants, and the walks were bordered with board fences. The gardeners who had been in charge had not been paid for some time, and had gained their living by raising vegetables in the interior of these flower gardens. They were paid regularly by the Americans from the first, and this illicit source of gain prohibited. Later it was necessary to discharge them as it was impossible to keep them from these corrupt practices.

The parks were finally taken in hand by Mr. Harper, the fences taken down, flowers removed, and the spaces thus exposed were made into fine grassy lawns, the first that had ever been known in Havana. The formation of these lawns was a mystery to the Cubans, who could not be convinced that the Americans did not have some secret method and kind of seed by which they were produced, and did not realize that it was simply the result of careful attention.

The parks, some of which had been shunned by decent people, quickly were utilized for places of rest and recreation, and no part of the American work in Cuba was more thoroughly appreciated. The transformations were truly wonderful. Mr. Harper took the greatest interest in his work, and inspired his employees with the same enthusiasm. The space in front of the palace occupied by General Ludlow's headquarters, was at first a mud hole. This was paved and a small park arranged for. On the Saturday evening following the first Fourth of July, General Ludlow had prepared to give a large public reception at his headquarters, and on the preceding day had said to the Chief Engineer how sorry he was that he had been unable to get some trees in the park in time for it. This was mentioned to Mr. Harper, who said nothing, and things remained as they were during Friday. On Saturday morning the General looking down out of his windows found the park filled with beautiful trees from ten to thirty feet high, and could not believe his senses. He turned to the Chief Engineer and said: " Where did you get your lamp?"

One of the extremely pleasant duties was the restoration of the grounds and ditch of the Fuerza to their ancient condition, and also the preservation of the ruins of the old city walls, in both of which works General Wood took great interest. Another was the transformation of the vacant space to the west of the Punta, and at the foot of the Prado from a receptacle for all sorts of garbage into a beautiful park, with a strong sea-wall on the Gulf front, forming the beginning of a bund, or waterside drive which, when completed, will not be equaled in the world. In authorizing the Engineer Department to do this work, General Wood has added, greatly to the beauty of Havana. This park faces directly on the open waters of the Gulf, with shores of rock which fall steeply into great depths, so that the waves of the sea roll in at full height, and to within a few feet of the promenade, where, in time of storms, they rear themselves and break with a vast upheaval of foam and spray. On calm afternoons the view from the sea wall along the crescent-shaped front of Havana, with its many tinted buildings, out to the Western horizon, where, over the dark blue waters of the Gulf the setting sun tints the sky with its greatest splendors, is entrancingly beautiful. The atmosphere is singularly pure and clear, and to the eastward, in the rosy sunset glow, the masonry of the Morro Castle, which seems to spring naturally from the rough rocks of its base, takes on colors which cannot be reproduced by art.

The Water and Sewer Department was organized by Captain A. W. Cooke, who remained in Havana after the departure of his regiment, the 2d Volunteer Engineers, and was its efficient head until he resigned in the summer of 1900, to accept a very advantageous position in the United States. He was succeeded by Mr. Ovidio Giberga, a Cuban engineer who had received his training in the United States. It seemed the irony of fate that, in the following fall, Captain Cooke, who had passed unhurt through the dangers attending the first cleaning up of the city, should have revisited Havana on business and should have died within a few days of his arrival, a victim of the dread yellow fever.

Havana is blessed in its pure water supply. Water was first introduced into the city toward the end of the 16th century, from the Almendares river, through an open aqueduct called the Zanja Real, which started from a pool formed by a dam placed about four miles above the mouth of the river. The Zanja ended in a ditch or moat outside the walls of the city, which it supplied with water. In 1837 a set of filter-beds was constructed on the banks of the river near the inlet of the Zanja, and was connected with the city by a 20-inch iron main. This was known as the aqueduct of Ferdinand VII. The works of the present system of water supply were constructed between 1880 and 1893. Five miles above the old dam, and about six miles from Havana, a spring of pure water, having a daily flow of about seventy million gallons, bursts from the west bank of the Almendares river. This spring was carefully walled in and protected from overflow by the river during freshets, and the surface of the ground was drained in such manner as to prevent contamination by surface water. From this spring, water is led through a covered brick aqueduct about six feet in diameter to the reservoir which is situated in the Cerro. The aqueduct crosses the river beneath its bed, close to the spring, and the masonry at the spring, in the tunnel, and in the aqueduct itself is a most creditable piece of work. This aqueduct is called the Canal de Albear. This name and a statue in the city commemorate the gratitude of the people to Colonel de Albear, an engineer in the Spanish Army, who constructed the aqueduct. The water is wonderfully clear,

ESCOBAR STREET, 1899

ESCOBAR STREET, 1901

and a small piece of silver thrown into the reservoir can be seen shining at its bottom through a depth of twenty feet.

The water department of the city was better organized than any other branch of the municipal service, but even the fine aqueduct had been allowed to fall in need of repairs, and work had to be done at the river crossing to prevent its destruction. The distribution system through the city, contained parts of the old system of Ferdinand VII. It was found that the water pressures in the houses were not what they should be, and an examination showed the cause. Leaks and stoppages existed everywhere in the pipes of the old system. One piece taken out and brought to the office was a curiosity. In this the workman had neglected to calk first with tow and had simply poured the lead solder into the open joint. When the joint was taken up there was a lump about the size of a derby hat in the interior of the pipe. This was simply a sample of the kind of work which was found. Water waste prevailed everywhere, and energetic measures had to be taken. There was nothing like an equal. system of distribution of water. Every legalized abuse existed and on the whole it was found that the equitable, proper and financially economical use of water was no more understood in Havana than in New York. Among the improvements made, were the supplying of the suburb of Casa Blanca and the fortresses of Cabana and Morro

179

with water by means of a 6-inch pipe, leading across the
harbor, with a small pumping station in Casa Blanca;
the construction of a main around the head of the bay,
for supplying Regla and the intermediate suburbs; the
construction of a pumping station for the high service
necessary for Cerro and Jesus del Monte, and Marianao,
and the installation in Havana of modern plugs for fire
service.

There were about forty miles of old sewers in Havana.
These had been constructed apparently on the shortest
line from some particular house or locality which was
to be served, to the bay or sea. They ordinarily were
situated just below the street pavement; were rectangular
in cross-section, with sidewalks and top of rough stone
and a bottom of natural rock or roughly paved stone.
They were totally unfit for carrying anything but storm
water, but as modern toilet arrangements began to be
introduced in Havana, the houses were necessarily connected with them, and at the time of American intervention the sewers were in a frightful condition. There was
no map in existence which showed their location or
course, and they were discovered usually by the odor
arising from a sewer opening. They were found and
cleaned, by tearing up the streets and removing the accumulated filth by hand. All possible precautions were
taken to prevent sickness in pursuing this most unpleasant, but most necessary labor, and it is gratifying

to be able to state that not a case of sickness was known to have resulted therefrom.

Together with this sewer work the installation of proper plumbing in the buildings of the city was taken in hand. When plumbing installations were ordered by the sanitary department, the plans were furnished, and in many cases the work done, by the Engineer Department. No plumber able to make a wiped joint was to be found in Havana, nor was there adequate knowledge of modern plumbing systems, so that not only the materials but also the men to install them had to be brought from the United States. Another improvement worked was in the night soil service. Odorless excavators were imported and put in use, to replace the filthy hand cleaning which had been done, or not done, prior to the American occupation.

As stated before, the subject of a proper sewerage system for Havana had been, from the first, under serious consideration. In the almost panicky condition of the people of the United States over the dangers of Havana, not only to the army, but to the cities on the southern sea-ports, the greatest haste was urged on the American authorities, and absurd propositions to install a complete sewerage system in Havana within three months received strong political backing. Under these circumstances it required a strong will and clear judgment on the part of the Military Governor to act wisely. There was no map of Havana in sufficient detail on which to make the proper calculations for designing a sewer system, and no experiments had been made looking to a proper and economical means of disposal. Prior to the American intervention, an individual had urged upon the city a plan for sewering and paving a portion of it, and formalities for the granting of a concession to him had been partially completed. He too, urged his claims on the Military Governor. After careful consideration it was determined, however, that Havana could be made clean and free from disease without a sewer system, and that such delay as might be necessary to permit surveys to be made and a proper system devised, with the aid of the best sewer experts attainable, was not only justified but was most to the public interest. This decision received not unlooked-for abuse from interested parties who had hoped to profit very largely at the city's expense. Its wisdom, however, was recognized by General Wood, when he succeeded in charge of the city, and the action has been abundantly justified by the completion of a contract which will afford a thoroughly efficient system of sewers and pavements for the whole of Havana, at a cost less than had been contemplated, in the proposed concession before mentioned, for providing sewers and pavements for a portion of this area.

The sewer system was devised by Mr. D. E. McComb, Civil Engineer, Washington, D. C., and the final project was made by Mr. Samuel M. Gray, of Providence, Rhode Island.

In gathering the data necessary, very interesting information was obtained relating to the tides and currents of the Gulf, and the Bay of Havana. Havana is situated in a bight of the coast, and in front of it the Gulf Stream forms an eddy, so that the flow of the water passes from the mouth of the harbor along the city frontage, to the westward, almost the entire time. There is but one real tide a day in the harbor, and the rise is about the same in the Gulf and at the head of the bay, averaging about eight-tenths of a foot. The surface flow at the mouth is almost invariably outward, the flood current entering from the east as a subsurface current and not showing on the surface until well within the harbor.

The works of the Port of Havana were formerly a State institution managed by a Junta with an Engineer Director in immediate charge. General Ludlow placed these works under the Chief Engineer, along with the municipal work. Captain A. H. Weber of the 2d Volunteer Engineers was placed in immediate charge, and in the conduct of these works, and all other works intrusted to him, Captain Weber added to the reputation which he obtained in his twenty years' service as an assistant engineer in the Engineer Department of the U. S. Army as a thoroughly reliable and clear-headed assistant, absolutely devoted to duty. In the many problems that arose it sometimes occurred that work was given to Captain Weber outside the line of his former experience, but in not a single instance did he fail to merit the full confidence that was reposed in him by his superiors.

The work of the port as found organized under the direct charge of Señor José Pujals, was the only really efficient organization which the Department discovered in Cuba. Señor Pujals was a most courteous gentleman, and an able engineer, and it was a great pleasure to the intervening government to retain so honorable a public servant in service. The same may be said of his assistants. Additions were made to the department, but almost all of the old personnel was retained. The work carried on by this department included the cleaning of the shores of the bay, and the periodical cleaning out of the vile Mateadoras creek; dredging in the bay, and the repair and construction of piers and bulkheads.

The Bay of Havana has been about the most maligned natural body of water known, but when the city was cleaned, and kept clean, the bay promptly cleaned itself. The worst portions are the shores at its head, for the bulkheading and clearing of which projects have been formed, but not yet carried out. Even the water in that vicinity was clean as compared with the Chicago river, and portions of the harbors of New York and Philadelphia. A portion of the staff of General Ludlow lived in a large building on the harbor front, a little over a half mile from its mouth, and it was a favorite diversion in the early morning to watch the schools of fish ply about the water directly beneath the house walls. The presence of the fish and the fact that they could be seen was a sufficient proof of the clearness of the water.

One of the busiest branches of the service was the Building Department which, under Captain T. H. Huston, formerly of the 2d Volunteer Engineers, who organized it and remained at its head until the fall of 1900, when he received a most advantageous position in civil life, reached a high degree of efficiency. Captain Huston was succeeded by Mr. G. W. Armitage, who had been his assistant.

All kinds of construction work were carried on by this department, and the records were so carefully kept that the unit cost of each class of work, both of materials and labor, was known accurately, so that work projected and estimated for was completed inside the estimates, and work done by contract was let under prices which exceeded the estimated cost only by the usual contractor's profit. The work of this department was very interesting. The better class of houses in Havana were solidly constructed of stone, with heavy side walls. The floors and roof had the same construction which usually consisted of a series of deep joists laid quite closely together. over which was placed, at right angles 2" x 4" strips spaced so as to support an ordinary flat tile, a layer of which was then set with mortar joints. Over this was from two to three inches of sand obtained from rotten limestone, called " coca." On this again was spread a layer of mortar in which the tile which formed the floor and roof, as the case may be, was laid. The roofs were flat as a rule, and the side walls were ordinarily extended about two and one-half feet above them, forming a parapet. The addition of another story was a simple matter. Smaller houses had roofs with a very steep pitch, covered usually with semi-cylindrical tile. The lines of these roofs were ordinarily slightly curved, the effect being very picturesque.

Many beautiful woods were found in the old buildings which, when stripped of their disfiguring coat of paint and given an oil finish had a lovely coloring. As an example of the profusion of fine timber formerly found in Cuba, it may be stated that the wharf at Santiago was decked entirely with mahogany planks. Woods of equal richness in coloring were used for railroad ties.

The plan of the houses was well fitted for the hot climate. Ordinarily a single depth of rooms with lofty ceilings was built around a patio or court, with corridors inside and out. This court sometimes was screened by awnings and ornamented with fountains and plants.

Nearly a million dollars was expended in this department up to December 30th, 1901. Practically all the public buildings in Havana received more or less attention

PALATINO ROAD, 1899

PALATINO ROAD, 1901

from it, and some were almost entirely reconstructed. The department must be given the credit for introducing into Cuba expanded metal concrete construction for the cheaper class of houses, a style of building well suited to the climate. In addition to this construction work, there were installed in hospitals, prisons and other public institutions, modern sanitary plumbing, lavatories, electric light plants, steam laundries and steam kitchens. One of its most extensive works was the transforming of the Hospital Militar, alluded to earlier. The skill and taste shown, as well as the economy and efficiency of management, were most creditable.

The office of the Municipal Architect was entirely distinct. Some of the building laws of Havana are very wise, especially those relating to the exterior construction, adornment and painting. Under these laws, private individuals desiring to build were compelled to obtain permits from the municipal architect in the usual manner. For this reason it was deemed best that the municipal architect's office which had the charge and supervision of this, should be entirely Cuban, and the Department was very fortunate in obtaining a fearless and honest head for it in Señor Luis de Arozaréna, a well-known citizen of Cuba.

On the arrival of the Americans in Cuba many maps of Havana were found. These all proved to be on too small a scale to be used in detailed municipal work, and almost all were quite inaccurate. Some of the maps appeared to be beautiful specimens of cartography, but a close investigation showed that they bore not a very close relation to the accidents of the ground which they were supposed to picture. This was notably the case with the Spanish engineer maps of the fortifications around Havana. Under these circumstances it was deemed best to make an accurate chart of Havana and its surroundings. As before stated, the portion within the city was made by the Street Department; the remaining portion of the original Department of Havana was mapped under the charge of Mr. Joseph A. Sargent. In carrying on his work Mr. Sargent had some forty different maps of the country for his guidance, but no two of them agreed. Almost all of Mr. Sargent's assistants were Americans.

To the force of Americans employed in the Engineer Department too much credit cannot be given for their faithfulness to duty. Where work was to be done and time was pressing, as was the case through that first year of stress, office hours were entirely disregarded, and when yellow fever appeared in Havana they remained at their posts. A very few were scared away. Happily the force was little touched by the fever; a few became sick, but only two died. Among the employees were several young American women, typewriters and stenographers, and their pluck was equal to that of the men. Our country owes a debt of gratitude to the men and women in this and the other departments of the intervening government for upholding its good name, and conducting a missionary work which will have most far-reaching results. It is a pity that the names of all cannot be recorded and made known.

After the arrival of General Wood in Havana, the Department of Havana was consolidated into the Department of Cuba, and the field of labor was correspondingly enlarged. One of the important works which fell to the Engineer Department, was the compilation of an organic law for the Department of Public Works of the island; the drawing up of its blank forms, and the translation of the whole into Spanish, not an easy task when it is remembered that differences in methods and work are always reflected in a language. For example, it was impossible to find a Spanish word corresponding to our term "public property" and the word "material" which had been used somewhat in that sense in branches of the Spanish military service, had to be adopted and defined.

Throughout Cuba was found the quickening hand of the Americans; roads and bridges built; hospitals and schools established; and prisons renovated, showed the work of officers of the various arms of the service. Cuba to-day is a very different country from what it was on December 31, 1898.

In the little band of Americans which formed the staff

189

of the Commanding-General, mention must be made of one whose name but rarely appeared, and who has never been associated with any particular work, but yet whose influence was felt everywhere, removing threatened friction between the heads of the various departments, and by wise counsel strengthening the hand of his commanding officer. This was the Adjutant-General, Colonel H. L. Scott, U. S. V., Captain 7th Cavalry. It is a sad reflection on the system of rewards in our military service that after the hard work, well done, Colonel Scott will finish his career in Cuba with exactly the same rank and pay in the regular service as that which he had before the war.

The details of Major Black's organization and its workings are so vast that it would require twice the number of pages at my disposal to set them forth, but one special item of unusual significance in the matter of the personnel of the Engineering Department is worthy of note. It may be added that in the assignment of work in all the departments now in operation in Cuba the same idea is followed out, and to such a degree that it may be said that almost every penny that has been expended in Cuba for the advancement of Cuban health and prosperity in the line of public works has gone into Cuban pockets. I quote from Major Black's report of May 1, 1900, published in the report of General Ludlow:

"In forming the personnel of the department, prefer-ence has been given to Cubans seeking employment. The absolute lack of experience of the natives of this island in general in modern municipal work has made it necessary to employ Americans to a great extent. It is believed, however, that this department has, at the expense of some money and a great deal of time, succeeded in placing in training a number of Cubans for advancement later to higher posts. It would have been possible to have made a better showing in cost had none, with but few exceptions, but Americans been employed in all positions above the grade of ordinary laborer, but it is not believed that that would have been the proper policy to be pursued. In the works promotions have been made from the lower grades to the higher, with excellent results throughout, and a number of excellent foremen and inspectors have been obtained thereby. As time passes, and as Cubans of the requisite training and acquirements become available, the number of Americans can be gradually decreased. To-day there are not in the island of Cuba enough trained Cuban engineers, architects, master-mechanics, master-workmen, stenographers, and type-writers to carry on the works that are required."

From the time when Major Black's report was made, and his relinquishment of his office in this particular respect he more than fulfilled the implied pledge of this paragraph. Cuba for the Cubans has been the key-note of American administration in that island, and those who state aught to the contrary do so either in ignorance or in wilful perversion of the facts.

With the results of the methods of this Department, we of the American public are much concerned to-day. Among those who comprehend the difficulties of the work that was undertaken by them the recognition of the admirable service rendered by the responsible heads of the various departments is inevitable. By those who see only the results equal appreciation will be shown, although these may fail to realize the intense application, the unremitting energy, the enthusiasm, and the discouragements through which the Cuban tree, grafted with American ideals, has been made to bear such good fruit. Havana of to-day is a redeemed Havana, and while of old it was said that Havana is not Cuba, it is true to-day that the same energy and spirit of upliftment which has shown such remarkable results in the capital city of the island, are typical of the work throughout. Those who left Cuba in former days, despite the enjoyment of the *dolce far niente* hours spent within its boundaries, left it with a sense of relief. To-day, after a brief sojourn, it is left with regret and with a positive sense of affection. Somehow or other Havana brought to myself the sensation which a glorious toy would have brought in my boyhood days, and I should not have regretted it had I been permitted to remain there indefinitely to enjoy its many charms. It is a smiling city. It is a clean city, and as a haven of

THE SEA WALL OF LA PUNTA

LA PUNTA, 1900

delight, of rest, and of pleasure it may be called without exaggeration a miniature Paris. The scouring it has received from the street-cleaning forces has made its highways sweet and fair to look upon. The rebuilding of these highways has made traffic throughout their quaint and devious length a delight. The harbor, once known as the natural home of all sorts and conditions of disease-breeding germs, has now some of the unspeakable charm that we look for along the Venetian canals. The public parks, the broad drives through the Cerro, the Vedado, the Palatine Road, the Esplanade of La Punta—all to-day suggest, even to an unimaginative mind, a municipal paradise, and whatever the future may hold for those who have wrought this transformation; whether they find or do not find that appreciation of the strenuous effort they have so self-sacrificingly put forth in behalf of the Havanese and the Cubans generally which is their due, the American rulers of the island, since January 1, 1899, may regard with pride and personal satisfaction the results which are obvious to any open eye and to any fair mind.

If Mr. Gomez prefers General Weyler, with his atrocities, to General Wood and his beneficent despotism, with the evidences of the great work accomplished before the eyes of the world, one cannot but feel sorry for Mr. Gomez; nor can we escape the conviction that if he represents any considerable portion of the Cuban public, then a considerable portion of the Cuban public is unfit to assume the responsibilities of self-government, and that, therefore, our obligations, not alone to humanity, but to Cuba itself may require us willingly or unwillingly to assume once more the responsibilities of the Trust.

In the matter of breathing-spots in cities, the record at Havana is typical.

Visitors to the Havana of former days look back with much sentimental pleasure upon the public squares and parks of that charming little city of which I have already spoken generally. Among the first questions that were asked of me upon my return by friends who knew the Cuba of other days was as to the condition of these breathing-spots, and most solicitous have all seemed to be for the Prado, which, once seen in its beauty and gayety, is not soon to be forgotten. It has been a pleasure not only to reassure these reminiscent folk of the continued maintenance of the Prado as an avenue of delight for those awheel, afoot, or on horseback, but to be able to add that American genius and enterprise have given to this broad and deliciously shaded boulevard in miniature a finishing-touch which leaves it little short of perfection. The chief trouble with the Prado of olden time was that it led to nothing in particular. It began at the Parque Central and ended there. The objective was eliminated, unless a vast space of rough and unimproved frontage on the Gulf, where careless people disposed of refuse articles at their pleasure, may be considered a spot worth going to see. It is not to be admitted that a sublime junk-repository, or a vacant lot unadorned, would be a fitting climax to such a broad highway as Commonwealth Avenue at Boston, for instance, and yet the famous drive of Havana was hardly better off than this. It was a pity that it should be so, too, for there is no more beautiful spectacle to be seen anywhere than the breaking of the waves of the Gulf of Mexico upon the seaboard at what is now the terminal point of the Prado. The most unsentimental of souls must yield to the seductions of that scene. There is an element of grandeur about it which we do not find in the breakers of the New Jersey coast, or even in those which lend to the rock-bound coast-line of Newport an indescribable charm. Both day and night it provides for the eye of man a glimpse of nature in a mood that thrills; or if not, at least soothes; and in my own particular case I found in a five minutes' contemplation of its beauties more real rest and relaxation from care than could be derived from a six hours' sleep upon my steel-ribbed mattress and wood-fibre pillow at the hotel. In spite of its vastness there is a spirit of friendliness about the sea that makes a man think just a little better of himself than he otherwise might, and there are few men who can be oppressed by a sense of loneliness if in some way they are able to establish a personal relationship with the restless waters of the earth. One gets down to the elementals of life in a contemplation of the elements in their normal estate, and I should say on general principles that in giving to the people of Havana a point of vantage whence they may look upon that beautiful body of water which nature has hitherto wasted upon them, the tyrants of American empire have accomplished a work of actual beneficence an appreciation of which is filtering into the consciousness of the beneficiaries. It makes little difference how bad a man may be or how unsusceptible to the fineness of the things that lie ready to the eye, there is an undeniable appeal in the glories of nature that must touch somewhere and at some time upon his latent sense of appreciation; and if a man be one of the weary—as so many of our Cuban brothers are—a vast wash of spray made prismatic by the wondrous colors of a Southern sunset cannot fail to bring relief to the tense nerves and rest to the tired mind.

I do not know if the American rulers of Cuba had in mind the philosophy of La Punta when they ventured upon this improvement. It is more than likely that they thought of it merely as a new outlet for their energies in the line of constructive public work. Nevertheless, they have accomplished a work in the building of this parklike terminal of this favorite and fashionable drive of Havana which makes of this highway not alone a perfect and exhilarating diversion

196

for those favored by fortune, but a haven of rest and
comfort and health as well for the care-burdened members of a semi-submerged class. It was not until an
administration capable of discerning the possibilities of
the situation came into control of their affairs that the
Havanese were permitted to see and to enjoy the natural
beauties of their environment, and in supplanting the
red glare of a vacant and obnoxious acreage with that
coign of health and restfulness La Punta, the soldiers
of the United States have conferred an actual blessing
upon the Cuban people. The use which the latter make
of it indicates their appreciation of its value to them.
The sea-wall on Sunday afternoons is crowded by Cubans
of all sorts and conditions; and of all ages, from prank-
some youth, romping, while the police are looking the
other way, along the coping of the wall itself, to the
solemn, sedate, and contemplative patriarch seated on
the benches, gazing out over the waters of the Gulf and
letting its beauties soak into the recesses of his weary
brain. At night, especially on moonlight nights, one
finds not a few evidences hereon that, however strict the
regulations of society may be, all Cuban maidens are
not required to sit under the espionage of duennas at
important crises of life—or if so required are sometimes
able to escape an irksome association; and as a substitute for the nightcap of Northern latitudes I found a
stroll to La Punta and a brief moment thereon shortly

before retiring a delightful and fitting climax to the day.

It was never my good fortune while in Havana to encounter Mr. Juan Gualberto Gomez, the most ardent opponent of American ideas in Cuba, upon the Esplanade of La Punta, and it is possible, though hardly probable, that he has never seen it. If he has not, however, I should advise him to hasten thither at the first convenient moment, and to take in all the suggestiveness of the scene. He may not be susceptible to the natural beauties of the Gulf that will strike his eye, but he will find himself able to take in at a glance the essential differences between Spanish and American militarism, since from this esplanade of peace, health, and pleasure, the work of the American military authorities, he will be able to look across the narrow entrance to the harbor of Havana upon the frowning heights of El Morro, re-enforced to the southward by the grim and tragic walls of the fortress of Cabaña—these both the outward and the visible signs of Spanish militaristic aspiration. If there is no object-lesson in this contrast for the distinguished statesman and his followers, he and they are past educating, and so far beyond the possibility of pacification that it would seem almost like giving the island over to renewed chaos for the American authorities to relinquish the responsibility for the future welfare of Cuba to such a leader and to such a party.

COLON PARK, 1899

COLON PARK 1901

Another notable improvement, along similar lines is encountered in Colon Park, some idea of which the reader may derive from a glance at the before and after photographs here presented. Both pictures were taken from practically the same spot, and show the precise condition of the northeast cuarton of the park as it was when our forces entered into control and as it appears to-day. The transformation is striking, and as far as any one can discover meets with the approval of all save those who may no longer profit by demoralized conditions. I have been informed that former care-takers of Colon Park were in the habit of devoting their best energies to the raising of vegetables for their own aggrandizement upon this public play-ground, the dense foliage serving as a screen behind which to hide the evidences of their unlawful industry. Under present conditions, of course, such enterprises as this are as impossible as they would be in Madison Square Park or on the Boston Common; but, after all, one can hardly blame the canny Cuban of other days for making a private enterprise of a public utility, since place from top to bottom of the official scale was regarded as a legitimate outlet for the activities of the plunderer. Surely if General Weyler was able to regard Cuba as his farm, the superintendent of a public park could hardly be expected to see anything reprehensible in the transformation of the people's play-ground into a market-garden. Men of this stamp are probably unfavorably impressed by American ideas in relation to the park system, but these are few in number, and are no more worthy of serious consideration than the cavilling critics of the cafés, or the politicians who for obvious reasons would like to have supervised the work.

The remaining photographs of contrast presented herewith are but additional evidence of the energy and sound sense of those who have had the physical regeneration of Cuba on their shoulders. The contrast between Monserrate Street as it once was, and now is, is interesting in the fact that the transformation involved an attack on what in this country we would call " Shanty-town." A large number of wooden shacks bordered the ruin of the old Havana wall, and were the natural resting-place of all sorts of unhealthful and revolting conditions. These have practically all been cleared away, and a locality which was to all intents and purposes a pest-hole of filth and disease germs is rapidly being turned into a further acreage for the rest and diversion of the people of Havana. The ruined wall is being retained as an object of historic interest, repaired where necessary, and restored where desirable, but the squatter's sovereignty is at an end and where once he built his shack we now see stretches of grass-bordered paths having all the attributes of a public parkway.

It should be added in a discussion of the park improvement of Havana that the special instances already noted are only typical of the work that has been done and is still being prosecuted throughout the whole city, as well as in the other cities of Cuba. It is not much of an exaggeration to say of Havana that it has become almost a park in itself. In spite of its business activities, which are great, there is an atmosphere about the Cuban capital which suggests the play-ground rather than the market-place. It strikes one as a city designed by nature to become a resort for men and women in search of rest and recreation, and just as Paris since the days of the empire has been in many ways remodelled and made over into a city of pleasure as well as of commerce, so is Havana being transformed in such a fashion that great profit must ultimately come to her people. Thousands of Americans flock annually to the State of Florida to secure a little surcease from the trials of business life, and not a few of the leisurely make a habit of spending their winters in that favored State. It is inconceivable that once the American people realize the wonderful interest of this developing section of the world they will not travel the very few hours longer that are necessary to bring them into those Southern latitudes across the Strait of Florida. Of what commercial value alone to the island of Cuba this influx of travel must ultimately become it requires no superhuman intelligence to estimate, and even those who find vent for cavilling comment upon the operations of the American military government in these improvements must admit that they are the necessary forerunners of a great prosperity.

Aside from this, the commercial aspect of the situation, however, are the greater considerations of the public health, and the immediate welfare of the general public. In the work which the military authorities have prosecuted in these improvements they have not only made Havana a city more healthful than many cities of a similar class in our own country, but have given work to thousands of laborers who without it would either have starved to death, or have become a charge upon the charities of the island. Viewed from any stand-point, then, these efforts have been along lines of the highest political wisdom, and as such should redound everlastingly to the credit of the American administration in Cuba.

# Chapter IV

THE DEPARTMENT OF CHARITIES AND CORRECTION. I.

ONE of the most pressing duties of the American Military Government upon assuming control of Cuban affairs was the immediate care of the destitute and homeless people of that unhappy country to the number of thousands. To exaggerate the condition of misery into which the rule of General Weyler had plunged those who were unhappily subject to his monstrous will is impossible. Adequately to describe their woeful condition is too hard a task for any pen. Weyler's successor, General Blanco, none too scrupulous himself in the matter of the humanities, was an angel of mercy compared to this High-Priest of Inhumanity, who brought things to such a pass on Cuban soil that it taxes the credulity even of those who witnessed them to believe that such conditions could have existed in any age, much less our own. The policy of reconcentration inaugurated by General Weyler in the province of Pinar del Rio was merciful only in that it was a policy of death; but there were some who escaped its mercy, and who lived to face an awful beggary in a land where the well-to-do had nothing to give, to face starvation in fertile fields which the policy of reconcentration had rendered unproductive, and whose only friend was the Cuban climate, which fortunately is almost always kind to the roofless and the naked. It is an old story, that of the corruption of the Spanish official. It is one of the few stories in history that compel the historian to set aside rather than to cultivate his imaginative powers, since in a mere narration of the facts he runs the risk of destroying that confidence in his periods which is essential to success. But the corruption of the Spanish monster was as an ant-hill beside the Alp-like heights of his inhumanity. Such open cruelty as was that of Weyler is terrible to contemplate. His subtle cruelties are beyond description and belief. Fertile fields were laid waste by fire, families were broken up, workers were forbidden on penalty of death to work, even while it needed but their effort to silence the cries of their starving little ones; children were separated from their parents; homes were utterly destroyed, both physically and morally; and where death failed to follow in the train of Weyler's endeavor to "pacify," a life that was worse than death ensued. The photographs of individual men, women, and children who suffered the horrors of this policy but who yet survived its monstrous requirements, are of so terrible a realism that I should not dare reproduce them in these pages. It suffices to say that they exist, and are actual pictures of living human beings, dwelling in a land so richly fertile that there is scarcely another like it in all the garden-spots of earth, reduced

MAJOR E. ST. JOHN GREBLE, U. S. A

to a condition of actual suffering and material misery alongside of which a contemplation of the sufferings of the famine-stricken people of India as shown in the photographs that now and then come to us from the East becomes a positive relief.

To give a faint idea of the destitute condition throughout the country side and merely to suggest the brutalities of the Spanish soldiery which left so much ruin in their train I reproduce some extracts made by Mr. Franklin Matthews from the notes set down by Gen. James H. Wilson, while upon his tour of inspection, immediately after the American occupation, as follows:

" SANTANILLA.—About 800 widows, girls, and helpless children left without male support.

JAGUEY GRANDE.—About 550 destitute widows, besides 850 destitute women and children.

LAS CABEZAS.—There are now about 300 widows and their families; total destitute, from 700 to 1,000.

BOLONDRON.—About 450 women and children without male support.

CORRAL FALSO.—About 100 widows and 400 orphans."

And so the list might be extended to town after town. Remember, this was the situation in small towns, mere villages, and only in one province.

Here are some notes taken by General Wilson as to the conduct of the Spanish soldiers:

"Las Cabezas.—After the people had planted and raised crops the Spanish soldiers would not permit them to gather them, but took them from them, and also stole everything they had—cattle, cows, and chickens.

Bolondron.—Spanish soldiers stole everything in sight, and told council to pay for it.

Jaguey Grande.—Eight hundred Spanish troops here for eighteen months; left 28th of November; went to Matanzas; they robbed the people of everything they possessed—poultry, livestock, vegetables, fruits—everything.

Cuevitas.—Spanish troops left here on December 17. They stole everything they could find every night; even broke into houses.

Cumanayagua.—About 800 to 1,000 Spanish troops left here on December 11; they stole right and left—everything and everybody.

Macagua.—The Spanish soldiers behaved in the blackest and worst manner. When traveling by train and they saw a herd of cattle, the train would be stopped, such quantity as they needed for use would be killed, and the remainder ruthlessly shot and left lying along the track."

And that feature of Spanish conduct could be extended indefinitely. Mr. Matthews makes another quotation from these notes, which General Wilson jotted down roughly:

" Nobody seems to have yet understood how far-reaching was the effort of General Weyler to starve the Cuban people. He took occasion to send to every town a garrison whose business it was to sweep in all the cattle and other livestock, and consume it, as well as the garden products; and also to destroy the bananas in the field, leaving the people absolutely without anything to eat or the liberty to procure more by cultivation or purchase. In explanation of the fact that no farm-houses are to be seen, General Betancourt says that while the custom of the people used to be to live in the country, the war resulted in the burning and destruction of all the houses, and the people were all forced into the towns."

What has been the course of the American Military Administration of Cuban Affairs in respect to these conditions? What has American Imperialism—this terrible bogey, which the negro leader of a shiftless Cuban element properly fears, and which our paler brothers of Boston mistrust with such fearsome outpourings of their eloquence—done for these suffering people? It is a very simple story, yet one which should give to every American a thrill of joy that he may account himself such, and of pride that the army which represents him, under such difficult conditions has produced men capable of achieving such marvelous results.

In January, 1898, when the American troops began the occupation of Cuba, they encountered, among other things, a large number of destitute Cubans who had been taken from their work and rounded into the cities by the order of reconcentration issued by General Weyler; in such a condition, in fact, as I have already indicated. Most of these people were "guajiros," many of whom had lost all the male members of their families, either in the war or through sickness after the reconcentration, and the percentage of women and children was exceedingly great. The homes of these people had been destroyed in the war, their little fincas were absolutely unproductive, and in many cases, where only small children had been left out of large families, these unhappy little ones did not know even the locality of their former homes.

The so-called hospitals were absolutely without equipment, without medicine, and without medical attendants or nurses. The houses where the women and children had been herded together were pest-holes, and as there was no work for the men, except such as was given them by the Spanish troops—building forts—and for which they received no pay, the families, even where the men were alive, were in the utmost destitution. The first thing necessary, therefore, was to devise some means by which these people could be fed, given medicines and some clothing. The Red Cross had undertaken to do this, and had supplied much clothing, medicine, and food for these families, and had established small orphan asylums

SOME RAW MATERIAL FOR THE SCHOOLS

THE SCHOOL ROOM AT GUANAJAY

throughout the country for the care of the little children. The United States government at once sent large numbers of rations to Cuba, and these were distributed abundantly to the people, and undoubtedly saved the lives of many hundreds of them. The continuance of this distribution, however, would have resulted in the pauperization of a large part of these destitute, and some means had to be devised by which the people who had at first been fed could be put to work. This was accomplished in various ways.

First, the Engineering Department and the Department of Public Works, in their various constructions, and especially in the making of roads throughout the island, furnished work for a large number of the men, and a careful inspection of the families applying for rations promptly cut off the supply to all those who could gain their own livelihood, work being furnished to many of the women in sewing on the sheets, pillow-cases, and clothing needed to equip the hospitals and asylums.

In Matanzas province, under General Wilson, two separate schemes were tried to start the families at productive labor, which would in a short time render them independent and self-supporting. One scheme started near Sagua la Grande consisted of buying a certain number of oxen, ploughs, wagons, and other appurtenances of a farming life. These were divided into four parts, and placed under the charge of men who were hired at salaries, and by them distributed among the families who were placed upon land which had been provided by the citizens of Sagua la Grande. The families were also divided into four groups, and given land surrounding the central station, at which were placed the animals and implements. Each central station would, in succession, plough and prepare for planting a small part of the land belonging to each family, and after thus serving each group would start at ploughing more land, and so on until enough of the land had been prepared for each family to plant crops sufficient to support them. This scheme worked well. The natives were rationed for three months, at the end of which time their crops began to come in. The total cost of starting the scheme did not amount to more than the cost of the rations for these people for about three months. The last reports from Sagua la Grande state that the beneficiaries are now self-supporting.

The other scheme started by General Wilson was to supply the families who had been receiving rations with oxen, ploughs, twelve chickens, a rooster, a couple of sows and other essentials of farm life, the total amount to be given to each family not to exceed $250. All these articles were branded, and the families receiving them signed a formal contract with the municipality, promising to pay for them in two years, the price being the cost at

CALISTHENICS AT THE GUANAJAY SCHOOL

GYMNASIUM AT THE GUANAJAY SCHOOL

which the articles were purchased by the government. Interest at four per cent was also charged, provided the articles were paid for in the two years. If it was found that for any reason the families could not make their payments in two years an additional year was granted to them, but the interest in this case was to be eight per cent. Eighteen or twenty such families received this aid most of them, however, taking only a yoke of oxen, which as a rule, were of low cost being unbroken, and costing eighty-eight dollars a yoke. The families broke these oxen, and the majority said they could provide all the other things necessary to start farms. These families have all done well, and many of them at the end of two years had paid for the articles furnished them.

General Wood, through the Secretary of Agriculture, continued this mode of helping the poor, and imported cows and bulls, which were distributed to those who desired them.

In the City of Havana, the reconcentrados and destitute found at the close of the war had been placed in the Fosos, and in the government buildings on Paula, Fundición and Monserrate Streets. These people had been furnished rations for nearly two years, and, being given shelter, there was no inducement for them to work. They were fast drifting into the pauper class. The distribution of rations to the families in the houses on Paula and Fundición Streets had been discontinued by April, 1900, but the women and children in the Fosos and the families on Monserrate Street were being fed by the Municipality and steadily refused to work, even when given it, and as a rule were dirty, shiftless and immoral. The Military Governor directed that they be returned to their homes at once or placed in rooms in the City of Havana, the rent for each family to be paid for one month, not to exceed $6 for the small families, and $9 for the larger ones. The women and children were to be equipped with cots, bedding, cooking utensils and clothing.

Miss Nevins, an employee of the Department of Charities, was intrusted with the work of breaking up the Fosos. She met with the most persistent resistance in her attempts. As long as the people were fed they seemed unwilling, or perhaps through long suffering were unable, to shift for themselves but finally the Mayor of Havana issued an order discontinuing their food, and the pauperizing system was destroyed.

As soon as these destitute, sick, and dying had been afforded relief, attention was turned to the hospitals and asylums. One of the principal needs in the hospitals was trained nurses. The only persons in the hospitals who pretended to look after the sick at all were the Sisters of Charity, but such a thing as a trained nurse was unknown in Cuba. If the sick could get medicines and food they did so themselves. Sometimes they were helped to these things by another sick person in the same

THE SHOE SHOP AT GUANAJAY

SOME OF THE WORK OF THE BOYS AT GUANAJAY

ward, who could crawl out of his bed and help a less fortunate companion. To relieve this condition trained nurses were brought from the United States and placed in some of the hospitals, and training-schools for nurses were started in six of the larger ones, with such results that it is confidently expected that a sufficient number of tolerably well trained Cuban nurses will shortly be available for supplying the demand. Gradually the hospitals have been supplied with equipment and medicines, and in most instances those which have continued in operation are able to give decent care at least to the sick.

These expedients for the immediate and temporary relief of the victims of Weyler's cruelty having been devised the Military Government took up the business of the complete and comprehensive organization of a Department of Charities. In July 1900, Gen. Wood issued an order providing, first for the organization of the Department; second a declaration of the policy of the island that destitute and delinquent children should be cared for and under what conditions, defining the meaning of the terms, destitute and delinquent; third for the establishment of a Training School for Boys, and another for Girls wherein should be taught such subjects or pursuits as should better fit them for the duties of their mature years; fourth for Reform Schools for children of both sexes in which the wayward and seemingly incorrigible might be persuaded from the paths of evil and have the highways of rectitude pointed out to them; fifth for the prompt organization of a Bureau for the placing of children in families; and sixth for the proper control of Hospitals and Asylums for the Aged and the Insane. The general powers and duties of the Department were clearly defined and the necessary powers to proceed at once to the work of placing it upon an active footing were conferred by this order. It was a very complete and comprehensive effort to meet the immediate and future needs of the island of Cuba in matters involving the humanities and was drawn up by Major E. St. John Greble, the Superintendent of Charities and Hospitals, assisted by Mr. Homer Folks of New York. Mr. Folks in this as well as in other matters pertaining to the relief of the downtrodden in Cuba rendered valuable aid to the American authorities, placing his wide experience in the Charities of New York at their disposal.

In dealing with the orphans, General Wood, the Military Governor, decided, along the lines laid down in the order of July 7th, to start three state institutions—viz., a reform-school for boys at Guanajay; a reform-school for girls at Aldecoa; a training and agricultural college for boys at Santiago de las Vegas; and to develop to the full a training-school for girls already established by Gen. Ludlow on Compostella Street, Havana, of which I shall speak specifically later. In addition

SCHOOL-ROOM

FIELD DAY AT GUANAJAY

to these there were large provincial asylums for boys and girls—one at Cienfuegos, two at Matanzas and two at Santiago de Cuba. The other homes for orphans, which had been started and which were little more than refuges, were broken up, the children being returned to their relatives wherever possible, or placed with good families who were willing to receive and care for them under the rules and system of supervision adopted by the New York Bureau for Placing Children. This system has worked well. Such children as have to be kept in asylums are congregated in some one of the large institutions, which are well equipped and provided with means for furnishing both mental and manual training for the inmates. The children taken from the other refuges have all been furnished with fairly good homes, and are growing up as part of the community which will eventually have to absorb them.

There are photographs in these pages showing conditions as they exist to-day at the Guanajay Reform-School under the efficient superintendence of Captain Robert Crawford, and before his retirement from Cuba of Major E. St. John Greble. If the reader desires a before and after photographic presentation of the good work done by these gentlemen, and of a work which is merely typical of what is being done throughout the island of Cuba, he need only look at the picture of the raw material herewith presented, showing the boys about to set forth on their journey to the school, and then to gaze upon the photograph of the products of the shoe-shop showing the material results of the instruction they receive.

THE BLACKSMITH SHOP

THE CARPENTER SHOP

# Chapter V

*T*HE fairest example, however, of the humane work for the little ones of Cuba that we can find in the roll of American achievement is the Compostella School. By no means least among the achievements of Major Black, of the Public Works Department, to whose work I have already made special reference, is the transformation of a filthy Spanish barracks into a healthful, cheery home for an orphan industrial school, which in its own habitat supplants with three hundred children learning a useful trade in life a regiment of Spanish light-artillery, to which, according to all accounts, the principles of cleanliness were absolutely unknown. I have chosen for special note the Compostella Barracks at Havana, because it represents to a peculiar degree the precise nature of the work that the representatives of American Imperialism are doing in Cuba to-day. I know of no especial achievement of our forces in the unfortunate island, for whose welfare we are immediately responsible, that is more thoroughly characteristic of the high-minded and great-souled men who have represented us there than this same transformation of a filthy barracks for unclean military folk into a sweet, wholesome, and edifying industrial school for the most truly helpless living beings in the Antilles.

If we can only bear in mind the fact that we ran to the assistance of a people racked by war, and living under conditions which, even now that they have been laid before us, are scarcely conceivable to the American mind in the nineteenth century, we shall be less inclined, I think, to find fault with our soldiers who have made the cause of humanity their first care. When men trained to warfare, trained either at the military academy or in the harder walks of military life in the far West, set aside the predilections of this training and assume the burdens of civil administration with actual results which the average civilian of brains, energy, and equipment for the work in hand might well envy, it ill becomes those of us who dwell far apart from the strenuous scenes into which they have been thrust to withhold from them the meed of praise which is their due, merely because, as civilians, we have little personal liking for that kind of authority which is said to be bolstered up by gold lace and brass buttons. In so far as my Cuban experience is concerned, I have yet to meet the civilian who could do better the civil work that our military representatives in Cuba have actually accomplished there. I am even willing to go so far as to express my belief that if our Anti-Imperialist friends, Mr. Atkinson and Mr. Winslow and Mr. Garrison, could be induced to desert the comfort of their firesides in New England to travel into Cuba they would come back with resolutions of such a character that we should never

THE GARDEN AT ALDECOA

hear from one of them again upon this subject. They would sacrifice speech itself in the face of American achievement in Cuba, and no greater sacrifice on their part than that could be expected of any man. It is not impossible that Mr. Garrison would even write a sonnet in exaltation of American Imperialism if he could only see this Compostella Industrial school as I saw it one afternoon in February, 1901, under the guidance of General Wood.

I do not know if all people are as much interested in children as I am. To those who are not I can only say that in a consideration of the Cuban question they cannot ignore them since the Cuba of the future will be the Cuba of the Cuban children of to-day; and with all due respect to the adults of that island, the children of Cuba to-day are almost all there is of human kind in existence there that is worth fighting for. The real hope of the island is in the juvenile element, and for a very good reason. Their elders are tired, wearied by the uncertainties of life, the exactions of war, the privations of strife, and, barring a few politicians like Juan Gualberto Gomez, who would turn Cuba into an opaque republic, and drag it down into a ruin worse than it has yet known in further-ance of their own ambition, the adults of the island care little what happens to them, provided the Cuban flag flies officially for a few moments over the palace at Havana, and a balance of trade for so long a time denied them flows into their pockets. But the children are worth while—they are bright, alert, interested, happy, and best yet saddest of all, represent the only class of individuals now to be found in the Antilles who are entirely trustful and wholly grateful. Wherefore I think the transformation of the Compostella Barracks into the Compostella industrial school for orphans a feat not only of achievement, but of conception.

The Compostella school, as stated in General Ludlow's report, 1899-1900, was the outgrowth of the efforts of the United States military authorities in Cuba, at the beginning of the period of occupation, to provide food, shelter, and instruction for an unhappily large class of helpless and dependent orphans in Havana. To provide relief for men and women, not an easy task of course, was comparatively less difficult than to care most adequately for the children, who, either by reason of desertion or the death of their parents, were left wholly dependent upon the charitably inclined. The men and women could be set to work after a fashion. The care of the young was as difficult as it was pressing. The first intention of the authorities was to transform the old Spanish barracks into an orphan asylum for both boys and girls. It was supposed that an institution capable of caring for four hundred of these would suffice, but the

AT ALDECOA

THE CHAPEL AT ALDECOA

numbers requiring aid were found to be so large that it became necessary to provide, in this institution, accommodations and instruction for girls only, and, considering the peculiar disposition of the unattached gamin of the Havana streets in those days of chaos, to send the boys off into the country, where such agricultural and mechanical pursuits as would give an outlet to their surplus energy, and at the same time make useful citizens of them, could be more successfully taught them. Having an eye to the future of these youngsters, the authorities decided that they should have not only a home and the ordinary instruction which a child requires, but that they should have also an opportunity to acquire a knowledge of useful industrial arts, lest they should remain indefinitely dependent upon public charity. The idea of pauperization has never commended itself to any of the American military governors of Cuba. Furthermore, to quote from General Ludlow's report of 1899-1900, in order that the institution should be one of advantage, not only to its beneficiaries, but to the whole island, it was essential that it be constituted as a normal school, or centre of instruction, where half-grown girls and young women, themselves orphans and dependent, could receive instruction in the methods and management of such institutions, and be prepared to inaugurate and conduct them elsewhere, so as to establish other centres in the several provinces.

# UNCLE SAM TRUSTEE

We must keep in mind the fact that the public-school system of Cuba does not include instruction in industries or trades. The means of employment for girls and women are extremely limited. A modicum of teaching a few nearly profitless uses of the needle, and, in individual cases, some music or painting, are about all the occupations open to girls of the better class in Cuba. An institution was needed where dress-making, millinery, housekeeping, domestic arts, kindergarten, type-writing, stenography, bookkeeping, and the like could be taught, and the ambition and capacity for independent self-support be inculcated an acquired. This within two short years was accomplished. Fortunately for General Ludlow and the Department of Charities and Correction, the services of Miss Laura D. Gill, of the Cuban Orphan Society of New York, now Dean of Barnard College, were secured, and it is due to her active participation in the work in hand and to her own personal endeavors on its behalf, both in Havana and in the United States, that the development of the original plan of the asylum, both in theory and in practice, has come to such a substantial realization. The school is now caring for all the orphan children within the sphere of its usefulness, and under the superintendence of Major Greble, as the official head of the department, under whose control this institution and others of a similar nature directly came, the Compostella school has thrived

222

SEWING CLASS AT ALDECOA

AT MAZURRA

until it is to-day one of the most successful ventures of its kind to be found anywhere in the world. Not alone has it developed healthful ideas in the minds of the children, but it has instructed teachers as well, who are of assistance not only in the administration of the institution itself, but are capable of going out into the island and taking charge of such other institutions of the same kind as the various communities of Cuba may require. The filth of the Patio, which was incredible, not only in the number of the cart-loads of dirt removed, but in the nature of it, has given place to the health of the courtyard, wherein we are enabled to see, through the photograph printed herewith, between three and four hundred orphan children at play. In pavilions where we might once have listened to the profane speech and questionable tales of Spanish soldiers we may now hear the happy voices of some fifty-odd little tots as they sing the songs and play the games and pirouette through the little dances of the kindergarten. It is a transformation as wonderful as it is appealing. No man or woman of feeling can look upon it without a thrill, without a lump in the throat and a suggestion of wetness about the eye. Nor can any student of humanity gaze upon these classes of girls who might in other days have been left to roam the city streets, exposed to dangers which we need hardly mention, now learning to sew, to cook, and to make themselves useful in the life that lies ahead of them, without the conviction stealing over him that this was a good thing to do, that the men who have done it are good men and strong men, and men worthy of our confidence, even if they sometimes fail to secure the endorsement of the hordes of political pot-hunters who once filled the air with their denunciations, the approval of the army of café loungers, or the commendation of the querulous correspondent who refuses to look at these things, since, forsooth, they have no bearing upon questions of State —as if this latter contention could by any possibility be true!

The Compostella industrial school is but one of many evidences lying before the eyes of those who visit Cuba of the wonderful energy, the deep sincerity, and the magnificent philanthropy characteristic of the work of the American military authorities in that island. It is not an easy task to cleanse the Augean stables. To not only cleanse them. but to transform them into an institution of high educational aims, into a home for the homeless and unprotected, into what may be termed a factory of a future citizenship which shall be uplifting and equal to the burdens of national existence, is little short of a miraculous achievement, and in this particular instance that is precisely what the Military Government of Cuba has done.

In taking the hospitals in hand similar vigor to that in

INSPECTION AT THE LEPER HOSPITAL

the formation of schools was shown and drastic changes were made in their administration.

Prior to January 1st, 1900, the Juntas de Patronos or Boards of Governors of the various institutions had been required to submit estimates for the support of the institutions pursuant to existing regulations, and allotments were made from Insular funds in accordance with the estimates thus prepared, but this was proven to be a most unsatisfactory method to those who were compelled to accept the responsibility for the proper expenditure of the revenues. The Department instituted a thorough system of inspection and auditing of accounts and within a few months had succeeded in devising a system of procedure which resulted in many economies and vast salvage of public moneys.

Up to this time the institutions were being conducted upon the plans originally in vogue, and no efforts had been made to establish them upon a basis more in conformity with the modern recognized methods of conducting such institutions. The Civil or District Hospitals were actually hospitals only in name, being little more than refuges where the destitute sick were collected and taken care of in a most primitive fashion. The asylums likewise were but gathering places for the large number of orphans and other children whose mothers were unable to afford them support.

225

The extreme devastation produced by the Cuban revolution and the large loss of life incidental to the reconcentration produced a large number of destitute women
and children, whom the American authorities found in
a demoralized and starving condition and for whom it
was necessary to provide an immediate refuge.  This
resulted in an unnecessarily large number of asylums,
all of which soon became overcrowded, and in most of
which there was little or no effort made to conduct them
upon any but the crudest principles.  Owing to the immense amount of sanitary and humanitarian work which
devolved upon the army during the first year of the military occupancy of Cuba, it was impossible to do more than
create these refuges, which ably fulfilled their missions as
emergency measures, but as hospitals they were lament-
able failures.

The whole internal system was in the usual state of
demoralization. Patients, such as there were, were almost
wholly neglected.  Food was improperly prepared and
of a kind utterly foreign to the requirements of a hospital.
There was hardly an institution of this character provided
with an operating room equipped to perform more than
the simplest operations.  In most instances the beds were
of a nondescript character, uncomfortable and unservice-
able, and the bedding and clothing were tattered and in
most instances filthy, by reason of the fact that the limited
quantity only allowed changes at long intervals.  The

IN THE LEPER HOSPITAL OF SAN LAZARO

THE DINING HALL AT MAZURRA

superintendent reported that he had seen one half of the men in some of the hospital wards lying naked on the beds, as there were not sufficient night shirts to supply them, and the clothing in which they entered the hospital was unfit for use.

The actual nursing in these institutions amounted to practically nothing. Many instances were observed where patients too ill to hardly lift up their heads were required to get out of bed to perform the required functions of nature because the simplest contrivances of a well equipped hospital were lacking. No efforts apparently were made to wash even the faces and hands of patients, many of whom would often be weeks possibly in a ward without that duty being even once performed.

All of these and many other of the more trivial abuses were gradually corrected. The lists of employees were carefully revised, many unnecessary ones eliminated, and others added, whose services were essential. Operating rooms have been amply equipped with surgical instruments and appliances, and a liberal amount of bedding and clothing has been distributed, and in all cases possible the bathing facilities have been improved. Training schools for female nurses have been established in two of the hospitals, and are giving extraordinary satisfaction. There seems to have been a genuine effort on the part of the hospital authorities to improve the condition of their institutions, and there was almost from the first perfect harmony and accord between the civil authorities and the Department.

The condition of the insane and of the lepers was deplorable. The former, irrespective of sex, of age, or of degrees of insanity, were herded together in a mass of Bedlam which is well nigh inconceivable and certainly indescribable; and the leper hospital was in no wise different from the other hospitals of the island—ill-equipped, filthy and unsanitary. To-day the hard fate of the inmates of these various institutions has found the amelioration which comes from a tender solicitude for their needs. The insane asylum at Mazzura is as well-conducted an institution of its kind as may be found anywhere; the victims of the mind disordered are cared for, and their unhappy estate is relieved in so far as it can be of its miseries; while the leper hospital of San Lazaro is a clean and efficient refuge for those suffering from this awful malady. If it is good that the victims of leprosy should be deprived of their liberty, it is not possible to imagine a better housing than that which has been set apart for them. but in this point lay my only serious apprehension as to the completeness of our phil-anthropic work in Cuba. Since leprosy is not contagious there seems to be no good reason why its victims should be placed behind, what are to all intents and purposes, the bars of a prison. Their sequestration might easily

A VIOLENTLY INSANE PATIENT AT MAZURRA

be made a happier one, and I should have been happy to be able to record the establishment of a leper colony in Cuba, where the afflicted persons might enjoy a certain degree of personal freedom and contact with nature in some more intimate fashion than that which is possible from a restricted interior court, or upon the roof of their hospital. There is a vast acreage in Cuba at the Government's disposal, and it would have proven no very difficult task to try some such experiment as that which appears to have succeeded in the South Seas, and in Hawaii. Nevertheless the condition of these sufferers has been materially altered for the better, and there is not one of the inmates of the San Lazaro Hospital at Havana, at least, who has not gained courage and consolation in his affliction from the vigorous and cheery presence of General Wood himself, who has personally visited the sick for whom he has had to care as if he were their personal friend and physician.

So has it been in all branches of this humanitarian department. The sick and destitute have been cared for; the orphan has been housed and clothed and started usefully along in life; the prisoner in the jails and penitentiaries has learned that the law is punitive, but not vindictive; the incorrigible have been placed within the sphere of corrective influences; the hospitals have been built anew, and the afflicted have found comfort in the arms of Uncle Sam—and they are grateful. I wish no more beautiful sight than that which repeatedly met my eyes when, while inspecting these institutions, either with General Wood or Major Greble, the soft little hands of the children crept trustingly into the brawny grasp of the soldier, nor shall I soon forget the glances of heart-felt gratitude that went out from the prostrate on many a hospital cot to those two Samaritan gentlemen, whose official and personal care it has been to relieve distress in all its forms, and to bring sunshine into thousands of darkened souls.

TRAINING CUBAN NURSES

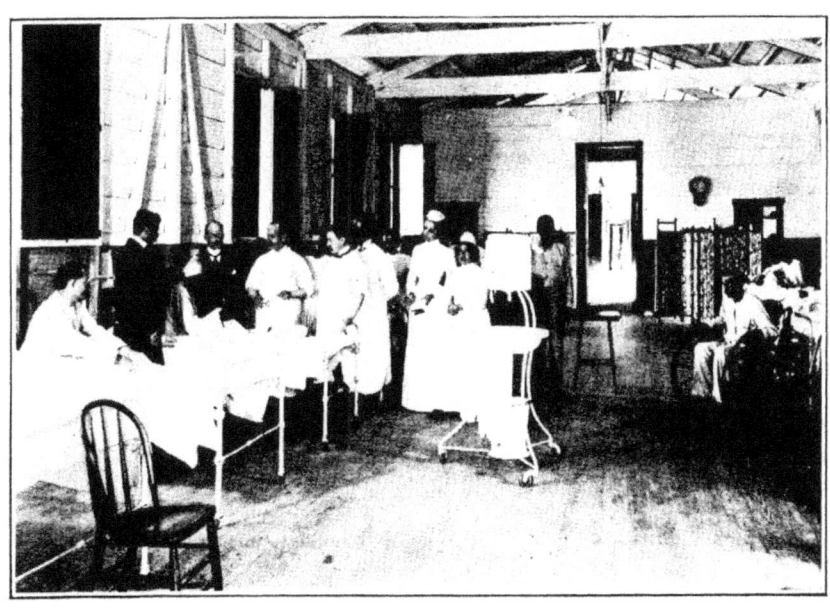

SCENE AT HOSPITAL NO. 1, HAVANA

# Chapter VI

*T*O the general rule of chaos which prevailed in Cuba at the beginning of the American military occupation, the cause of public instruction was no exception. Indeed, there was every reason why it should not be excepted from the rule of chaos, since it was the one branch of public work which Spain by choice preferred to hold in a chaotic state. The Spaniard from the first, with few exceptions, as is shown by the records, seems to have taken as his educational platform for his colonies, the sentiment of Charles IV., who " prohibited the establishment of the University of Merida, in Maracaibo, on the ground that he did not deem it expedient that enlightenment should become general in America." As one considers Spain's endeavor to keep her colonial subjects in a state of dense ignorance, one's chief source of surprise at the present moment is that at the beginning of the American military occupation there should have been any system of public-school instruction in that then unhappy island susceptible to demoralization, yet such was the case. There was a system of education in vogue in Cuba before our army people took charge, but it was typical of Spain, not of the United States; was a source of abuse and profit to politicians, rather than of profit and learning to the

231

young of Cuba. In fact, it was the logical result of many years of application of Spanish ideas. The chaos into which it was plunged at the end of the war was not the chaos of strife, but was its inevitable and intrinsic desert, as any one who has ever studied the history of school-work in Cuba under Spanish administration must admit. The history of Cuban school-work, private or public, ecclesiastic or secular, primary or collegiate, is not exactly a page of plumage for the Spaniard. On the contrary, it but emphasizes the very natural contempt which most well-ordered persons of Anglo-Saxon origin must feel for the essentially degenerate race who desecrate the beautiful peninsula by their ocupation thereof. It is, of course, true that prior to the nineteenth century education was everywhere at a low ebb as a national asset, and it is possible that among the then great nations of earth, learning in its primary sense was cultivated no more by France and Britain in their colonial enterprises than by Spain, yet there was a vast difference. In Cuba, Spain pretended to give and gave not, and made of the thirst and aspirations of a subject people merely another graft for the growth of Spanish corruption. The last period of Spanish rule in Cuba was characterized by the most absolute neglect of everything connected with instruction. Popular teaching had sunk to the lowest level. There was not a single public school-house in the island; the teachers, always badly paid, lived in penury; school

LIEUT. MATTHEW E. HANNA,
*Commissioner of Public Instruction*

furniture and appliances were out of the question, the school attendance was almost insignificant, and the greater portion of the school population was illiterate.

Prior to the nineteenth century education in Spain as well as in other European countries was within the reach only of those who could afford to pay for it.* The free school as an institution was rather an abstraction than a tangible reality, and necessarily the educational needs of a colony did not appear particularly pressing to a home government that paid little attention to the subject in its immediate vicinity. Nevertheless the desirability of free schools in Cuba did manifest itself to certain unofficial minds and we find numerous instances of private individuals placing their own resources at the command of their fellows for the purpose of teaching the young certain rudiments at least which might suffice the better to fit them for the duties of man and womanhood. Until the eighteenth century was far advanced, beyond the founding of seminaries under the control of the church nothing worthy of note was accomplished along educational lines and in these efforts more attention was paid to the pretentious form than to the substance, and the title of academy or institute was given to institutions which

* For the historical statement concerning the growth of schools in Cuba under Spanish rule, I am indebted to the excellent record thereof prepared by Mr. R. L. Packard, United States Commissioner of Education, and published in his report on Education in Cuba, Porto Rico and the Philippines for 1898-99.—J. K. B.

233

were hardly more than primary schools, which held out
inducements of a speedy preparation for the university.
At that time, it should be remembered, the natural sciences
had not reached the importance they subsequently attained, and the study of philosophy required the royal
permission, so that secondary instruction was reduced to
a superficial study of the humanities, especially Latin,
which occupied the leading place on account of its use
in fitting for the university and because teachers of Latin
were easily found among the clergy, who were the principal factors of education at that period. All this may
be said without detracting from the praiseworthy efforts
and antiquity of some institutions like the Chapter of
Havana, which in 1603, convinced of the need of a teacher
of grammar, voted a hundred ducats for the support of
one who should teach Latin; but as the plan did not
meet with the royal approbation they were obliged to
drop the project, only to revive it afterwards with a
larger salary. In the same year the municipality provided for continuing classes in grammar by a monk of
the convent, which had been suspended. In 1607 Bishop
Juan de las Cabezas Altamirano founded the Tridentine
Seminary, the citizens offering to pay part of the expenses annually. The secular clergy also gave lessons
in Latin and morals, as Conyedo did, who prepared students for the priesthood in Villa Clara, and later Fr.
Antonio Perez de Corcho, who gave lectures on philosophy

in the monastery of his order. By the bull of Adrian VI of April 28, 1522, the Scholatria was established at Santiago de Cuba for giving instruction in Latin, and by his will, dated May 15, 1571, Capt. Francisca de Paradas left a considerable sum for the foundation of a school in Bayamo, which in 1720 was intrusted to the charge of two monks of San Domingo, in whose hands the estate increased. In 1689 the College of San Ambrosio was established in Havana with 12 bursarships for the purpose of preparing young men for the church, but it did not fulfill its purpose, and subsequently received the severe censure of Bishop Hechavarria Yelgueza on account of its defective education, which had become reduced to Latin and singing. Fr. José Maria Penalver opened a chair of eloquence and literature in the convent of La Merced in 1788, which also was not a success.

After these attempts the foundation of a Jesuit college in Havana gave a new impulse to education. From the first, the priests of this order had observed the inclination of the inhabitants of Havana toward education, and Pezuela states in his history of Cuba that the municipality in 1656 wished to establish a college of the order, but the differences between the Jesuits and the prelates in the other colonies had been so frequent that the bishops and priests in Havana opposed the plan. But as the population increased the demands for the college multiplied, and in 1717 a citizen of Havana, Don Gregorio

Diaz Angel, contributed $40,000 in funds for its support. The necessary license was obtained in 1721; three more years were spent in selecting and purchasing the ground, when the institution was opened under the name of the College of San Ignacio. The old college of San Ambrosio, which had been under the direction of the Jesuits since its establishment in 1689, was then united with it, although the old institution still retained its distinctive character as a foundation school for the profession of the church.

As early as 1688 the *ayuntamiento* (or city council) of Havana petitioned to the Royal Government to establish a university in the city in order that young men desirous of study might not be compelled to go to the mainland or to Spain. This request was furthered by Bishop Valdés. and finally, by a letter of Innocent XIII of September 12, 1721, the fathers of the convent of S. Juan de Letran were authorize1 to found the institution desired, and after some years of preparation it was opened in 1728. This University of Havana which consists at present of an academic department together with professional schools has had a varied and by no means useless career, and like all other institutions of Cuba, at the close of the war was found to be in a state bordering at least upon collapse. It was ill equipped with books, material and apparatus. A great many of the professors were entirely unfitted for their positions, which had been obtained in many instances in an irregular manner and held very much as a sinecure without any feeling of responsibility as to either the amount or quality of services which they rendered in return for the salary paid by the Government. The University was, in short, in a condition of demoralization, and after a few months it was apparent that if it was to become in any way efficient a thorough reorganization combined with radical changes in the personnel was necessary.

The condition of the Institutes of Secondary Instruction was equally demoralized. They were such only in name, and as the report of Secretary Varona points out, " nothing was taught in them, but on the other hand, they were the scene of the most barefaced traffic in certificates of excellence and degrees granted to the pupils. There were Institutes, like that of Havana, where such certificates were subject to a regular tariff. Students would leave these Colleges, duly furnished with Bachelor degrees, but could not write a fairly well spelled letter. When the war came on, the classes in the Institutes of Pinar del Río, Santa Clara, Puerto Príncipe and Santiago de Cuba were entirely suspended. The University dragged on a sickly existence, without influencing in any way public culture. It never showed that its Faculty was composed of men who lived in contact with outside civilization. Not a single work can be mentioned, as having been written by them, except some compilations

without criticism, and they cannot be credited with
original work of any kind. Most of them looked upon
themselves as privileged office-holders, members of an
irresponsible bureaucracy. Some lived in Spain and were
substituted by assistants, drawing, however, their salaries
with due regularity; others enjoyed practically limitless
leaves of absence."

The task of reorganization was a difficult and unpleasant one, the Military-Governor confesses in his
report to the Department of War. Many of the chairs
were held by venerable gentlemen whose days of activity
and capacity for teaching had long since passed. The
old institution was surrounded by an atmosphere of help-
lessness and inefficiency. To intrude upon its traditions
with modern ideas or purposes of reform was regarded in
a way as something almost sacrilegious. No one seemed
to doubt the fact that the University was thoroughly inefficient, but no one was willing to put his hand to the
work of reformation until the matter was actively taken
up by Señor Varona, Secretary of Public Instruction in
the Cabinet of Gen. Wood. This gentleman with singular
courage and devotion to the improvement of the University and the elevation of University teaching in the island,
regardless of the storm of personal abuse which was
poured upon him, taking at times the form of most insulting letters, and indifferent to the loss of personal
friends or the creation of enemies, proceeded to mark

COMPOSTELLA BARRACKS, HAVANA, in 1898

COMPOSTELLA BARRACKS, HAVANA, in 1901

out what he considered a straight line of advance and improvement and adhered to it. In this he was given the full support of the Government and the result was the re-examination of practically all professors of the University as well as those of the Institutes of Secondary Instruction. In all such the professors who had obtained their positions by competition and were still efficient and able to render good service were retained. Those who either by virtue of eminent attainments or conspicuous ability were deemed worthy of appointment or retention without examination were also continued. Among those of this latter class were included several secretaries of the insular cabinet who were professors in the University. All other chairs were declared vacant and competitive examinations held to fill them. The result was many new men, bringing with them new energy and ambition to make the University one in fact as well as in name. Certain qualifications were prescribed for admission to the University and the University course was rearranged and modernized, making it practically a four years' course in the academic department. Admission to the professional schools was prohibited for students under eighteen years of age and it was required that they should be either graduates of the academic department of the University or able to pass certain preliminary examinations sufficiently severe to indicate that they possessed a liberal education.

239

Besides this reorganization of the University as a whole especial attention was paid to the needs of the Medical School, which is one of the most important branches of an institution of this nature in a country for so long ridden by pest and disease due to a careless attitude toward sanitation. This Department of the University has been well established in one of the former Spanish barrack buildings, which has undergone considerable alterations and repairs to render it suitable for school purposes. Other similar buildings in a very desirable portion of the city have been equipped as thorough laboratories with all modern conveniences and apparatus. These laboratories are the first of the kind ever constructed in Cuba. They furnish ample space for a large class in general Chemistry, a separate laboratory for general and advanced work in Histology and another for advanced and general work in Bacteriology. Large lecture rooms containing a thoroughly modern equipment have also been provided. The best of microscopes and all necessary special apparatus have been supplied for the laboratories in Histology and Bacteriology. Plans have been drawn to erect, adjoining these buildings, one for general lectures and a library for the medical school, thus assembling this department of the University. The location selected is an excellent one, in one of the most desirable portions of the city, and almost equi-distant from the important hospitals. With

the completion of the buildings of the medical school it
is the purpose to remove the Institute of Havana, which
is now occupying a portion of the University, into the
building at present occupied by the medical school, giving
to the University the rooms now used by the Institute.
This will give them sufficient space for necessary laboratories and some additional class and lecture rooms.

With the present sincere interest in the welfare of the
University, says Gen. Wood in his annual report for
1900, there is no reason to doubt that it will soon be on
a prosperous footing and its capacity for useful work
taxed to the utmost.

Important as the work of the University may be considered to be however it is the more elementary institutions that come closer to the real needs of the people and
while we may feel a certain measure of pride in the work
of Uncle Sam's army officers in this reorganization of the
college and professional schools of the Cuban University
it is the work along public school lines of which I fancy
the reader would most like to hear, and the story is a
pleasant one to tell.

Until the 17th century was far advanced the Cubans
had not a single public institution where they could
have their children taught to read and write, says Commissioner Packard in his report of 1898-1899. The first
school was that of the Bethlehemite fathers in Havana,

and was established through the generosity of Don Juan F. Carballo. He was, according to some authorities, a native of Seville, and according to others, of the Canary Islands. He repaid thus generously the debt of gratitude he owed the country where he had acquired his wealth. Already, in the sixteenth century, a philanthropist of Santiago de Cuba, Francisco Paradas, had afforded a like good example by bequeathing a large estate for the purpose of teaching Latin linguistics and Christian morals. The legacy was eventually made of avail by the Dominican friars, who administered it, but when the convents were abolished it was swallowed by the royal treasury, and thus the beneficent intentions of the founders were frustrated, to the permanent danger of the unfortunate country. Only these two institutions, due entirely to individual initiative, are recorded in the scholastic annals during the three first centuries of the colony. The thirst and scent for gold reigned supreme. The sons of wealthy families, in the absence of learning at home, sought schools and colleges in foreign parts. On their return, with the patriotic zeal natural to cultured men, they endeavored to better the intellectual condition of their compatriots. This enforced immigration of Cubans in quest of learning was fought against by the Government, and finally *the children of Cuban families were forbidden to be educated in foreign countries. This despotic measure was adopted without any honest effort being*

THE COMPOSTELLA SCHOOL CHILDREN

DAILY DRILL AT THE COMPOSTELLA SCHOOL

*made to establish schools for instructing the children of a*
*population already numbering nearly 500,000 souls.*

The Sociedad Económica was founded in 1793, during
the time of Las Casas, whose name has always been ven-
erated among Cubans. Then, as now, the members of
this association were the most talented men of the country, and their best efforts were directed toward promoting public instruction. It gave impulse and organization
to the school system in Cuba. It established inspections,
collected statistics, and founded a newspaper to promote
instruction and devoted its profits to this cause. It
raised funds and labored with such zeal and enthusiasm
that it finally secured the assistance of the colonial government and obtained an appropriation, though but of
small amount, for the benefit of popular instruction.

In 1793 there were only seven schools for boys in the
capital of Cuba, in which 408 white and 144 free colored
children could be educated. From this privilege the slaves
were debarred. The seven schools referred to, besides a
number of seminaries for girls, afforded a means of livelihood for a number of free mulattoes and some whites.
The schools were private undertakings, paid for by the
parents. Only one, that of the reverend Father Senor,
of Havana, was a free school. Reading, writing, and
arithmetic were taught in these schools. Lorenzo Len-
dez, a mulatto of Havana, was the only one who taught
Spanish grammar. The poor of the free colored classes

243

were on a par with the slaves. The Sociedad Económica then founded two free schools, one for each sex, but the bishop, Felix José de Tres Palacios, nullified the laudable efforts of the country's wellwishers by maintaining that it was unnecessary to establish more schools. From 1793 to 1893 the society was unable to accomplish even a part of its noble purpose; it was found impossible to obtain an official sanction of popular education. In 1817 there were 90 schools in the rest of the island—19 districts—all, or nearly all, founded by private individuals. In 1816 the section of education of the Sociedad Económica was established. It afforded a renewed impulse to the cause of education, thanks to the influential support of the governor, Don Aliquando Ramirez. The schools improved, the boys and girls, both white and black, were taught separately, literary contests were opened, annual examinations were made obligatory, prizes were distributed, and a powerful incentive was created among all classes for the cause of education. But the concessions obtained for the society by the influence of Ramirez were revoked by royal order of February, 1824. In this year the municipality of Havana loaned the Sociedad Patriótica $100 for school purposes.

So we see that after many years of fruitless experimentation the first real impulse and organization given to school-work in Cuba was by the foundation, in 1793, of the Sociedad Económica, but that it merely bettered conditions by a degree, it did not remedy them, and in thirty-three years the net result of its efforts was 140 schools in the whole island, of which only sixteen were free. In 1860 there were 285 schools in operation, a growth of which the authorities seemed to take some note, since the secretary of the governor in 1863 began to make " recommendations " for school reforms which tended "to keep the population in ignorance *in order to keep it Spanish.*" As an example of the Spanish attitude toward the movement in Cuba, it is not without interest that I should quote Mr. Packard's digest of the preamble of the decree reforming education in Cuba, published by the government at Havana in 1871:

" It states that the insurrection of 1868 was due to the bad system of education; that while the old methods were slow, the new are prompted by eagerness for hurry, and the child is taught a number of things, whereas its mind is unable to comprehend many things at a time. A number of subjects should therefore be suppressed. Balmés is quoted as the authority for the psychology and pedagogy of the preamble. The latter goes on to say that this haste to teach many things has made religious instruction secondary to that of the arts and sciences, a fatal error which has produced fatal consequences. It refers to statistics to show that crime has increased with education, and states that Aimé Martin found the remedy for this evil in educating instead of merely instructing. But as there were many religious sects, Martin unfortunately selected an irreligious religion as the means of educating, and consequently there was no decrease in crime. Señor Lasagra is quoted to prove that suicides are more numerous in Protestant than in Catholic countries, and more so in the capitals than elsewhere. This is due to too great individual freedom of thought and consequent changes in social and economic conditions, which have produced dissatisfaction, despair and suicide. Philosophical and religious sects have multiplied, and the multiplicity of these has always and everywhere produced doubt and scepticism, which in their turn have engendered a materialism whose only offspring is disbelief in virtue and morality. Under its influence some are tortured with unhappiness without hope of the future, while others are filled with envy. Religious instruction has been too much neglected or too carelessly performed, and the real remedy would consist in Christianizing or Catholicizing education by putting the government and municipal machinery of education in the hands of the religious teaching orders, when the evil would disappear. It goes on to say, with severe condemnation of the schools where they had taught, that many of the insurgents had been teachers, and mentions particularly the school formerly conducted by José de la Luz. Instruction must be supplemented by moral and religious education, and great care should be taken to prevent access to (politically) evil literature. Even in text-books of elementary geography, it declares, have wicked documents been inserted. In one of them we read that the greatest event of the present century in America was the revolt of Bolivar. 'See under what seductive forms the minds of children are predisposed to treason.'"

A finer example of Spanish hypocrisy than is here presented it would be hard to find, and that under such a *régime* even the rudiments of education should ever have come within the reach of the people as a mass is little short of marvellous. Yet such was the case. The Spanish hide was penetrable in spots, and in the ensuing twenty-seven years—up to 1898—a school system grew up which, the authorities state, was in itself unassailable, but in its administration so abominable that it was worse than none at all.

The precise situation was that in order to make a superficially good impression, the Spanish authorities devised a school system that in honest and competent hands would have worked well, but which, having no sincere desire to uplift the masses back of it, was allowed to lapse into failure. The laws made ample provision for the free education of Cuban children, but the administration of the laws was corrupt. Through the failure of the administration to provide funds for the proper maintenance of the schools, only a small fraction of the boys and girls of the school age, six to eighteen, were cared for. In 1895 there were 904 public schools in the island, conducted by 998 teachers with 36,306 pupils. But even with this showing the advantages to the children were practically *nil,* since the festering sore of corruption at the top spread down through the trunk of the educational tree, and infected even the teachers. These were supposed to be appointed after a competitive examination, but the practice was not along the lines of the theory. Nothing ever was with these haymaking Spanish, who farmed out instructorships in the schools and professorships in the colleges on the basis of personal friendship, or for political considerations, without regard to the intellectual or moral fitness of the appointee. An additional obstacle in the way of the struggling Cuban youth with a thirst for knowledge was the failure of the state to provide school-rooms. The teachers themselves were looked to for class-room accommodations, so that the larger number of the schools were conducted in the homes of the fortunate " instructors." " Of school furniture," says the Census Report for 1899, " such as desks, books, slates, blackboards, maps, etc.—there was frequently none, and the pupils, without respect to race, blacks and whites mixed, sat on benches with no backs for five or six hours consecutively, the instruction being usually given simultaneously to the classes, study and recitation being exceptional and impracticable." But a single teacher was allowed the elementary schools, no matter how many pupils, although the superior elementary schools were sometimes provided with assistants. The school-rooms provided by the teachers were badly lighted, ill-ventilated, with insufficient and foul toilet accommodations, and the idea of a playground was unheard of.

Among the further evils of the public school system as it then existed, the Census Report continues, were the provisions for substitute teachers and pensioners. A teacher requesting a leave of absence for any purpose— for example, ill health, or private business—was permitted to propose the name of a substitute, who was paid by the regular incumbent of the office. After being formally appointed substitute, he was supposed to receive one-half of the compensation assigned to the school, the contributions of the children whose parents could pay, and the amount allotted for school supplies—usually one-fourth the amount of the salary. On the surface this would appear to be a very fair arrangement; but, as a matter of fact, the salary, fees, and allotment for supplies were handed over to the regular incumbent of the office, who paid his substitute whatever sums had been agreed upon when he paid him at all. It is said that in this way schools were without their regular teachers for years, and meanwhile were left in charge of persons without a single qualification for this most important duty. In other words, just as the politicians sold positions in the public-school service to their favorites, so these men in turn farmed out their offices to others of their own selection, retaining for themselves a comfortable margin of profit.

Confronted by such conditions the American military government of Cuba began its work of upbuilding the Cuban school system.

A GROUP OF CUBAN TEACHERS
*Compostella School*

THE COOKING CLASS, COMPOSTELLA SCHOOL

# Chapter VII

*I*N taking up the school work in Cuba, the authorities were confronted with many difficulties. It was not as if they had entered a field where everything could be done *de novo,* and without regard to the prejudices of the beneficiaries. Added to the difficulties of reorganization on every hand were the obstacles which are never wanting to impede any great measure of reform. There were the jealousies of those who had profited under the old system. There were the prejudices of the parents to be overcome. There were the tremendous difficulties of getting the children into the schools, and, after that, of keeping them there. Some one was needed to take hold at this particular juncture of peculiar temperament, of indestructible enthusiasm, full of patience, having a knowledge of school requirements, and no fear of hard work. Providentially such a man appeared in the person of Mr. Alexis E. Frye, who, singularly enough, possessed almost all the qualities enumerated; and upon the request of General Brooke, then Military Governor, this gentleman undertook the difficult task of drawing order out of chaos. Whatever criticism may be made of Mr. Frye as a master of detail in the administration of his office of Superintendent of Public Instruction—and much of it appears to have been wholly just and well directed—there is no denying that he was the man for the moment, and for the particular work in hand, just as Funston was the man for the capture of Aguinaldo. As a permanent factor in the educational development of Cuba it is doubtless true that Mr. Frye was impossible. It rarely happens that one of so great enthusiasm as was his ever becomes a permanently useful wheel in a great human machine, but without the preliminary efforts of Mr. Frye in the reorganization of Cuban schools, it may be doubted if the showing of to-day would have been so creditable in its comprehensiveness. The ex-superintendent went at his work with an almost fanatical zeal, and within six months he had succeeded in getting the schools reestablished upon a reasonable basis at least; the attendance had been increased to a marvellous degree, and throughout the corps of instructors there had spread the contagion of Mr. Frye's personal enthusiasm. Whatever Mr. Frye's limitations, it soon became evident that the extension of popular instruction had received a vigorous impulse. With great rapidity school-rooms were opened, even in places which had never heard of a school. The whole island was covered with them in a few months. Although little discrimination could be exercised in the selection of teachers, the latter displayed, as a rule, real interest in the duties confided to their care, especially the women, who distinguished themselves from the start for the activity and zeal they put into their work. But for the first year of American occupation in the nature of things not very much of permanent character could be done to remedy existing evils.

The close of the year 1899 showed only such immediate betterment of conditions as the opening of the schools under the old system, which, it is pointed out, was merely a lack of system. These were without desks, chairs, textbooks, proper school furniture or other materials. " The children were perched on benches without regard to size. No attempt was made to grade or classify them, nor was there any settled procedure in the school methods; in short, public instruction was without organization and of little value." The end of the year saw the change in the Military Governorship. General Wood succeeded General Brooke and immediately after taking charge, separated the Departments of Justice and Public Instruction, which had hitherto been combined, showing thus the intelligent interest he took in a matter so vital to the prosperity of Cuba. There was never any sane reason for combining the Departments of Justice and Public Education, and it did not take the thoughtful mind of the new Governor long to perceive how particularly inexpedient in Cuba was the union, and how necessary the divorce, if indeed anything of permanent value in the way of a system was to be obtained.

The union of the school system and the politics of an island like Cuba, was a mesalliance of the worst kind, and General Wood acted promptly. The operation performed, a new Department of Instruction was organized, and the serious consideration of the Cuban school problem began.

"It was evident," says General Wood, "and had been ever since the military occupation of the island, that if a stable government was to be established in Cuba, opportunities must be given the children to obtain an elementary education and with this object in view vigorous measures were instituted looking towards the organization of public schools and supplying them with books, materials, etc. One of the first things to be done was to settle the question of salaries, concerning which there was already much discussion, and explain to the teachers, who were opposed to the salaries as being too small, that the salaries proposed by the new school law were most liberal and in excess of those paid by most cities in the United States."

To this end a circular note was written and sent to all the teachers, signed by Gen. Chaffee at that time Chief of Staff to the Governor-General, explaining the reasons for the financial adjustments required by the situation, and demonstrating by illuminating comparisons that they were rather better off, if anything, than the bulk of the teachers in the public schools of the United States. The note closed with an appeal to the patriotism of the teachers in the following terms:

" Having in mind the great task of preparing the Cuban children for citizenship—a task which calls for the highest effort of every patriot—the teachers are earnestly advised to cease further agitation concerning salaries, and devote their entire time to organizing their schools, thus proving which among them are worthy of the highest rank as educators."

The appeal was not made in vain, for the salary agitation as a disturbing factor ceased, and the great majority of the teachers " displayed great willingness and anxiety to faithfully carry out the work entrusted to them." The Administration has been criticized on the other hand for the liberal amounts paid to teachers, but as the Governor has well said, the work required of them had to be of high character, and to obtain proper persons to act as teachers it was necessary to pay a sufficient amount to maintain them properly.

The next important step was the proper equipment of the school-rooms that were already in operation, and to provide for those that should be started. The precise needs were ascertained, and under the superintendence of Mr. Frye, Maj. Chauncey B. Baker of the Quartermaster's Department and Lieut. E. C. Brooks, one hundred thousand desks and chairs, and a vast amount of other necessary material were obtained and properly distributed. Books and materials, together with the furniture, cost approximately three quarters of a million of dollars, but results soon began to show, and at the end of January, 1900, 635 schools were in active operation, and in June of the same year this number had been increased to 3,313 schools, with 143,000 pupils actually enrolled.

But it was not alone upon the children and their urgent necessities that the representatives of Uncle Sam had their eye. The needs of the teachers themselves began to attract attention, and they were soon made aware that the fount of learning must be of crystalline clearness if the stream that flowed therefrom was to be of the required purity. Of the Cuban teachers, Lieut. Hanna, Commissioner of Education, in his report for 1900, speaks as follows:

" The teachers of Cuba have been so written about and talked about, and advertised to the world, that it would not be at all strange if they had misjudged their powers and abilities, but through it all they have remained calm and self-possessed. The most promising feature in the outlook of the public schools of Cuba to-day is the simple modesty of the teacher. He knows that he has much to learn. and his eagerness to learn is most encouraging. It is no reflection on the teachers of the island as a body, to say that they are but poorly fitted for their work. The

PARADE OF SCHOOL CHILDREN
*HAVANA, February,* 1901

RECESS

fact is denied by no one, and the teachers are free to acknowledge it. But when the past is considered, the very poor advantages there were for training teachers, to say nothing of educating them, and the present is considered, the sudden increase of their number from a few hundred to nearly four thousand, it is no less a fact that cannot be denied that the progress the teachers have already made is remarkable. They were almost totally without any knowledge of the theory and practice of teaching; modern methods were unknown to most of them. In the United States, a bright boy or girl who is educated in the public schools may make a fair teacher, for he is able to perpetuate the methods followed by his teacher. In Cuba there was almost a total lack of such example, and nearly all the teachers, up to the present time, have had to depend mainly upon their own good sense and judgment, without the aid of past experience under a good teacher to guide them. Some, however, are born teachers and the instruction they are giving is of a high order. Others, who need the assistance of the ideas of others are doing their duty in a way that no one can complain of seriously."

To meet such conditions as are here indicated, and in order to broaden the minds of those to whom the actual work of instructing the youth of Cuba was committed, early in the spring of 1900 the plan of sending a certain number of teachers to Harvard was taken up and actively discussed. The idea was first suggested to the Military-Governor by Mr. Cameron Forbes of Boston, and Mr. Ernest L. Conant of Havana, and Gen. Wood at once assured them of his hearty approval of the project and promised the substantial cooperation and support of the Government. Mr. Frye had also been actively engaged in promoting this plan and pushing it forward. In March Mr. Frye went to the United States to arrange the details of this expedition and returned in May, having, in connection with President Eliot of Harvard and others, completed the details of the plan. The War Department at Washington, through the Quartermaster-General, arranged to transport all teachers, send ships to the ports of embarkation and return the teachers to Cuba at the completion of the summer work. The entire project was a success. The teachers sailed in the latter part of June, returning in August. The authorities of Harvard University deserve the greatest credit for the deep and generous interest which they took in this great work, and for the liberal provision which they made for the care and maintenance of the visitors. The work of caring for them in Cambridge was conducted with the greatest attention to detail, and was in charge of a committee of intelligent young men under the supervision of Mr. Clarence C. Mann. At the conclusion of the work at the University a trip was made to New York, Philadelphia and Washington, after a brief stay in each of which the teachers returned to Cuba. The entire expedition was without accident and practically devoid of unpleasant or unfortunate incidents. In addition to the technical information acquired, all members of the expedition came back with new ideas concerning the United States, its people and their feeling towards Cuba.

In addition to this educational outing for the Cuban teachers Summer Schools were established in the capitals of the different provinces for the benefit of those who were unable to go to Harvard and every effort was made to give them in these institutions courses of lectures containing useful and practical information on the subject of teaching. The courses included practical talks upon Reading, Language, the History of Cuba and its relations to the countries of Latin America and the United States, School Hygiene and other subjects of signal importance in the fulfillment of the work they had undertaken to perform.

As the work in hand grew in magnitude, and as its importance to themselves began to be realized by the Cubans, it was seen that certain changes were essential if the labors of the Americans in Cuba were to produce the best results. The number of schools had increased in six months from 312 to 3,313, but Mr. Frye's system, excellent for the beginning of things, proved deficient for the constantly enlarging business of the school department. To be superintendent, commissioner, and all else, considering the vast amount of detail to be attended to, was too much to expect of any man, and especially of one who was not a little of an idealist. It became necessary to somewhat restrict the functions of the superintendent, and to remodel the school act to a very considerable degree. Mr. Frye, regrettably, resigned wholly from further participation in the work, and General Wood appointed to the head of his Educational Department Lieutenant Matthew E. Hanna, of the regular army, a gentleman of broad culture, and of actual previous experience as a school-teacher.

In July, 1900, a new school law prepared by Lieut. Hanna was published, the old one having been found to be thoroughly inefficient and lacking and faulty in many essential features. The new law was framed upon lines which are practically those of the school law of the State of Ohio, which was selected after careful consideration as the basis upon which the needs of Cuba might be most satisfactorily met. It was of course adapted to meet conditions existing in Cuba, which do not exist in Ohio, and in many points differs not a little from the original. Yet in the main it is the Ohio law, and it has worked with entire satisfaction and is giving most excellent results.

Gen. Wood states that "it was at first, of course, extremely difficult to organize and put in harmonious operation over three thousand new schools with new teachers, and in a country where public instruction had hitherto been practically unknown. To those dealing with only one or a few schools, the difficulties were not so apparent, but for those charged with the organization, maintenance, supplying and payment for over thirty-three hundred schools, together with the leasing of buildings, etc., the confusion and vastness of the work was not only apparent but almost appalling. The teachers, janitors and owners of houses were all required to submit their monthly statements as to salaries, rent, and so forth. The agents of the Finance Department of the Government, charged with the payment of these salaries and expenses, found innumerable errors in the method of rendering accounts; mail facilities in many localities were extremely poor, and as a result an immense amount of confusion arose in the early months of the school year; in fact, it was not until the close of the summer vacation that the innumerable tangles had been thoroughly straightened out." In addition to these, such other difficulties arose as the distaste of teachers for new methods the opposition of existing Boards of Education, and greater still, the passive resistance to the new law when the Board of Superintendents, in the month of September of the same year, modified several of its Articles and took away the presidency of the Boards of Education from the Alcaldes. The reason for this modification was that municipal mayors, with very praiseworthy exceptions, paid very little heed to the interests entrusted to them and others no heed whatever. For some of them it may be advanced as an excuse, that, with the multifarious duties of their office, they could not possibly give to this important part of the public administration the attention it required, and in order to do away with a state of things with such evil and unhealthy consequences, the modifications were introduced. True it is that this step made the resistance to the new law still greater, so great that the government had to appoint Inspectors, whose duty it was to see that the law was enforced throughout the island, but the end has justified the act. In place of active or passive opposition to the regulations by those to whom the work was entrusted and in marked contrast with the indifference then manifested by the public generally, the records of 1901 show that there are now in the island of Cuba one hundred and thirty-five Boards of Education; five in city districts of the first class, nine in city districts of the second class; and one hundred and twenty-one in municipal districts, and everywhere exhibiting the most sincere interest in school matters. Their energies are not in every instance directed in the right channels, but the enthusiasm that they display, if under careful control and rightly directed, will result in the end in preserving public interest in the schools of the island of Cuba, and will make permanent a school system of which any country might well be proud.

# RESULTS

Lieutenant Hanna gathered his forces into a cohesive and compact body; reorganized his department from top to bottom; gathered up the loose ends of official threads which were a part of his heritage from Mr. Frye, and in the closing days of his Administration of his Department was the master of as well-organized a school department as may be found in this Hemisphere of Enlightenment. Controlled by this department are 3,650 teachers, conducting schools in 2,800 buildings, educating in all branches of school work, from primary through grammar grades, 172,000 children.

In other words, in less than four years American energy has planted upon a worse than barren soil a public-school system which would be a credit to any portion of New England, and by labor almost incredible in its demands upon those who control the situation has placed within the reach of the young of Cuba opportunities the like of which have been denied their ancestors from time immemorial. The schools, which are as far from perfection as such institutions will always be, and by no means measuring up to the ideals of the men who have made them, are none the less in efficient operation where four years ago they were in a state of chaos. Where there was a corps of teachers irresponsible, unfitted, and of political cast to the great wrong of the young entrusted to their care there is to-day a band of instructors both trustworthy and faithful, who make up in devotion to their labors that which they may lack in technical knowledge of methods, and what is best of all there are discernible everywhere in the island an interest among the people for educational work, a thirst for knowledge, and a manifest desire to aid the authorities in their efforts to extend the beneficent influences of a public school system at whatever proper cost to themselves to the rising generation.

And as for the rising generation no one can look into the faces of the thousands of youngsters in the schools of Cuba to-day without invoking the blessing of a divine Providence upon these men of War who have built up almost in a day, this wonderful engine of civilization. It has been my good fortune to see the public schools of Cuba in operation at close range and I have paid more attention to the raw material to be found there than to the methods which were the care of wiser heads than mine. Among the Cuban children I found much that was inspirational of hope for the future, a real interest in and even an enthusiasm for their work, and back of many a bright eye there seemed to me to flash the light of a soul capable of great things and worthy of the best that can be done for man by man. With the introduction of the Gill School City into the schools of Cuba and its proper management, one cannot but be hopeful for the future citizenship of the island.

The object of the School City is " to teach citizenship by practical means and to raise its quality to the highest

A GROUP OF CUBAN TEACHERS

CLASS ROOM FOR GIRLS

standard; to increase the happiness of student life; to add effectiveness to the teacher's work; to set forth in clear relief, before the teachers and students, that there is another object of education, greater than merely sharpening the wits and storing the mind with general information, which is that the individual while young shall be led to form the habit of acting toward others honestly and generously, to govern himself fearlessly and wisely always, and to use to the best educational and economic advantage, time, energy, tools and materials. for this is essential to best morals and best citizenship:

First. By engrafting into the character and habits of all its citizens that principle which is the necessary foundation of all successful popular government, that one should love his neighbor as himself, and do to others as he would have them do to him.

Second. By leading its citizens to more fully appreciate and utilize the benefits of education and other privileges of citizenship.

Third. By leading its citizens to use carefully and economically the books, supplies and other property entrusted to them, both for the public thrift, and that by means of a wholesome public spirit, their characters shall be guarded from that injury to which they are made liable by their being made recipients of such free bounties.

Fourth. By training its citizens in the ordinary duties of citizenship.

Fifth. By affording instructors and students the opportunity and means to check every tendency toward wrong thinking such as results in profane and indecent language, hazing, bullying and other unmanly and cowardly conduct and forms of anarchy.

Sixth. By getting such good for the community as may be gained by enlisting the active co-operation of the students with the public authorities for various purposes; such as preventing the littering of the streets, the defacing of private and public property, and improving the general health and the esthetic conditions of homes and public places.

Seventh. By relieving instructors of the police duty of school government, that their undivided attention may be given to the work of instruction and inspiration, and thereby to give them fuller opportunity to lead their students to the attainment of a higher scholarship and more noble character."

Surely, with a system of instruction inculcating such principles as these placed upon a solid and permanent foundation one must indeed be hard put to it to vent his spleen if he finds aught herein at which to cavil.

Of course the politician of Havana who could not profit from its financial administration and who would take to the woods before he would avail himself of its educational advantages, has viewed this work with disfavor, as has also the café critic, who writes letters for the American anti-Imperialist press, the clouds of smoke from his cigar being too thick to permit him to get anything more than a very hazy view of this very healthful situation. But to those of us who realize the difference between a civilization founded upon the Spanish Inquisition, or a Tammany Hall, and that which finds its rockbed in the school house, the Educational feather in Uncle Sam's Cuban cap must appear to be a bit of plumage of divine beauty, to which he may point with honest pride, and for which he may devoutly thank the high-minded American soldiers who have done the work so successfully and accomplished results so marvellous. The Military Government of Cuba in this Department at least has benevolently oppressed the victims of its despotism with the blessings of enlightenment.

# Chapter VIII

## THE CUSTOM HOUSE AND THE POST OFFICE.

*I*N a community for which so much needed to be done at the outset, and for which necessary funds were instantly required—it being understood, of course, that the Spanish, in their inglorious exit, left little that bore semblance to ready cash behind them—the reorganization of the custom house became a matter of immediate importance. In Spanish times there was no department that was more corrupt than this, and under American rule there has been none that has been better administered. For this important undertaking, Col. Tasker H. Bliss of the regular army was chosen, being made collector of the port of Havana and placed in charge of all the other custom houses in the island, under the supervision of the Department of War. For his assistant Mr. Walter A. Donaldson, a gentleman who had more than a score of years' experience in custom house matters—largely in the City of New York—and who, during Gen. Leonard Wood's early administration of the affairs of the province of Santiago, had successfully reorganized the customs service at that point,—was selected.

These gentlemen made an immediate and thorough investigation of their problem; and to say that they found matters in a state of chaos and of incredible corruption,

# THE CUSTOM HOUSE

is but a meagre description of the situation which confronted them. They took charge of the customs service of Cuba at noon on the first day of January, 1899, under the authority of an order dated December 9, 1898, which formed the island of Cuba and all other islands evacuated by Spain and lying west of the seventy-fourth degree of west longitude, into a customs collecting district, with Havana as the chief port of entry. Later orders established fifteen additional ports of entry in Cuba, and collectors of customs, reporting to Col. Bliss, were appointed to each, from among the commissioned officers of the United States army.

Results immediately began to make themselves apparent, for, as Mr. Franklin Matthews testifies: "Only a few days had elapsed after the Spanish evacuation of Havana and after the United States army officials had taken charge of the government in all its branches, when the merchants of Cuba began to realize that the strangest thing in all the world had happened—the custom house was being run honestly."

The tariff which was adopted for immediate use was a literal translation of the existing Spanish schedule with such modifications as the condition of the island demanded, consisting chiefly of reductions in the rates. The Spanish rates, as we have seen, had been excessive in many instances, more particularly upon such articles as Spain herself could not supply. The maximum reduction was

269

seventy-five per cent. and reached an average of nearly sixty per cent. Special modifications were made in the tariff on the necessities of life; and for the hastening of the work of reconstruction and of placing the people upon a basis of self-support, all farm implements were put upon the free list; and the livestock necessary for the farmers' work, as well as for that of the various departments of street cleaning, sanitation and others, were taxed only the minimum duty; enough merely to meet the cost of passing them, properly inspected by veterinary surgeons, through the custom house.

The average duty under the modified schedule was less than twenty-two per cent., while under the Spanish rule it had approximated fifty per cent. Differential rates favorable to Spanish imports were abolished. No preferential provisions of any kind were made, and the United States was granted no more privileges under the new schedule than those possessed by all other nations.

Col. Bliss and Mr. Donaldson naturally met with many irritating obstacles in the way of opposition, not only from employees of the department, who had come to regard lax methods as one of their inalienable rights, but also from merchants, who found the strict enforcement of the law not wholly to their taste, and certainly not as much to their individual profit as the dishonest practices of the Spanish collectors. The new officials, however, were not to be deterred by any such opposition as this,

COLONEL TASKER H. BLISS, U. S. A.

*Chief of Customs and Collector of Port of Havana*

and Col. Bliss, having conceived the idea that the way to
" collect taxes was to collect them, set himself to finding
out what he had to collect and then to doing it in the most
direct and straightforward fashion." It must be borne
in mind that under Spanish rule the custom house was
the chief source of revenue for the captain-general and
other high officials, who had been appointed to their lofty
positions for the purpose of securing their individual en-
richment. The system in vogue had been described by
Mr. Robert P. Porter, the tariff expert, as having been
" made by Spaniards for Spain in the interests of the
Spanish." Mr. Porter added that on any other theory,
it was inexplicable.

Col. Bliss did not begin by turning out all the old
officials. He kept as many of the old force at work as
was possible. He instituted a new bureau of audit;
placed the book-keepers in a different room from the
cashiers; placed gates at such points of the custom house
as were necessary to keep the clerical force from coming
into contact with the merchants and their agents; and,
best of all, broke down the barriers of " red tape " which
hitherto had existed between the person of the collector
and the public. No honest employee was discharged,
and no man under suspicion was discharged unless upon
actual proof of his dishonesty. The principles of civil
service reform were applied, but in such fashion that the
hold-overs from the previous administration were not led

into the comfortable belief that once in office, it was impossible for anyone to get them out.

Many instances of blackmail manifested themselves early in the administration; but by degrees the firmness with which such underhand attacks were met convinced those who were attempting by nefarious methods to impede the honest performance of the functions of the collector's office, that blackmailing was, after all, an unprofitable business.

One of the principal difficulties in the beginning was the management of the appraisers, or avistas, as they were called in Spanish times. These individuals had come to believe that they were after all, the custom house; and that the custom house existed more for the purpose of supplying them with funds than for that of supplying the government of Cuba with revenue. Perhaps this misconception was not wholly unnatural, since they received salaries which were not at all commensurate to the services they were supposed to render; and, taking their cue no doubt from the regularly accredited officials of the home government at the palace, they deemed that a certain large proportion of the funds which came into their possession was the perquisite of their own pockets. In spite of the smallness of their salaries, it is stated that these persons " earned " annually enormous amounts of money, there being a double source of revenue, comprising that which could be got from the funds of the government and that which could be extracted, as a matter of friendly interest, from the importer.

Apropos of the devious methods of the former Spanish officials to enrich themselves, a story is told of a Spanish customs inspector who was asked by an American captain if he could see if a gold doubloon were placed over each eye. He replied by stating that under such conditions he could not see; and that if one were placed over each ear and his mouth he could neither speak nor hear.

Another story illustrating the easy attitude of the Spanish customs officials toward their work, related to the port of Manzanillo. This until the ten years' war was simply the port of Bayamo, a charming little town located in the hill country, forty miles away from the coast. It was considered a very pleasant place for the Spanish officials to spend the summer months. Duty possessed no compelling force for these officers, and finding Bayamo so pleasing a resting place, when summer came they departed one and all, including the captain of the port, for its precincts, compelling every ship's master who entered the port of Bayamo, if he wished to get his clearance papers, to take a horse and ride there and back to get them, a distance altogether of eighty miles.

The new system placed into operation by Col. Bliss and Mr. Donaldson brought these " avistas " to an unpleasant realization of the fact that a hitherto profitable business was in imminent danger of being one of the ruined industries of Spain; and in consequence of this realization —they struck. The strike was met simply, directly and promptly. The leaders were discharged. Some of the minor malcontents were requested to resign; and at the end of a quarter of an hour, the remainder were expressing their willingness to go back to business again.

A more serious revolt, because harder to cope with, came later, when the merchants of Havana and Cuba ventured to disapprove of the new honest methods of the customs department. They refused to abide by the system which had been adopted, and threatened to leave their goods in the hands of the custom house until there was a return to the old system of dealing directly with the appraisers. They complained also of what they considered the "red tape" of the department, which consisted merely of organized effort where there had been haphazard methods, and their ultimatum was that modifications of the new system should be made at once, else the commerce of the whole port would be tied up.

These gentlemen were met in a spirit of tact and diplomacy which was wholly admirable; and which, considered in all its bearings, would probably prove very disappointing to anti-imperialistic friends at home, whose idea of an army officer in power is that he is an arbitrary despot, who does by force of arms and without respect to the rights of citizens, that which could be accomplished by finesse. Seeming to yield to all the demands of the merchants, Col. Bliss and Mr. Donaldson by a process of ad hominem argument soon managed to convince a sufficient number of the reputable among the remonstrants of the impracticability of their demands. Mr. Donaldson laid before them the various planks in the platform of the new management, proved to them the necessity of modern business methods for the proper protection of the interests of the department, and showed them very briefly that the only desire of the collector and himself, after having protected the interests of the department, was to be helpful to the merchants in their business, and to place them in a position of being not victims but customers of the custom house.

There were practical methods of doing this, and the collector availed himself of them. From that time to this, it has come to be recognized among the merchants of Cuba that the department is run solely with regard to its own requirements, and without involving any interests of a purely personal consideration.

As time went on, many inequalities in the tariff schedule manifested themselves; and in the spring of 1900, a second revision was ordered. This was made and went into effect on the fifteenth day of June, 1900, and is still in operation. The main principles of its predecessor were maintained. The average rate remained the same—about twenty-two per cent., and its net results have barely

275

differed from those of the preceding instrument. Its provisions levy a moderate, equitable and uniform duty on all imported articles, irrespective of their source; and they have been administered in the same spirit of unvarying, uncompromising impartiality.

Another early problem which the singular condition of affairs had interjected into the situation, Mr. Matthews notes was that of an " open door." Col. Bliss and Mr. Donaldson, as well as Mr. Porter, our tariff commissioner in Cuba, saw that if Cuba would be rehabilitated the ports must be open to ships of all nations. There were not enough ships under the American flag to deal with its commerce as if the island were our own possession. Had it not been for the open door policy, the mines at Santiago could not have been started up, and commerce at most of the ports of the island would have stood still.

In a report as far back as December 1, 1898, to Gen. Wood at Santiago, Mr. Donaldson said: " It is to be remarked that the policy of no discrimination in intercourse extended to the vessels of all nations in the matter of entering and clearing at this port, as well as at the various other ports within this province, has greatly facilitated the reestablishment of commercial relations.

This policy, adopted at the beginning has been extended since then to all ports, and the " open door " has been of inestimable value in the rehabilitation of the island.

Another somewhat curious complication arose in the early days of Col. Bliss's administration, and that was as to the flag under which Cubans might engage in their coast trade. Their vessels not being vessels of American register, the flag of the United States could not be used upon them; and, since there was no Cuban nation, clearly the Cuban flag was useless. The Spanish flag naturally was not such a one as, under prevailing conditions, the coasters cared to use. To meet this complication, the President of the United States ordered "that a blue flag with a white jack" should be used for such vessels. Owners were required to take an oath renouncing allegiance to all former governments. Some of the captains of the vessels thought they had a right to fly the United States flag, and it took a long time to convince them that the only flag they could fly would be that blue field with a white patch on one corner; and that the forces of the United States would be used, if necessary, to protect them from being considered pirates or as belonging to a fictitious nation. That flag, Mr. Matthews states, is the only flag of Cuban sovereignty or semi-sovereignty that the United States up to this writing has recognized, and so far as this country is concerned officially that is the present Cuban flag.

Physically, the task of the collector and his aids was a very difficult one. The custom houses were in a frightful state of dilapidation and filthy beyond description. The

Havana custom house was without adequate furniture, there was no stationery of any kind, and for some reason probably well known to themselves, the Spaniards had taken care before departure to remove or to destroy important records. Conditions at other ports were in a similar condition of demoralization. Then, too, the question of sanitation intruded itself upon the vexations of Col. Bliss, followed by the necessity for countless repairs and improvements indispensable for the proper conduct of business—a situation for which there seemed to be little prospect of immediate relief, since the requirements of the island for improved hospitals, new roads and school houses were so pressing that such things as improvements to the custom house itself and the construction of new wharves seem to be matters that might be allowed to wait. Time and patience, however, have brought about necessary reforms in this direction; and at the present time, while far from perfect, the material conditions under which the custom house is operated have taken a long stride in the direction of adequacy.

The customs service of Cuba as it exists to-day is the work of the military representatives of Uncle Sam. Its personnel is made up of men who had had no experience in the business of the custom house prior to the period of intervention, with, of course, a few exceptions. Requiring good business knowledge, as well as business sense, and a knowledge of customs laws and regulations, the

THE HAVANA CUSTOM HOUSE

DRILLING RAW RECRUITS, HAVANA POLICE

collectors of the sixteen ports of entry have practically had to acquire these qualifications by untiring application; and that their service has been constant and intelligent and fruitful of results speaks volumes for their faithful and efficient labor. Eternal vigilance has been required of the heads of departments, unremitting attention to their duties has been exacted of the subordinates. And when we consider that the coast line of Cuba is more than 2,000 miles in length, the enormous work of this department in the administration of its affairs, in the suppression of smuggling, in the instruction of the incompetent, and in the rooting out of corruption becomes little short of marvelous.

Every kind of organized smuggling was resorted to in the old days, from bribing the inspectors, and appraisers to making false entries. Scarcely a trick of the professional smuggling fraternity but was a common practice under Spanish rule. An amusing instance of this is found in the employment of a certain negro expert in former days, when there was a big differential duty against American flour. Spanish and American flour were interchanged on the dock, for the purpose of avoiding duties, by the simple process of changing the labels. This change of label was brought about by this expert, who had the proper brand upon the seat of his trousers, and entertained the appraisers by cleverly sitting the brand on the sacks on the open dock.

Many changes have been made in methods by which great advantages accrue to the business interests of Cuba. The original orders provided for sixteen ports of entry, of which three were sub-ports reporting respectively from Havana, Manzanillo and Trinidad. In order to facilitate the business interests of the island, especially its exportations, other sub-ports have been established. As Col. Bliss has said, " to have limited the trade to sixteen ports would have done much injury to the trade of the island, especially its export trade. Fruit and wood and iron ores are now loaded at sub-ports and taken directly to their destination in the United States, and since export duties have been abolished there is no danger from exportations in this practice."

Unorganized or sporadic smuggling has practically been eliminated, if, indeed, in the sense in which it is ordinarily known, it was ever practiced outside of the regular channels of business. In a country lacking high-ways and railroads and other facilities for carrying smuggled goods to market, the ordinary business of the contraband was not particularly profitable. What little remains has been got under control by a revenue cutter service, which was established in 1901, at a cost of about $50,000; and which, in addition to restraining the illegal traffic of the smuggler, gives protection to the sponge and turtle fisheries of the coast.

As to the personnel of the Cuban customs service, which

includes the employees of the office of the Surveyor of the Port at Havana, Col. Bliss states that it is a varying quantity, but at the present time contains a number slightly in excess of 800. Of this number it is estimated that 700 are about equally divided between the Havana custom house on the one hand, and all other ports on the other. The remainder are engaged in the general work of the whole service. And in the whole service the Americans still engaged at the moment of our departure from the island barely exceed 100, the rest are Cubans, with the exception of eighty men who were born in Spain. This has been a marked feature of American military control in the island. As in the other departments, " Cuba for the Cubans " has been the guiding principle of those having public place to bestow. The military government has not been one of " carpet-baggers; " but, on the contrary, has made it its constant concern to develop along lines of utility to the public and to themselves the capabilities of the real owners of the island of Cuba. It is estimated that less than one per cent. of the personnel in the various offices of the insular government are Americans. Of the Americans holding places in the customs service, twelve are officers of the United States army; the remainder, Col. Bliss tells me, are employed in the bureau of correspondence, as special agents, in the department of statistics. and in the revenue cutter service; and perform duties that none other than Americans could

render for so long a time as our military government remains in charge. Precisely what service this small army
of workers has performed can best be determined by a
brief retrospect of the business operations that have been
transacted at the customs houses of Cuba since January
1, 1899.

The duties collected by the American administration at
all ports up to the first of January, 1902, were somewhat
in excess of $39,000,000, at a cost of less than $1,825,000.
The moneys thus received were of an interestingly varying kind. At the port of Havana at the end of the fiscal
year, ending June 1, 1901, six different kinds of money
were paid to the cashier. Of the $11,538,949 taken in
by him, $7,409,139 was in paper currency of the United
States; $1,366,871 in American gold; $108,775 in American silver; $2,084,795 in Spanish gold; $21.45 in Spanish
silver; $567,316 in French louis; and $2,032 in half-louis.

These transactions involved the execution of about
180,000 entries of declarations on importations, of which
number a trifle over 120,000 were handled at Havana
and the balance at other ports; and, as evidence of the
fairness and accuracy with which this was accomplished,
it should be stated that fewer than 2,600 protests were
filed by importers during a period of thirty months. About
one-fourth of these protests were sustained, and the
over-charges refunded—a system which has been most

astonishing to the Cuban, who rarely, if ever, got anything back once paid to a Spaniard.

The total value of all classes of importations into Cuba up to the first of June, 1901, approximated $180,000,000, and the exports exceeded $145,000,000. At a time when we are considering the interests of the Cuban ward, who, even when he has assumed charge of his own affairs, may still need some assistance from his old-time guardian, we should note Col. Bliss's comment upon the thirty-five million-dollar balance of trade against the island. "This," Col. Bliss states, "is no doubt an additional price that Cuba must pay for the ravages of the late war. Princely sums have been realized for sugar and tobacco during this period—more than sixty millions for each of them; but it was not enough to meet the extraordinary outlay which the war entailed upon this people. For the necessaries of life and for the rehabilitation of their homes and farms, they expended $65,000,000 for articles of food, including wines and liquors; nearly $25,000,000 for livestock—1,000,000 animals of all kinds, including 825,000 head of cattle having been imported; $24,000,000 was paid for cotton, linen and woolen goods; $5,600,000 for shoes, hats and other articles of clothing; $7,000,000 for manufactures of metal, such as structural iron, railroad material, hardware, tools and implements; $45,000,000 for machinery, of which nearly $10,000,000 was for sugar and brandy machinery; $12,341,671 of gold and $236,166 silver coin, a total of $12,576,837 was imported."

Three-fourths of the products of Cuba the records of Col. Bliss show have been sent to the United States, and one-half of Cuba's importations have come from the United States. The United States have supplied $83,-250,000 worth out of a grand total of $180,000,000 of imports, or forty-six per cent.; and has bought $108,000,000 worth out of a grand total of $145,000,000 of exports, or seventy-five per cent.

The most important item of Col. Bliss's figures may be set down to be the fact which they prove that most of the food stuffs and livestock, nearly all of the manufactures of metal, implements, machinery, hardware and railroad material, and the bulk of the coin—all the necessities— were imported there from the United States.

The United States has received practically all of the sugar of the island, more than 2,000,300,000 pounds. at a cost of $63,000,000; barely 300,000 pounds have been shipped to all other countries. America has purchased most of the Cuban tobacco, comprising sixty-four million pounds of manufactured leaf, 540 million cigars, and twenty-eight million packages of cigarettes. All other products. fruit, vegetables, fibres, fine woods—of which there are countless varieties in Cuba—and various ores were sold to the value of $13,500,000, of which $12, 000,000 worth found its way to the United States.

Surely it would seem as if there was in this vast volume
of business an adequate basis for mutually satisfactory
reciprocal relations between the new Republic and ourselves.

In marked contrast to the administration of the Custom House, has been that of the Post Office Department
in which we find the only blot upon the escutcheon of
Uncle Sam's work in Cuba. Yet even the difference is
illuminating, for the work of the Postal Department was
the one branch of American endeavor that was not under
the absolute control of the Military Government. Its
high places were farmed out from the political wing of
the Department at Washington, on the good old Spanish
principle, apparently, of take what you can get and get
away with it if you can—at any rate political services
were paid for by its emoluments and as a result the
calibre of the men selected was of inferior grade. The
revelation of the corrupt practices of the postal stewards
has been a humiliation to those who have cared for Uncle
Sam's good name under circumstances so peculiar, but
the swift retribution which has overtaken the criminals
while it does not wipe out the disgrace of the peculations,
nevertheless in a measure emphasizes our insistence upon
honesty in public office. Viewed in this light the be-
trayal of their trusts by the convicted men of the Cuban
Postal Service is not an unmixed blessing. For malfea-
sances for which Spanish officials would have gone un-

punished, the American thieves have been sentenced to heavy fines and prolonged imprisonment—a lesson in contrasts which may not be without value. It is curious in this connection that in Mr. Franklin Matthews' book, *The New Born Cuba,* one of the illustrations of his article on the Postal Service bears the title " The Present Post Office Building." As a matter of fact the illustration is not that of the post office building, but of the penitentiary. A more prophetic forecast of the natural abiding place of the then Administrators of Cuba's posts could not have been devised.

Apart from the peculations of these " opportunists," the Administration of the Cuban posts has been efficient. I do not care to go into details concerning it since it is of the Army work in the civil administration of Cuba that I wish to speak more particularly. The Army's chief connection with the office has consisted of seeing that its corrupt heads have not escaped the punishment their crimes have merited. Gen. Wood can stand all the criticism he will receive from high political quarters for his " complicity " in the conspiracy which has brought Neeley and Rathbone and Reeves to justice. In this as in other matters that would have inconvenienced men of lesser build he has shown himself sternly inflexible in the face of a plain duty; fearless as he is just, and unafraid in the presence of the majesty of the political machine.

# Chapter IX

## THE POLICE, THE LAW, AND THE CHURCH.

*T*HE maintenance of public order under the principles laid down as guiding ones by the American administration in Cuba, in which the civil rather than the militant idea was to prevail, was one of great and immediate importance. The chief effort in the direction of organizing a well-equipped constabulary was made in Havana.

Preparations for reforming the police department were begun by General Francis V. Greene, who engaged the services of ex-Chief McCullagh, of New York, to organize the new force. On January 6th, a mounted force of 350 men was created for the policing of the district lying outside of the built-up portions of Havana; it was formed mainly from the Cuban troops and proved very efficient. The organization and equipment of the municipal police was begun at once but it was not until the first of March that the city was placed entirely under their protection, and the American sentinels withdrawn.

Much praise is due to the American soldiers for the police work done by them during these early days. Complete order was kept, though the bewilderment of the men in trying to calm and direct the excitable Cuban was frequently laughable, and sometimes the methods employed were not strictly in accordance with any recognized code. On one occasion one of the sentinels saw a mule, attached to an overloaded cart, which had fallen and had one leg over the shaft. Its brutal driver, without dismounting from the cart, tried to make it rise by beating it. The sentinel remonstrated in plain English but without any effect, whereupon, seeing that the situation demanded other measures, he leaned his gun against the nearest house, walked out to the cart, knocked the driver off with a blow of his fist, picked up the driver, and with his assistance got the mule to his feet and started, then resumed his gun and went on patrolling his beat without further words. And here it may be remarked that our soldiers were a continual source of surprise to the natives. They looked so big and so burly, and while apparently so rough in their ways and ready to use their fists, were withal so honest and kindly.

Shortly after the police force was organized, the United States patrol in going its rounds saw at the far end of a block a couple of soldiers, evidently out on a lark, who had just stripped one of the new policemen absolutely naked and neatly piled his uniform, with his revolver on top, beside him, and were apparently about to give him some lessons in deportment. By the time the patrol reached the spot the men had disappeared, and the policeman was rehabilitated and sent on his way. Later, these policemen learned their authority and learned to exercise it properly. They learned another lesson also, and that was the value of the club. The Cubans do not seem to be afraid of a pistol shot or of a sword, but they could not stand a blow of the fist or of the club. In the early days of the force the club was left sheathed and the pistol drawn in case of a disturbance, and on at least one occasion quite a skirmish ensued, with wounds on both sides. Afterwards the mobs were handled easily by the club alone.

The courts of first instance having proved to be very slow and very uncertain in the administration of justice, it was found necessary to establish a police court in Havana on lines similar to those existing in the United States, for the prompt trial and punishment of minor offences. The Spanish system of jurisprudence contained no provision for police or correctional courts, such as are known in the United States and elsewhere, for the speedy disposal of police arrests and minor offences. When judicial action was required, recourse was had to the regular city magistrates' courts, having mainly inquisitorial and reportorial powers, and later to the courts of first instance, with limited jurisdiction, above which were the provincial courts, designated "audiencias." The punishment of minor offences, collections of fines and penalties, and the like were therefore attended by the inconvenience and injustice of prolonged delays in completing trials, involving unnecessary detention of offenders and witnesses, frequent failures to reach conclusions at all, and the multiplication of opportunities for corrupt practices in connection with the courts and their respective functionaries, high and low. During the anomalous conditions obtaining at the outset of the American occupation in Havana, and prior to the organization of a local police, and when soldiers were performing police duty, the number of arrests and the variety of offences, as well as offenders, complicated the situation and caused much embarrassment in their disposition.

For this reason Gen. Ludlow established at the vivac (the police jail) a summary police court with an officer of his staff in charge, who sat every morning for the purpose of disposing of the police arrests of the preceding day.

The first incumbent was Major Evans, U. S. V., inspector-general on the staff of Gen. Ludlow, who conducted these novel proceedings with tact, judgment, and good humor, so that in fact the institution furnished both instruction and entertainment to the public, and became a popular feature even with the victims, who preferred paying their $2 to $10 fines to being detained for two or three months awaiting trial and judgment.

Major Evans upon leaving the United States service was succeeded by Captain (now Major) Pitcher, of the Eighth Infantry, who still further enhanced the renown and usefulness of the court until its repute extended all over the island. Major Evans was succeeded by Captain (now Major) Louis V. Caziarc, 2d U. S. Artillery, under whose later management of its affairs, the Havana Police Department reached its highest efficiency.

When the administrative reorganization of the city government had been fairly accomplished, and matters were proceeding with smoothness and regularity, practically the only arbitrary military feature remaining was the police court, which had approved itself thoroughly as both a convenience and a practical necessity in the conduct of the city affairs. This court, which was organized through necessity, and without any local foundation, proved not only beneficial but popular, and later, was made by General Wood a part of the judicial system of the island. The officers presiding over these courts performed their novel duties with much tact and discretion, and it is a curious fact that they became very popular, even among the more turbulent elements of Havana, who highly appreciated the fact that they were sure of a prompt trial and punishment for any offence that might be committed and were not, as in the old days, to be kept in prison until they or their friends could raise the amount of money demanded. Captain Pitcher, who held this position the longest, became well known in Havana, and in his rides around the city would be saluted by the street urchins with, "Ho! Meester Peecher, ten dollahs or ten days!"

The "Vivacs" or principal city police stations in which prisoners first arrested and those convicted of the minor offences were confined, were vile holes, with little pretence of sanitation of any kind. One of the first tasks of the officers in charge was to see that this was reformed. There were three buildings used for this purpose; two for males and one for females, the latter being the well known "Recogidas" from which, during the war, the sensational escape of Miss Cisneros took place. One of the others, a rented building, was what had formerly been a palatial dwelling; this was subsequently abandoned. The third was an interesting structure built in the eighteenth century by convicts under the direction of a monastic order which, at that time, had charge of the prisons. As quickly as possible this last building was cleaned and repaired by the Engineer Department, and is to-day a model police station. When the repaired building was first opened it was dedicated, after truly Cuban fashion, with a reception and promenade concert given under the auspices of the police of that precinct. Cleanliness was strictly enforced in this and the other police stations, so that the Vivac became not only a correctional, but also an educational institution for the class of people who most needed this kind of training. Later, the building formerly used as a barracks and known as the "Dragones barracks" was also transformed into a police station with all modern improvements. The old

THE VIVAC, HAVANA

castle of Atares was made into a workhouse for prisoners under sentence. In all of this work Captains Pitcher and Caziarc took the very greatest interest, and under their care the police force of Havana became a model of neatness, respected by the law-abiding and dreaded by the law-breakers.

The work performed by former chief of police McCullagh of New York in the reorganization of the Havana Police, forms one of the most interesting stories that are told of the early American days in Cuba. The ex-chief arrived in Havana on the fourteenth of December, 1898, having, upon the suggestion of Gen. Greene, the first military governor of the city under the United States, been appointed by President McKinley a committee of one to assist in the reorganization. Col. Moulton of the Second Illinois Volunteers had already been appointed chief of police, and with the promised assistance of Mr. McCullagh had undertaken the complete reconstruction of the department. The system already in existence was seen to be a mere farce. It comprised about 1800 men, of whom 300 were municipal police appointed by the city council to enforce city ordinances, 300 were government police appointed by the authorities of the province, and 1200 belonged to what was called the *orden publico*, and were really soldiers of the Cuban army. There was so much ' red tape ' about the performance of the functions of their office that comparatively little in the way of preserving public order was possible. There were no station houses in existence, and all of the prisoners upon arrest were taken to the city jail. A record was made of an arrest, and Mr. Franklin Matthews states " that was as far as all police records went. There was no record of criminals kept, and after a man was sent to jail, all sight of him was lost so far as the police were concerned." The hard lot of the prisoner is further indicated by Mr. Matthews who continues his story as follows: " The policeman after an arrest took his prisoner to his captain, whose office was in his residence. The captain committed him to jail and sent the case to a magistrate. There were twelve magistrates, six of whom were judges of the first instance. The salary of these was $5,000 each, and they adjudicated felonies. The other six judges received no salaries, and they sat in misdemeanor cases. They simply lived on blackmail. Those prisoners who had money never went to jail to stay. After from one to three days, the prisoner's case was heard, and then came jail or a fine. The police knew no more about the case, except as an unusually intelligent policeman kept a record for himself. The man who went to jail got out afterwards as best he could, either from expiration of sentence or through corruption. The system was thoroughly Spanish in its operation, and corruption was its corner stone."

After four or five days of drastic investigation, Mr.

Major Louis V. Caziarc, U. S. A.

McCullagh reported to Gen. Greene the results of his observations, and laid before him a full and complete scheme of reorganization. By this plan he divided the city into six inspection districts and twelve precincts, and recommended that 360 night posts and 180 day posts be established. He divided the force which was necessary, in his judgment, as follows: one chief, one deputy chief, eight inspectors, twelve captains, forty-eight lieutenants, eight hundred and thirty-four patrolmen, ten detective sergeants, fourteen detectives, twelve precinct detectives, and twelve doormen. One hundred of the patrolmen were to be mounted for duty in the suburbs, and the total force was to consist of about one thousand men.

Gen. Greene immediately approved Mr. McCullagh's report, and applications for membership began to pour in. Equipments were secured, similar in kind to those used upon the force in the city of New York, to which the United States government added, at its own cost, a sufficient number of revolvers for department use. Designs for uniform and buttons were made, and all other details necessary for the turning out of a complete policeman, so far as externals went, were completed in about a month. The necessary stationery, consisting of desk blotters, arrest books, complaint books, transfer books, and other essentials, were printed; and a set of 180 rules and regulations for the instruction of the new police was printed both in English and in Spanish.

Gen. Menocal, formerly of the Cuban army, now succeeded Col. Moulton as chief of police; and friction began for the first time to show itself in the department. It became necessary for complete authority to be vested in some one individual, and Mr. McCullagh, finding his hands somewhat tied by the authority of Gen. Menocal, refused to go further without full and exclusive powers. These were given to him by Gen. Ludlow, who had succeeded Gen. Greene in command of the department of Havana, and the work began to proceed toward completion with gratifying rapidity.

On the 16th of January, 1899, the first applicants were examined. It was required of the men that they should be at least five feet, six and one-half inches tall, in good physical condition, and able to read and write. 2700 men applied for examination, of whom 800 were accepted. Whereupon drills were begun, the measurements of every man were taken for uniforms, and the officers required by the system were appointed. So far as possible the responsible officers were appointed from the ranks of the natives.

The personnel of the force selected, it was now found somewhat necessary to instruct its members in the topography of Havana. There was, in fact, no correct map of distances to be found among the city records. This shortcoming was speedily remedied and within a week the posts of patrolmen were laid out for the entire city in feet.    The salaries paid were $4.000 for the chief, $2,000 for the deputy, $1,800 for inspectors, $115 per month for captains, lieutenants $90 per month, rounds-men $65 per month, patrolmen and door-men $50 per month; and each member of the force was required to pay for his equipment in deductions from his salary.

The infinite patience of Mr. McCullagh in the drilling of his men was something wonderful to look upon; and it is greatly to his credit that at a peculiarly irritating period he was found to be so fully in sympathy with the work in hand that he set for the men in his charge an indubitably useful and admirable example in self-restraint.

As in the other departments, at the time of the relin-quishment of American control, the number of Americans employed upon the police force of Havana and in the other branches of the constabulary throughout the island, was barely one per cent.    The opportunities of the force were placed in the hands of the Cuban people and they quickly availed themselves of them.

It may be said of the men who constitute this municipal guard to-day that they will bear favorable comparison with the police of any other country in the new or the old world.    They are efficient and courteous always; physically not of any particular distinction they, nevertheless, are a most presentable body of men.    They seem to be under-sized compared to the police of New York or London, but they make up in soldierly bearing and general cleanness

of cut and of person what they lack in physical proportions. It may be said to their credit and with truth that
they take a sincere, honest and even ambitious view of
the work they have in hand. The police band of the
city of Havana established under American auspices is
one of the best military bands I have ever had the
pleasure of listening to, and its concerts in the city of
Havana on Saturday nights, as well as the afternoon per-
formances upon the Prado and at fêtes of a public nature
are a delight to the ear. There seems to be among these
police officers of Havana the smallest—if indeed there is
any—of that natural tendency toward corrupt practices
which would appear to be characteristic of the police
officers in more experienced communities ; and, whether or
not this condition of affairs will last, it is certainly to the
credit both of the force itself and of those who have
had charge of the selection of its members that to-day
Havana seems to be possessed of an ideal constabulary.
Speaking to this point Maj. Pitcher in his report of April
20th, 1900, says : " The police officers are men chosen from
the better class of Cuban citizens, many of them belonging
to the best families in Havana. They learn their duties
well and make good officials.

" I believe that in their work the police, as a general
thing, have acted honestly and conscientiously. I think
they have done all that was required of them. There have
been some cases in which the police have arrested citizens

for attempting to bribe them. They have brought the citizen as a prisoner to the police court, handed over to the police magistrate the money offered as a bribe, and have made charges against the citizen for attempting to corrupt the police force. In most cases the money offered as a bribe was confiscated and the citizen punished for attempting bribery of the force."

In addition to the municipal police the needs of the outlying districts required attention and in the early part of the occupation of the Department of Havana by the United States it was found necessary to organize a rural guard for the protection of the suburban districts between the city and the boundary of the department. This force was established for the protection of the suburbs of Havana, as well as of the outlying municipalities of Regla, Guanabacoa, Santa Maria del Rosario, Puentes Grandes, and their vicinity. The force included 200 officers and men; about one-half of them mounted. The men were selected from among the Cubans who had served in the war, and were equipped with a machete and carbine. They were under the orders of the chief of police of Havana and were located in seventeen different stations. The principal stations are Santa Maria del Rosario, Jesus del Monte, Luyanó, Guanabacoa, Puentes Grandes, Cerro, and the Vivac. These men have done excellent work. Frequent inspections of their daily rendezvous, showed the force to be painstaking and clean and their equipments and horses well taken care of. They have prevented a great deal of stealing and disorder in the rural districts.

In the administration of the laws of Cuba, no little difficulty has been met with by the American authorities. The laws which prevailed there were naturally the laws of Spain, and were based upon a civilization radically different from that which we call our own. The American authorities, in so far as they have been able to do so, have enforced the existing statutes, except in such cases as it was clearly evident that they wrought injustice rather than justice. It is to the credit of the thinking element of Cuba that they were among the first to realize the embarrassments by which the authorities were confronted in the enforcement of laws which they felt to be iniquitous; and, sensitive as these people are in most matters involving a departure from their own established customs, they have been more than usually helpful in upholding the arm of the American representatives in Cuba in what they recognized as a sincere effort to administer justice to those who needed it. As Señor Jose Varella Jado, Secretary of Justice for the island of Cuba, has said in an interesting essay on legal jurisprudence, " The movement which broke out in February, 1895, called for the exercise of what is known as the American policy in its relations with the Antilles, and particularly with the island of Cuba, whose geographical location made it a serious and constant menace to the interests of the United States.

A SERGEANT OF POLICE, HAVANA

# INNOVATIONS

It is not strange that one who so believed should advise in good faith that we by aiding in the fulfilment of the laws of expansion, assimilation and progress, should endeavor to secure for our country all that is recognized as good in the United States. Let at least the generation that succeeds us, in place of the sad heritage that has always fallen to our lot, enjoy in every field of activity the full benefits which this transcendant social and political change will bring to us."

The first innovation which was introduced into Cuba by the military government was in the correctional courts, already referred to at some length, which, it is the testimony of this eminent Cuban whom I have just quoted, " has already produced magnificent results and will prove an important factor in the moral education of the masses, teaching them the respect due to the law, to each other, and to the general interests of the country."

The administration of Justice, has been on the whole, the most difficult problem the authorities have to deal with. They were from the first short of suitable personnel. The population of the island is small and almost every judge has been a lawyer and every case which comes up for trial is one in which his own friends are mixed up in one way or another. However, the time which prisoners formerly spent waiting trial has been reduced nearly two thirds, and there are few, if any men, held in prison without just and sufficient reason. The

Habeas Corpus is in force and gradually becoming understood. There was not one change that was more opposed by the secretaries and the lawyers than this. The points of view of Cubans and Americans are so different as to be remarkable, and one who was present at the preliminary discussions between Gen. Wood and his Cuban secretaries says that he was filled with surprise over the reasoning of the Secretary of Justice when he was opposing it. The Secretary seemed to think that it carried a reflection on the judiciary which would in the end defeat the purpose of justice and the penal clause for the judges filled him with horror. Not once in his whole discussion did he refer to the rights of the accused. The privileges and dignity of the judges were all that could come into his mind. But the American idea prevailed in the end with gratifying results, although as yet the writ has not been taken much advantage of except by resourceful Americans.

The railroad laws have recently been re-written and what is thought to be an excellent general railroad law substituted. A general law, very comprehensive in its scope, has been prepared, regulating the division of common lands—" Haciendas Comuneras "—a subject which has been most vexatious and which has been under discussion for a hundred years.

The " Haciendas Comuneras " were the outcome of the crown's habit of granting principalities to its best friends. The best friend came over to Cuba and standing on a certain spot and with a good generous radius described a circle which he claimed his own by royal grant. As the king had a good many friends to be rewarded these circles began to intersect so that for a hundred years there have been many long and weary fights over the different lines. The situation has been still further complicated by a provision of the law of inheritance which prohibits the heir from selling any part of his estate without the full consent of all the co-heirs; so that these old royal grants are still intact in many parts of the island, especially in Puerto Principe and Santiago, but belong to dozens of descendants of the original grantee not one of whom knows what part is his.

The general law which at this writing is about to be published is the result of the work of the present judicial commission and with the experience of a good many other such for the last hundred years clears up this difficult situation. It was extremely important that this question be settled while there was arbitrary power in Cuba to do it legally, as it would take years of discussion, probably a hundred years more, before any number of legislators more or less interested could be expected to agree on a proper solution. Of course a good many of the people over a good part of the island will feel injured by this arbitrary action, but it is the only way to cut the gordian knot and clear up most of the titles of the island. After a title has once been made clear it is a very simple matter to keep it so, as the system of land registration in Cuba is of the very best.

Summing up this phase of our subject in reference to the attitude of the American administration towards the existing laws in Cuba, it may be said, as a general statement, that little has been done in the way of radical changes in the law as a whole; the principal changes having been made in the procedure. An attempt has been made to do away with the fee system, which led to so much corruption among the clerk employees and officials. Police courts have been established throughout the island for the summary trial of minor offences. Habeas Corpus has been put in operation. Perjury has been defined and made punishable under the law. A marriage law has been put into effect, with the full co-operation of the Catholic Church, which recognizes marriages by all religious denominations and also recognizes duly performed civil marriages. The Catholic Church, is referred to because prior to the establishment of American control it had practically the monopoly of religious marriages and any changes adverse to this monopoly might be expected to arouse its opposition. Just and equitable laws, giving due protection to the ruined estates have been prepared. Cruelty to animals has been made punishable.

In looking over the orders which have been issued by the military authorities, one's first impression is that there may be some justice in the criticism of the Governor-General for having made a large number of changes in the laws and in the promulgation of new ones; but when this criticism arises in the mind of the investigator, second thought comes to the rescue and when it is remembered that in the Governor-General has been vested the whole law-making power; and that in making changes, he has been forced sometimes into expedients to meet certain immediate contingencies, a failure to meet which would have outraged his sense of justice, one's cavilling turns to approval concerning the ends which have been accomplished by the means criticized. Closer investigation will also develop the fact that there have been comparatively few changes in the fundamental laws of the land, and that most of the orders issued from the Palace have been those affecting appointments and other matters relative to the administration of the country's business.

To illustrate in some minor detail the absurdity of the laws, I may call attention to one or two instances of the operation of the Spanish laws framed for Spain, introduced into and enforced in Cuba upon the " rule of thumb " idea. One of the old game laws provided that deer could not be tracked when snow was on the ground—this is a land where snow is as rare as in Central Africa. There was another which answered very well for cool and comfortable Spain, by which in opening up streets they were limited to a very narrow width, which, upon being applied to Havana, left matters in a very unsanitary and unpleasant condition. One of the aides of Gen. Wood said to me that it looked for a while after the American occupation " as though we were rapidly wiping out all of the old Spanish customs without regard to the wishes of the people, such as stopping cock fighting and bull fighting," and for this the Administration has been severely criticized by the liberal minded at home, but the bull-fighting was only appreciated by the Spaniards and its abolition was highly approved by all classes of Cuban society. As for the Cuban national sport of cock-fighting that was abolished on the earnest solicitation of most of the prominent people of the island and has met with the full approval of all of the educated people.

Beyond such changes as these, the military authorities have not ventured upon any large scheme of reconstruction, feeling perhaps that this was a matter best left to those who might succeed them in the administration of Cuban affairs. But busy and able minds have been at work upon the subject, and Gen. Wood has succeeded in getting some of the best legal talent of Cuba so far interested in the subject of reforms that already many comprehensive schemes for the betterment of the courts, of one kind and another, have taken material shape. What will be done with these remains to be seen. The newly constituted republic cannot claim, however, if inequalities

A MOUNTED POLICE OFFICER, HAVANA

prevail, that the way has not been pointed out for them by their Trustee.

The attitude of the best elements of Cuba toward these changes is best indicated by the statement of Judge Gener of Havana, upon the general subject, who speaks in the following terms: " With the disappearance of the secular sovereignty of Spain, all our judicial institutions were disorganized, as they had their roots imbedded in the said sovereignty. Law regulates the life of countries. Law is essentially social. Law governs and controls social life. And if this is true it could not be conceived that, after the secular political moulds were broken into which Cuban society was cast, our legal institutions should remain permanently and intangibly intact. The political order of things which for four centuries prevailed in Cuba having been essentially modified, the sovereignty that served as a foundation having been destroyed, the necessity of modifying legal procedure became and continues to be absolutely needed. Cuba cannot easily and methodically make progress in political advance hampered by embarrassing legal methods. Judicial forms should not be the same in countries subject to the colonial system, as in countries that have succeeded in freeing themselves from the dominion of the nation that controlled them from the fact of the latter being the metropolis. The judicial forms that were perchance good or at least adequate for Cuba as a colony of Spain, could not be so in a like manner for Cuba emancipated from Spanish control.  Thus doubtless the matter was understood by the former Secretaries; for which reason they took in hand the judicial organisms, at times modifying them, and at times adapting them to the necessities or conveniences of the new order of things brought about by the ruin and disappearance of Spanish power.

" From this point of view the work of the former Secretaries was essentially revolutionary, as is and must be the case with the work of the present Secretary and of those who may succeed him in his thorny and difficult position.  The Cuban revolution, like all other revolutions, destroyed many things that were not in accordance with the spirit that brought it about.  But at the same time that destruction was carried out, it was necessary to go on rebuilding.  The reconstruction due after demolition should immediately follow it.  Two methods could be followed for the renewal of the legal status of the country; one consisting in conjointly reforming our institutions; the other consisted in making partial reforms as required by the public necessity or convenience.  This latter method is the one that must necessarily be followed, because it is the most convenient and most proper.  The most practical, because the study and preparation of an entire Code would be evidently a most complex and complicated work, requiring much time, perhaps entire years, to complete. On the other hand, there are less difficulties in the partial reformation of the law. Besides, the new order of things upon which Cuba has entered offers new necessities, brings up new problems to be solved quickly in order that collective or private interests may not be caused to suffer injury. Therefore, the necessity of slowly commencing the reformation of judicial institutions of colonial times was demanded, in the direction of a new political organization, a new judicial organization and new laws for new times.

" This necessity of changing the colonial laws was demanded besides, by a high political ideal. If here the colonial laws should be left intact, if the old judicial régime were adhered to, it would result that the revolution would be exclusively limited to the expulsion of Spain from Cuba; to a mere, although transcendental, political change in the government of the island. If this were the case the people would not receive from the revolution all the benefits to which they are entitled, inasmuch as in essence the laws of the vanquished régime would continue to exist.

" The effects of the Cuban revolution and of the war that the United States engaged in against Spain to save Cuba to the cause of humanity, liberty and of civilization, re-establishing in our island the reign of order and conscience must of necessity be felt in all parts of our legal life, as the revolution in Cuba was not solely for the purpose of putting one government in the place of another, one bureaucracy in the place of another bureaucracy, but was for the purpose of establishing some institutions in the place of other ones."

If the Government of Intervention needed any justification or apology for its few changes in the laws of Cuba, surely it would find this in this testimony of the Secretary of Justice in General Wood's Cabinet as to the necessities which compelled them.

The Church question in Cuba has been met upon broad and generous lines. In reference to the church property the situation was about as follows. In 1841 the church property was generally seized by Spain and practically confiscated. This led to a long and troublesome conflict between Spain and the Holy See. Finally, in 1861, the Pope acting as the temporal power made a treaty or Concordat with Spain to the effect that Spain would return to the Church all those properties which she had not actually sold or put to secular uses which could not be given up, and in lieu of this latter property she agreed to pay the church a certain sum per year, which amounted to $470,000 in Cuba; this amount varied from time to time. When the United States entered Cuba the authorities declined to pay this rental and at the same time held on to the church property. Gen. Wood's work with the church has been to settle the contingent dispute amicably and after a great deal of arduous labor and an infinite amount of talking this has been accomplished. All the Capellanias (mortgages on masses for souls) and censos were paid off for sums varying from $0.50 on the dollar to a few cents according to locality. This payment frees thousands of titles all over the island of church claims. The government has acknowledged the title of the church to such property as a judicial commission, appointed by Gen. Wood, decided to be the property of the church; and the bishop and archbishop and the Governor have agreed upon a price to be paid for this property, which, as a rule, is about one-fourth to one-half the original price asked for it. At these figures the state has an option on the property for five years, during which period she can buy it at the figure fixed: but as long as she holds it she pays a rental for its use of from three to five per cent. interest on the fixed price, according to locality. In case of purchase twenty-five per cent. of the rental paid is returned. The demands of the church were fair and it is thought by those most interested that the United States have dealt fairly with them, and very advantageously for the future government, since by the terms of the agreement an endless amount of trouble and discussion will be avoided.

# Chapter **X**

## THE DEPARTMENT OF SANITATION

*O*F prime importance, not alone to Cuba, but to the United States, in her Southern ports particularly, has been the work of the Sanitary Department of Havana. To say that that charming city was nigh unto a pest-hole at the close of Spanish control is far short of exaggeration. With the exception of its water-supply, which was excellent, the city had nothing in the line of public or private works which was above suspicion as a breeder of disease, and this fact, allied to the naturally filthy habits of the great mass of the people, rendered the sanitary crisis confronting the American officers at the beginning of the occupation exceedingly acute. When it is remembered that General Weyler himself, as a mark of special distinction to a guest, was wont to take him confidentially aside and show him his newly installed bathtub in the Palace as one of the chief objects of interest in Havana, and with all the prideful manner of a London Tower Beef-Eater exhibiting the crown jewels of the British Empire, one begins to get some idea of the standards of personal cleanliness that prevailed at this centre of Cuban civilization. Even to-day, in one of the leading hotels of Havana, the bathroom consists of a wooden shed on the roof of one of the

312

inner buildings, and the tub itself—having to do duty for the occupants of at least twenty rooms, or say thirty people—is a rectangular tank constructed of brown tiles, and fed by a single spigot, through which in the course of a half-hour a sufficient quantity of water to saturate an ordinarily large bath-sponge will flow. The floor of this lavatorial gem would not be tolerated in a third-class bath-house on the coast of New Jersey, and it was my personal experience that when I desired to use the apartment it usually required from half to three-quarters of an hour to find the key, which, I regret to say, was rusted, and turned hardly in the lock as if not accustomed to the function for which it was designed. I may also personally testify to the fact that after my first bath in this place I promptly hired a cab and went to the headquarters of an incorporated bath company and took another. All of which I mention merely to give the reader some idea of that inherent love of personal cleanliness with which American authorities in Cuba have had to grapple even in high places. If a bathtub was a curiosity at the Palace, and had become merely a lure for advertising purposes in a "first-class hotel," it is not difficult to conjecture how such a thing would be regarded as one descended the social scale.

I have already attempted to describe in these pages some of the difficulties which Major Black had to contend against in his reconstruction of the external Havana. On the outside, as we have seen, that city was not the fair and pleasant thing it has since become. Internally it was indescribable. It is the testimony of reliable witnesses that there was scarcely a building in the whole city —and the 250,000 citizens of Havana live in 26,000 houses of one kind and another—that was not an offence to the olfactories of those who have no liking for smells. The sewer system, such as it was, was antiquated, and the refuse of thousands of dwellings was carried into cesspools constructed immediately underneath the buildings themselves, which were never cleaned, and in rare instances even adequately covered. As a result the city was literally infested with "black holes," so called, from which nothing but the most frightful and unspeakable emanations could be expected, and to what extent germs of disease were bred and reveled in this environment it takes no superhuman intelligence to guess.

In connection with this chapter are printed two photographs of models constructed for the Cuban exhibit at the Buffalo Exposition, from a glance at which the reader may gain some idea of internal sanitary conditions as they existed under presumably favorable conditions in the old days. These models represent two views of a typical residence block in Havana. On three sides run sewers, on the fourth there is none, and the total number of connections with the sewers in this whole square was nineteen. Within-doors, located directly beneath the dwellings themselves, more often under the kitchen than elsewhere, having no outlet whatsoever, and depending wholly upon natural seepage for relief, were no less than twelve cesspools, into which flowed all the refuse of these houses. As long as the contents of these sink-holes kept below the kitchen floor they were left unattended and regarded with unconcern. When they overflowed it was the habit of the health-loving Havanese to remove a portion of their contents to make room for more, but not completely to clean them out, and in certain cases, in other portions of the city, there is evidence that some of these plague spots had not been cleaned out in fifty years. It is not without interest, too, that I should add that in this whole square there is no outlet from any of the buildings to the street excepting through the front door, and what that means when it comes to the unpleasant process of "cleaning up" scarcely needs to be described. As for the sewers of Havana, they were and still are hardly worthy of the name. Their condition is such that the Sanitary Department has not dared to compel the owners of buildings to connect their premises with them, since in construction they are wofully weak, in dimensions inadequate, and as a matter of fact hardly different from the cesspools, except in their form and location. A heavy rainfall fills them to overflowing, and aggravates rather than relieves

315

their condition, bringing up into the streets and through the vents substances that might better remain below.

From 1890 to 1898, inclusive, comprising the last nine years of Spanish rule, in spite of all its natural advantages, and the essential salubrity of its climate, the average death-rate per thousand in Havana was 46.71. During a portion of this period, however, conditions were not normal, owing to the insurrection, so to be quite fair to the Spanish we should take the six years of peace from 1890 to 1895, inclusive, when from carefully revised statistics we find that the death-rate was not less than 33.21 per thousand, high enough in all conscience, and comparing unfavorably with that of the principal cities of Europe and America during the same period. Nor was this due to virulent and widespread epidemics, but to the general diseases operating in large cities.

Here, then, were all the potentials of yellow fever, tuberculosis, small-pox, typhus, and other fevers, within ninety miles of the coast of the United States, and in a city whose chief commercial outlet was through the ports of the American republic. Into this atmosphere, furthermore, the fortunes of war thrust a large body of American soldiers, who, even if the beneficiaries of their service cared nothing for their own health, were entitled to the protection which a well-ordered sanitary condition could afford them.

The remedial efforts in relief of these conditions have

AFTER A SHOWER IN HAVANA

A TYPICAL HAVANA RESIDENCE BLOCK FROM TWO
POINTS OF VIEW

(*Photographed from the Models Constructed for the Cuban Exhibit
at the Pan-American Exposition*)

fortunately been from the first in the hands of men of energy, of experience, and of ideas. As the work of transformation of the external Havana was carried through, with wonderful results, by the persistent and intelligent application to his task of Major Black, so has the inner transformation of the city been wrought by Major John G. Davis and his successor, Major William C. Gorgas, assisted by Major V. Havard, chief surgeon. It was under General Francis Vinton Greene, Military Governor of Havana, that Major Davis gave to this work its original impetus and force, organizing his department and making the reconnoissance so to speak, upon which all subsequent effort has been based. Major Davis has been described as " one of those military officers who do things," in which respect he appears to be like the rest of those army men who have gone into Cuba on duty as soldiers and acquitted themselves with so much credit as administrators. He took hold of the situation with a firm grasp, was full of initiative, and constructive in every minutest detail of his work. What he and his successor have done has been the result of a scientific consideration of the situation, and in no wise the haphazard effort of men suddenly confronted with a hard proposition firing wildly in the dark with the meagre hope of scoring. In the face of opposition—not official, happily, for from General Greene, General Ludlow, and General Wood nothing but encouragement and helpful advice has been received—these men have carried through their arduous purpose to a conclusion which has been not only of lasting value to the Cubans, but of practical worth to the whole civilized world. The figures for 1901 show that under the American military régime the average death-rate per one thousand population has been reduced to 22.11—a marked improvement over the Spanish rate of 33.21. Furthermore, the report for the last month of 1901 showed this great reduction to have been still further bettered to a rate of 20.47 per thousand. Yellow fever has been materially checked. Infant mortality has shown a marvelous decrease, and along the whole line of diseases to which the Havanese were subject the reduction has been equally marked. These facts and figures tell the whole story far better than it can be set forth without them, and to those Americans who would deny to their representatives in Cuba the feathers to which their caps are entitled, they are respectfully commended as worthy of study.

The Department organized by these gentlemen at the conclusion of the Government of Intervention was under the direct supervision of Major W. C. Gorgas, Medical Corps, U. S. A., assisted by two principal assistants,— one being in charge of fines and remittances in connection with sanitary improvements: the other supervising the direct and indirect destruction of mosquitoes. For purposes of administration, the Department is sub-divided into divisions, the more important ones being the General Inspections, Engineer Inspections, Mosquito-Destruction, Disinfection, Hospital Inspection and Tuberculosis Division. The general office force consists of an Executive Officer, Chief Clerk and Divisions as follows: Correspondents, Record, Statistical, Accounts, Property, Fining, Purchasing and Time-keeping Divisions.

To give the reader a more comprehensive idea of the workings of the department, and its present condition, it is thought best to state the duties and the general character of the work performed by some of the more important of these sub-divisions, as brought out by the most recent inspection of its various branches.

Beginning with the Record Division, it was found that it files and forwards all official communications, such as notices to owners and tenants, relative to sanitary condition of premises, copies of sanitary ordinances, legal correspondence with the various municipal judges and the prosecution of the sanitary work, etc. The general records kept are very voluminous, but in good condition, under the supervision of Mr. Alfredo Silvera, a Cuban-American and an efficient officer. What is known as the card system is used, which insures prompt reference to any paper that has entered the office under the present management. Formerly the records of the Sanitary Department were few and, it is claimed, were loosely kept. Many of these old records have been gradually classified and indexed in such a manner as to render them available for immediate use. A check, in the form of a receipt from house owners and others, is kept to refute claims often advanced that papers sent out are not received.

The General Inspections Division follows the Record Division in order of importance. The chief of this division assigns the various inspectors to their duties, and makes necessary recommendations on the reports submitted by them. He also makes personal inspections in exceptional cases. The inspectors are required to make daily house-to-house inspections and to render such reports as they may consider necessary in the interest of efficient sanitation. For a better understanding of this part of the work, it seems proper to give an outline of the methods pursued.

The City of Havana, including Jesus del Monte, Cerro, Vedado, Guanabacoa and Regla, is divided into twenty-two inspection districts, to each of which is assigned an inspector. As a precaution to insure good work, these inspectors are changed frequently from district to district, and each in his district inspects every house in it three times a year, and renders reports embracing the results of his observations respecting the sanitary conditions. These inspections average about 1,000 to the district. It frequently happens that re-inspections are made of places for which sanitary improvements are ordered. The direct and re-inspections cover about 60,000 yearly.

Besides the district inspectors, there are ten sanitary inspectors, whose duties are to investigate and make full reports on such places as require special attention on account of unusually bad conditions. In the case of these special reports orders are issued to owners of property for the necessary sanitary work. Re-inspections and check inspections are made until the orders of the Sanitary Department are complied with. In extreme cases where the property owner or tenant shows no disposition to comply, fines are imposed.

The report of the sanitary inspector is rendered on a printed form, giving information in detail concerning the subject of inspection. Upon receipt of this report at the Sanitary office, a notice is sent to the tenant of the premises, giving him seven days in which to perform the work. At the expiration of the seven days a re-inspection is made to ascertain if the orders have been complied with, report of which is rendered on a blank form for filing. At the time of this re-inspection, if the Department's orders have been disregarded by the occupant of the premises, the inspector serves a notice to the effect that cognizance has been taken of default. About ten days thereafter, what is called check inspection is made, and if it is then found that the work has not been done, a notice is sent to the responsible party to the effect that he will be fined ten dollars American money unless the matter is attended to within fifteen days. At the expiration of the fifteen days, if the work has been neglected, a final notice is sent, stating that the fine will be enforced and the work done at his expense. The following day a communication is addressed to the judge of the municipal district in which the property is located directing him to collect the fine. If the work is done immediately, even after judicial action, the judge is usually instructed to remit the fines and costs. Should the facts so justify, notice is sent to the judge instructing him to remit the fine, but to exact the costs. All fines collected by the judge in this way are turned over to the Ayuntamiento and receipts taken therefor, which are transmitted by the judge to the Chief Sanitary Officer as evidence of settlement.

The above are termed unlicensed inspections, and deal principally with cleaning, whitewashing and removal of unsanitary matter.

To the Engineer Inspections Division are referred all cases where extensive alterations and new constructions are required to meet sanitary conditions. Its first step is to send to the responsible party a notice requesting him to call within seven days to arrange with reference to certain sanitary work required on his premises. If he fails to call within the specified time, notice is sent allowing him three days in which to comply with the request. If this elicits no response, a notice is sent, stating that he has incurred a fine of $10, for failure to obey said order. A circular letter, is then sent to the judge of the municipal district in which the property is located, for collection of the fine imposed. If the party calls at the Sanitary Office and arranges to do the work he is required to sign a paper making application for a license. After the license is granted the party is notified by the Sanitary Office to call and pay for the same. This having been accomplished, he is required to sign a pledge, to the effect that he will begin the work on a certain date therein stated.

Specifications for all licensed work are prepared by the Engineer Department of the City of Havana, which supervises the work until completed, when it is inspected and passed upon by the Sanitary Department, which also inspects the work from time to time during its progress, to see that it meets with the sanitary requirements. It sometimes happens that a place is in such bad sanitary condition as to necessitate the placing of the matter in the hands of the Chief of Police, who posts a notice on the door to the effect that the house will be closed if the evil is not remedied within thirty days. After a house is closed by the Police, it is inspected at short intervals by the Sanitary Department to see that it is not reopened. Occasionally houses of inferior character have been destroyed by the Department on account of unsanitary conditions, but such cases are rare.

The object of the Mosquito Destruction Division, is to

prevent the propagation of infectious diseases through the medium of the mosquito, first by the direct destruction of the insect, second by destroying its breeding places, in still water by petroleum, and by draining low lands by ditching. The department embraces two divisions, namely, the oiling and ditching. One branch, the oiling, inspects around premises in the city to see that there is no still water left where mosquitoes could deposit their larvæ; the other is engaged in draining by ditches, all the low lands lying around the bay.

The most important work of this division is done in and about private houses. Here there are forms of letters, circulars, notices, etc., issued in profusion. If still water where mosquitoes can deposit their larvæ is found around premises, the owner is called upon to comply with the orders issued by the Department. If the order is not complied with he is fined ten dollars, American money. This order is quite explicit in explaining to property owners and tenants that the yellow fever mosquitoes prefer clear still water in which to breed, and directs that all wells, cisterns, tanks, etc., containing standing water should be tightly covered. The oiling brigades follow up the inspectors of these houses to remove all water found in uncovered receptacles and to apply petroleum wherever needed. The inspections for this purpose reveal the fact that most of the houses in Cuba keep jars of water standing, called Tinejons, which are found to be favorite breeding places for this insect. In all cisterns, sewer connections, pozos negros, infiltration basins, etc., oil is used freely.

It has been learned from experience that the yellow fever mosquito, contrary to former supposition, habitually breeds in clear water, whereas the malaria mosquito prefers shallow water underlying grass. Another discovery is that the last variety is partial to hill-tops where the soil is clay, covered by shallow water, shaded by vegetation. This division claims to have destroyed ninety per cent. of the breeding places of mosquitoes in and around Havana.

The Disinfection Service disinfects or fumigates all places in which contagious and infectious diseases have occurred. In case of infection from yellow fever, all mosquitoes in the house, and in those adjacent thereto for a block, are destroyed.

This division is subdivided into three special brigades, each one of which is further sub-divided into sections. One of these sub-divisions has for its object the disinfection of houses as well as stables, from whence animals with glanders have been removed. Houses that contain cases of yellow fever, glanders or diphtheria are isolated and guarded until released by the Sanitary Officer. The major number of brigade sections clean houses when necessary, and disinfect others wherein have occurred contagious diseases, as well as distribute petroleum where needed. A monthly report is rendered, showing the work accomplished by each brigade during the past thirty days.

Under this division all clothing taken from infected premises is listed on a form kept for the purpose and sent to Las Animas Hospital for disinfection.

A most valuable section of the Department is the Statistical Division, which collects and compiles statistics relative to all classes of disease, births, marriages, deaths and immigration. It receives and files all statistical reports from the large cities of the world, which are used for comparison. It also classifies all data and prepares material for the monthly reports issued by the Chief Sanitary Officer. It notes all infectious and contagious diseases treated by resident physicians, who are, by its order, directed, under penalty of fine for disobedience, to report all such cases coming under their observation.

The records kept are:

1. A Yellow Fever Record.
2. Record of Typhoid Fever.
3. Record of Measles and Scarlet Fever.
4. Smallpox and Varioloid Record.
5. Record of Puerperal Fever.
6. Diphtheria Record.
7. Record of Glanders and Leprosy.
8. Pernicious Fever Record.
9. Book containing numbers of houses in which yellow fever has occurred since the year 1890.

10. Record of Tuberculosis Cases.
11. Record of Births.
12. Record of Marriages.
13. Record of Deaths.
14. Records of Births, Marriages and Deaths received from the various municipal judges.
15. Book and newspaper clippings from Island press in regard to various diseases, sanitary work, etc.

The Property Division keeps a record of all unexpendable property, showing amount of articles, cost per unit, and total cost, number of articles transferred, dropped or condemned, and total remaining on hand. A record of expendable property is kept, showing the date of receipt thereof, date issued, amount, balance on hand, and to whom issued. In connection with these records is a book containing a consolidation of monthly abstracts, kept in order to ascertain at the end of the year the quantity of property of various kinds purchased, expended, transferred and remaining on hand.

The Division of Tuberculosis was established in the month of March of 1901. Its object is to collect sputum, blood specimens, etc., from patients suspected of suffering from tuberculosis, typhoid fever, diphtheria, malaria, glanders, filariosis, etc., for microscopic examination in the City Laboratory. There are twenty drug stores, located in various parts of the city, that act as culture stations. This division has distributed circulars of information relative to the prevention of tuberculosis, diphtheria, glanders, malaria and filariosis. The Department has taken all precautions possible to extirpate the disease of tuberculosis by arousing a sentiment among the inhabitants against the evil practice of expectoration in public places. All correspondence and records pertaining to this division are kept separate from the general office files. The system used is the card index with envelopes containing original papers in each case, which are referred to by number.

There are other smaller sub-divisions, not treated specifically because closely allied to larger divisions of similar purport.

Such in general has been the organization of the Department.

The best idea of the results of the American system obtainable, can be derived from the report of Major Gorgas, Chief Sanitary Officer, for 1901, from which I quote as follows:

" All the tables of this report show a steady and general improvement in the sanitary conditions of the city, but the great work done this year by the Department, has been the extirpation of yellow fever from Havana, and, as I believe this has been due to measures for the first time adopted and carried out here, based upon certain scientific facts established by the Army Board, of which Major Reed was President, I will confine my remarks almost entirely to this subject. If we are right in our belief that, by measures taken for the killing of infected mosquitoes, we have rid Havana of yellow fever in a few months, when it had been endemic in the city for the past 200 years, it is of vast importance that these facts should be made known to the world as extensively and rapidly as possible, and this is particularly true with regard to the United States. For it may happen that during the coming summer, yellow fever might be introduced into our Southern cities, and, if it could be controlled as it has been in Havana during the past year, it would save many lives and prevent inconvenience and financial loss to the States so affected. The above reasons are sufficient, I think, for dwelling so much on this one topic.

"To make clear our claim that Havana has been purged from yellow fever during the past year by the destruction of infected mosquitoes, I will run over, in brief, the history of Havana with regard to yellow fever during the past 100 years and point out that yellow fever has always been endemic in Havana. up to 1901; that sanitary measures, which had reduced the excessive death rate of Havana to that of healthy cities of civilized countries, had had little or no effect upon yellow fever; that general disinfection, as carried out for other infectious and contagious diseases, had been most extensively and faithfully tried; that yellow fever had suddenly and sharply disappeared, upon the introduction of a system whose object was killing infected mosquitoes, based upon the theory that the Stegomyia mosquito is the ONLY means of transmitting yellow fever; that from the 28th of September to February 15th, the time of making this report, there has not been a single case of yellow fever in Havana, a condition of affairs so unusual that all question of chance can be dropped from consideration."

In the body of Maj. Gorgas's report will be found a table giving the deaths from yellow fever for the past forty-five years. From this it is seen that in these years, with scarcely an exception, some deaths have occurred from yellow fever in every month of the year; that the maximum,—2058 deaths,—occurred in 1857; the minimum, fifty-one deaths, occurred in 1866; average 751.44. For the year 1901, in which the new system was adopted, there occurred only eighteen deaths. And twelve of these eighteen deaths occurred before the new system was put into effect. It is equally well established that yellow fever existed in just the same way, before the time covered by this table. We have pretty definite data warranting the belief that it has been endemic in Havana since the English occupation in 1762.

The report goes on in substance as follows: " The general sanitary methods adopted by the American Administration, upon its occupation in January, 1899, had a rapid effect in reducing the general mortality as will be seen from the following figures. In 1898, the last year of the Spanish Occupation, Havana had 21,252 deaths; in 1899, the first year of the American Occupation, 8,153 deaths; the next year, 1900, 6,102 deaths and 1901, 5,720 deaths, which would be a small number for cities of similar size in any civilized country. This is a much smaller number of deaths than had ever occurred for a year in Havana before. In the body of the report will be found a table giving the number of deaths since 1870. For the past thirty-one years, this table shows that the maximum death rate during this period, occurred in 1898, when it was 91.03; the minimum in 1885, 29.30; average 41.55. In 1901 we have 22.11. The data above given would indicate that the hygienic conditions of Havana, at the end of 1899, were better by far than they had ever been before; but, when we consider the table for yellow fever, our conclusions will be very different as to that disease. From the figures just quoted, it will be seen that there has always been a considerable number of deaths from yellow fever in Havana every year.

" In 1898. on account of the Spanish War, there was very little immigration to the city, and therefore, there were few non-immunes to contract yellow fever; we had during this year, only 136 deaths from the disease. The next year, 1899, there was little or no immigration during the first six months, and consequently, few non-immunes, and we had only five deaths. During the last six months of that year, over 12,000 immigrants came in, and ninety-eight deaths from yellow fever occurred. The winter epidemic for 1899 was unusually severe. The next year, 1900, there were 310 deaths from yellow fever. This demonstrates that the general sanitary measures had had a marked effect upon the general death rate, but very little upon the death rate for yellow fever. Neither labor nor expense was spared. The floors and walls of the room occupied by the patient were washed down with a solution of bichloride, applied with a force pump; then the room was carefully sealed and filled with formaline gas. All the fabrics were taken to the disinfecting plant and passed through a steam sterilizer. Every case was carefully isolated, and the quarantine enforced by an employee of this Department, who was on guard at the room quarantined. Three men in eight hour shifts were assigned as guards to each case. By the end of 1900, the authorities were convinced that general sanitary methods could not, in a short time, eradicate yellow fever from Havana. In the smaller cities and military camps, entire success had resulted from the deportation of the non-immune population, together with general sanitary methods; but in a city the size of Havana, with a non-immune population of between 30,000 and 40,000, such a measure was entirely impracticable.

"At the beginning of 1901, the prospects, as far as yellow fever in Havana was concerned, were very unfavor-

MAJOR W. C. GORGAS
*Chief of Department of Sanitation*

able. There was a large non-immune population, probably larger than it had ever been before. The city was thoroughly infected, cases having occurred in all parts. During the preceding year, there had been 1,244 cases and 310 deaths, and all cases of non-immunes had suffered severely. On the staff of the Military Governor, the Chief Commissary, the Chief Quartermaster and one of the Aides had died.

" January commenced with an unusually large number of deaths from this disease, the record showing twenty-four cases and seven deaths; February was equally severe, eight cases and five deaths occurring during that month. The Military Governor, being determined that no precaution should be omitted, directed that, in addition to former measures, work be started on the line that the mosquito was the cause of the transmission of the disease. This work went into effect about the first of March, with the result that during the whole year we had only eighteen deaths from yellow fever and twelve of these eighteen deaths occurred before the mosquito measures were started.

" This is still better shown by taking the table of deaths, which estimates the yellow fever year as commencing April first. In this we see that, for the past eleven years, the maximum, 1,385 deaths, occurred in 1896-1897; the minimum, 122 deaths, in 1899-1900; average 467. For the year 1901-1902, up to February 15th, there were five deaths. This difference is too marked to be any matter of chance. That the yellow fever year of 1901-1902 had only 1-25 the number of deaths that had occurred in the minimum year of the preceding eleven years, must be due to some cause that did not act during these years. Still more marked is the fact that since September 28, 1901, no cases at all have occurred, particularly when it is considered that October and November rank among the worst months for yellow fever.

" Not only was this result obtained with the city full of non-immunes, with infection in all parts of it, but there were half a dozen infected towns in railroad communication with Havana. Constant intercourse was kept up and no interference with commerce occurred. Goods of all kinds were allowed to come into the city freely. No restriction was put upon bringing in clothing, bedding and so on, from those infected points. The only infected material from the towns looked after, was the sick man, who was carefully sought out and screened from mosquitoes. The number of other infectious and contagious diseases have been small during the year. There has been very little diphtheria and typhoid fever. The tuberculosis rate is about that of most cities of civilized countries."

Surely with such a record as this Major Gorgas is justified in pointing out some of the sanitary differences between the " then and the now " as he puts it, in the following terms:

" The Army took charge of the Health Department of Havana when deaths were occurring at the rate of 21,252 per year. It gives it up with deaths occurring at the rate of 5,720 per year. It took charge with small pox endemic for years. It gives it up with not a single case having occurred in the city for over eighteen months. It took charge with yellow fever endemic for two centuries, the relentless foe of every foreigner who came within Havana's borders,—which he could not escape, and from whose attack he well knew that every fourth man must die. It found Havana feared as a thing unclean by all her neighbors of the United States, and quarantined against as too dangerous to touch, or even to come near anything that she had touched, to the untold financial loss of both Havana and the United States. It leaves, after careful study of the question of yellow fever by its officers, undeterred by personal risk,—for several of the investigators have died of the disease, contracted at their work. It has established the fact that yellow fever is only transmitted by a certain species of mosquito, a discovery that, in its power for saving human life, is only excelled by Jenner's great discovery, and as time goes on, it will stand in the same class as that great boon to mankind."

In many ways the showing of this Department is the greatest feat of American achievement in Cuba if not in the world in so far as its benefits to mankind at large are concerned, and certainly the *New York Medical Journal* states the case mildly only when it says that " the sanitary revolution that has been accomplished in Cuba as a consequence of the American occupation must ever count greatly to the credit of American medicine and of American discipline." There is at Havana a small plaza and a handsome marble statue to the memory of General Albear, a Cuban engineer to whose initiative and energy and skill Havana owes its most excellent water supply. It is a fitting recognition of a worthy achievement. How much more fitting would be some such material expression of their loving gratitude of the Cuban people to the men who in the brief period of intervention have enabled them to drink of the crystalline fount of health; ridding them of the scourge of the slave-master, of the devastating fires of war and bringing to their impoverished bodies food for the soul and for the mind, and in a noble spirit of self sacrifice standing between them and pestilence and starting them along the highway of happiness with a clean bill of health!

It is a common and somewhat childish fashion among those who have been unable to bend him to their own purposes in Cuba to refer to Governor Wood as Doctor-General Wood. These persons are too shortsighted to see that after all this epithet which they speak in contempt and derision is rather a high distinction than otherwise. Certainly Doctor-Major Gorgas need not hesitate to take such a designation as a tribute, nor should Surgeon-Major Havard feel unhappy to be so called. The hyphenation is merely a further distinction for them all, since it indicates that to their unquestioned fitness as men engaged in the pursuit of arduous military duties they have added to their equipment those qualities of mind, of character, and of usefulness in the service of mankind which belong to the recognized guardians of the health of man.

The Cubans have cause to be grateful to the United States government for having so happily placed these doctors where they may do the most good. Without them there might not have been so many Cubans left alive to-day to dream of the new republic.

# Chapter XI

CONCLUSION

*A*ND so in meagre fashion the story of the Trust is told. Have we kept the faith and has the Trust been administered properly and well? Only a portion of the great painting has been sketched in here. Scores of the details of organization must perforce have escaped our attention. The work along lines of finance, under Maj. Eugene T. Ladd who as Treasurer of the island filled the arduous duties of his responsible office with signal fidelity and distinction, the thousand and one little things which go to make up the whole fabric, the difficult labors well accomplished by the silent hundreds who follow but without whom the leaders could hope for no results—all these things may only be surmised and may properly be left for some less rapid survey of the work than I have undertaken. To sum the whole story up however Uncle Sam may felicitate himself upon the facts that he found Cuba unhealthy and he leaves her healthy; he found her without an adequate system of charities and hospitals and he leaves her a well established one; he found her without schools and he leaves her with a good school law and a good school system established; he found the island filled with beggars and with an empty treasury; he leaves it without beggars, its people with enough to eat, and with a reserve of about a million and a half dollars in the treasury. He found her without any knowledge of popular elections and without an electoral law; he has given her both. He found the insane without any systematic treatment whatever, caged up like animals; he leaves them assembled in one large hospital under the best available treatment. He found her prisons indescribably bad and leaves them as good as the average prisons of his own country. He has built up a good system of sanitary supervision throughout the island. He has built and put into commission a small fleet of coast guard launches, or revenue cutters. He has collected the revenues at a figure which compares favorably with the cost of collection in the United States. He has buoyed the harbors and has added very largely to the lighthouses and lights of the island. An immense amount of road and bridge building has been done. He has organized a system of civil service for the municipal police throughout the island in order to protect them in their rights and secure them from arbitrary dismissal. He has enlisted, equipped, trained and thoroughly established a Rural Guard which will compare favorably with any similar force, and not over one per cent. of those employed to help him in his work has come from within his own borders. For the first time in history the carpet-bagger in a situation of this kind has been held in subjection and every penny of the

Trust has been administered for the benefit of the ward. It has been a wonderful showing and serves only to confirm me in an impression of a year ago, after a visit to the island that it would be a good thing for the credit of the United States at this moment, if we could only have a Floating University for the education of those gifted individuals to whom is entrusted the molding of public opinion. There is often a sad need of information on the part of a great many good people who write advice by which our rulers should be guided and through which public opinion should be formed; and in no connection does this fact become more obvious than in the published opinions throughout the country as to the Cuban situation and the work that has been done in connection therewith. It is difficult to say what one would surely do if possessed of unlimited wealth, but *a priori* my own opinion is that if I were Mr. Andrew Carnegie at this moment, I would scale down my library gifts about ten per cent., charter a ship and after placing aboard of her a selected number of students with minds like clean slates, enforced by a good digestion, re-enforced by an ability to see straight, and having a proper degree of patriotism, send them off to Cuba to see things as they are. The dullest clod among them would come back with impressions the proper presentation of which to the American public would inspire in the latter a pride so great that it could hardly be adequately described.

# A BRILLIANT SHOWING

After some observation of men and affairs in Cuba, I am satisfied that the only people of American birth in the island who know anything at all about the situation, who because of the American policy in Cuba are ashamed of being Americans, are those who, judged by any reasonable standard of fitness, should be ashamed of themselves. They have been trouble makers from the start. The administration at Havana, however, from top to bottom, has at no time had anything to fear from an inspection of its work by any man who approaches his task with a clear conscience, a good liver, and, if he be a newspaper man, with no instructions from the home office; or, having these, no carping, cavilling, bilious editorial policy to justify.

Despite these persons the manly men in authority have gone their way resolutely to the work in hand undeterred by the snapping and snarling of the jealous and irresponsible, and now that the end has crowned the work they have the satisfaction of knowing that they take rank among the strong and great figures in the pages of history whilst their envious critics have slunk back into the tobacco scented purlieus of the cafés where their ignoble energies have found their chiefest outlet. To Gen. Wood and the noble band of men who have fought side by side to help him and his predecessors in this regeneration of a fallen people the gratitude of the United States goes out in fullest measure, and when in future days they come to

341

look back upon the events of four years of discouragement and toil they will see I fancy merely the outlines of that enduring monument to their own nobility of character and purpose which step by step and hour by hour they have builded up. And Cuba? If Cuba in the remotest hour of the remotest century to come forgets this service and the names of these men who have rendered it, then will she be guilty of an ingratitude which is inconceivable, and to be likened only to that of the serpent, who, warmed by the fire of his benefactor, turned and stung the hand that brought him back to life.

END

# Reprint Publishing

FOR PEOPLE WHO GO FOR ORIGINALS.

This book is a facsimile reprint of the original edition. The term refers to the facsimile with an original in size and design exactly matching simulation as photographic or scanned reproduction.

Facsimile editions offer us the chance to join in the library of historical, cultural and scientific history of mankind, and to rediscover.

The books of the facsimile edition may have marks, notations and other marginalia and pages with errors contained in the original volume. These traces of the past refers to the historical journey that has covered the book.

ISBN 978-3-95940-077-0

www.reprintpublishing.com